A Rake's Redemption

*Other Five Star Titles
by Donna Simpson:*

Lady Delafont's Dilemma

A Rake's Redemption

Donna Simpson

Five Star • Waterville, Maine

Sim

Five Star Romance Series.

Published in 2002 in conjunction with Zebra Books, an imprint of Kensington Publishing Corp.

The text of this edition is unabridged.

Cover design by Thorndike Press Staff.

Set in 11 pt. Plantin by Elena Picard.

Printed in the United States on permanent paper.

Library of Congress Cataloging-in-Publication Data

Simpson, Donna.
    A rake's redemption / Donna Simpson.
      p. cm.
    ISBN 0-7862-4444-5 (hc : alk. paper)
    1. England—Fiction. I. Title.
    PR9199.3.S529 R35 2002
     813'.54—dc21   2002069331

A Rake's Redemption

One

One single bead of sweat trickled down the young man's domed forehead, passed his fluttering eyelid, and crossed his downy cheek to his receding chin. It dropped onto the rumpled and stained neck cloth that had been pulled from its owner's waistcoat some time before. Lord Hardcastle could almost find it in his heart to pity the young cub. Almost.

"Your turn, Fossey," Hardcastle said for the second time. The elegant card room of the Apollo club was unusually hushed. Generally there was a murmur of voices, but it seemed that this particular card game had captured the interest of many.

Young Baron Fossey, trembling, plucked a card from his dwindling hand and laid it down, rallying a little as he did so. It was a queen, but a queen of the trump suit. He glanced up at his particular friend, the equally young Mr. Hawley who stood by him smoking a cigar, and nodded. His eyes were wide and bright, and he clearly had hope. He had two out of the three tricks he needed to win this hand, the hand that would win or lose the game.

The tension of the onlookers perceptibly heightened as Hardcastle appeared to deliberate over his last two cards. The atmosphere of the club was smoky and revelry could be heard in a distant room, but here, all were silent. Until Hardcastle finally threw down his card with great aplomb—it was a king of that same trump suit—took Fossey's, and slapped down his last card, an ace. Then a sigh whispered through the crowd of some fifteen or twenty gentlemen. Fossey stared at the card and licked his lips. His gaze wandered the room for a moment, as though he were looking for relief from some agency, but his gaze was unfocused, hopeless.

Then, with a shrug of his shoulders, he slid his remaining card across the table.

"My trick, I believe," Hardcastle said, not bothering to hide the triumph in his voice.

"Your trick, my lord, and y-your game," Fossey said politely. He stood, though his knees buckled slightly, and bowed before Hardcastle.

Well done, young 'un, Hardcastle thought, standing and offering his hand. Fossey returned the courtesy, though his hand lay as damp and limp as a flounder as the older man shook it.

"Shall I visit your rooms in the morning, Fossey, to settle up?"

"Y-yes, sir. The Claridge, sir." The youthful baron, not above two-and-twenty, Hardcastle thought, turned and shambled away, stumbling and reaching out blindly for the support of a chair as his friends surrounded him to commiserate with his loss.

At least it was not alcohol that made him lurch that way. Hardcastle drew the line at gambling with drunken opponents. No, it was likely just an excess of emotion.

"You've beggared him, Hardcastle. You know that, don't you?"

"Mercy, old man!" He turned to greet the speaker. "How are you? Haven't seen you this age."

Mercy Dandridge, a friend of Hardcastle's since school

days, nodded in answer to the other man's greeting but repeated his first words. "You've taken everything he owns," he added, with a serious look in his mild blue eyes.

Hardcastle shrugged. " 'Twasn't me who made the terms."

Dandridge pressed on where many a man would have let it drop. "But you set your own. You and everyone in this room know how mad young Fossey is for horseflesh. And knowing that, to wager the entire contents of your stable? It was irresistible. He must have had visions of Derby Day and himself as the proud owner of your Theseus and Pegasus and Arcturus. Intolerably tempting to one so green, and one who has, perhaps, not seen you at the euchre table before."

Hardcastle gave his friend a look warning him that some imperceptible line was about to be crossed. Before answering, he made an attempt to master his flash of anger, tossing a guinea on the gambling table for the waiter and signaling for his coat and hat. He was not a man to be chastised, not by anyone, not even his closest and oldest friend, but his tone, when he spoke, was temperate. "And what purpose is the gambling table if what one gambles does not matter? I would have been sorely put out to lose my stable. That is the work of a lifetime, and Pegasus's sire was my father's horse, and a champion."

"But you would have had the wherewithal to purchase other horses; they are only animals, after all. You would still have had your fortune and your properties. Fossey gambled away his birthright!"

Hardcastle's dark eyes flashed. "Mercy," he said, his voice low and grating, "you know the rules and so does young Fossey. No man should wager so much if it is more than he can afford to lose. It is a lesson we all must learn."

"My friend," Dandridge said, putting one square hand on

9

Hardcastle's shoulder, "I know that old pain still rankles, what your father did to you, but you must—"

Hardcastle shook away his friend's hand. "Not another word, Dandridge, or so help me God, I will call you out for insufferable insolence!"

The other man drew back and stiffened. He was silent for a long moment, but then he said, "I will never fight you; you know that. But I am compelled to speak on, regardless of how you choose to hear me; if you thrash me for it, then so be it. I hope you will *think* before you destroy that poor fellow's life, Lawrence, my old and valued friend. I just hope that there is some angel out there who will speak in your ear. What happened to you was not right, but it was a long time ago, and you need not visit your wrath upon other poor young fools."

It was unconscionably early, considering how late he had been out the night before, but Hardcastle was ever punctilious in the pursuit of his rightful winnings. He rapped on the door to the young man's suite with the silver head of his elegant ebony cane.

A very correct gentleman's gentleman answered the summons and bowed before Hardcastle, who handed him a card.

"Tell your master that I have come to settle up our account."

The man glanced at the card, and said, "Lord Fossey has left London, my lord."

"Left . . . What the devil do you mean?"

"He has gone, my lord. Left. Just this morning."

Hardcastle felt fury well up inside him. The cheat! The filthy, despicable, dastardly cheat! Above all things, he could not abide a sniveling, sneaking, lying knave.

The man looked at the card again, and said, "I believe he left you a note, sir. If you will just wait one moment?"

Hardcastle could see into the room as the valet retreated. It was in wild confusion, as though Fossey had overturned all of his possessions as he scuttled off to his mouse hole. The man came back and handed Hardcastle a note, folded over many times and with "Hardcastle" scrawled in execrable penmanship on the outside. "Did he—"

But it was too late; the valet had already closed the door.

Outside the hotel, Hardcastle unfolded the letter.

My lord, it read. *I know this is unforgivable, but circumstances are such that I must beg for time. I will be in contact.* It was signed simply, *Fossey.*

Hardcastle crumpled it into a ball and tossed it down on the pavement with a sharp exclamation of disgust. Time? One did not ask for time, and Fossey must know that. No, the cawker thought he could weasel out of his rightful debt. Well, he would soon learn to his detriment that one did not put off the Earl of Hardcastle with weak excuses and whimpering lies. He would pay his rightful debt or he would feel the tip of the sword.

Just hours later, with nothing more than an overnight bag strapped to his horse, Hardcastle rode out of London in the brilliant light of the spring sun. So bright a day was it that it pierced the perpetual gloom that shrouded London. The air, as he rode Pegasus out of the city, certainly got noticeably cleaner and purer as one moved away from the coal fires and miasma of horse dung, rotting vegetation, and the ineffable smell of the Thames that clung to the city streets and alleyways like an expensive whore's cloud of sandalwood. The earthy scent of ploughed fields and burgeoning green vegetation freshened the May air and Hardcastle found himself breathing in deeper, filling his lungs with the purifying draught of country breezes as he hastened his gait from an easy post to a more invigorating canter.

He always forgot how much he liked riding in the country when he was caught up in the frenetic pace of London living, and he would have enjoyed the day if it were not for that insufferable pup's reneging on their bet. That rankled and nagged at him like an aching tooth.

If there was one lesson he had learned early and hard, it was that a gentleman always told the truth and stood by his bets. To renege was as bad as to cheat. A man's measure could be taken in the value of his word; he would hand on that bit of wisdom to the youngster, who would someday thank him for the knowledge about life's cruelty.

He rode throughout the day, Pegasus gaining enthusiasm once he shook off the lethargy that immured him in London. Fossey's country seat was in Oxfordshire, Hardcastle thought. He had some vague idea of where, and trusted to the invaluable help of innkeepers along the way. With any luck, and the light of the full moon that would rise that night, he would make it to Fossey's country seat by morning.

Lord, but it had been an age since he had ridden so long and so hard! Eventually even Pegasus, champion that he was, grew weary. Hardcastle stopped to sup at the Lazy Bullock, a Tudor inn on the other side of High Wycombe. The evening was a lovely one, mellow and mild, and he took his meal outside looking over a verdant valley while he slaked his thirst on a respectable home brew. The landlord, astute about the value of catering to one such as Hardcastle, and yet not obsequious at all, informed him, as he refilled the earl's tankard, that he had heard of Baron Fossey's estate. He thought it was some twenty miles or more northwest still.

Heartened by the shortened distance, but still not quite sure where he was going, Hardcastle paid his shot and asked the most likely way to an inn close to the Fossey estate. Receiving directions to an inn called the Pilgrim's Lantern in Ainstoun, a tiny village just north of Thame, Hardcastle retrieved Pegasus, who had, like his owner, been rested and well fed, and man and beast were soon on their way.

The sun slid behind the undulating hills, and for a while, as darkness enfolded him, Hardcastle feared he would have to stop. But the moon began her ascent as he clopped through the quiet streets of Thame, and by Luna's shimmering light he made his way over the smooth-packed road until he came to the turnoff indicated by the innkeeper. This was the way, the man had indicated, to the Pilgrim's Lantern in Ainstoun, where they would certainly be able to direct him to Baron Fossey's estate.

Trees closed in the country lane like a vaulted ceiling in a caliginous cathedral, and Hardcastle had to slow his pace because of the encroaching gloom. Any sensible man, he supposed, would have stopped for the night at an inn and continued his journey on the morrow, but on this point he was not sensible. There was a bitter anger that roiled in his gut at the mere thought of being cheated, and he would not sleep; he knew that of himself. Still, he would not allow Pegasus to hurt himself out of haste, though he chafed at the delay their slower pace produced.

And so he walked his mount down the thoroughfare. To pass the time he imagined the weak explanation Fossey would no doubt try to give him, seconds before the sound thrashing Hardcastle would deliver. He had thought the young man admirably collected considering that he had just lost his birthright, the Fossey baronial estate, but now he could see that the young man never intended to hand over the deed and right to the manor. Even then he must have been planning his flight, though how he thought it would benefit him, he could not imagine. He must know Hardcastle would pursue his

13

rightful winnings, and that society—and yes, even the law— would support the earl.

He rode for another couple of hours, quickening his pace when he could, slowing when the trees closed in overhead. Surely the small village of Ainstoun would be somewhere close! Pegasus was weary after a day-long ride that broke the laziness of a London season filled with little riding other than a trot down Rotten Row in the morn. But if beast was weary, man was even more tired. His back ached, his bones felt like they had been jolted from his skin, and every point of contact with the saddle chafed as though it were on fire.

He tried straightening his back, but it helped not one bit. Could it be he was getting older? Lord, but he hoped not. He would *not* descend into one of those sad-looking older men who still clung to their routine of going to the club and staying until dawn, becoming maudlin over a bottle of port while they reminisced about "the good old days" to any younger man who would listen. But what was he thinking? He was in his prime, barely into his thirties—well, into his middle thirties. He could gamble and drink and wench all night long and still go riding at dawn. He had proved to be better at that sport even than his friend Byron, who became riotous and un- controllable after a certain point, the second or third bottle of wine, while Hardcastle just became more disciplined and colder.

Ah, ahead there, it looks like a clearing. He leaned over Peg- asus's neck and peered into the gloom. Damned country lane was completely overgrown with trees. No doubt that was lovely and refreshing on a hot summer's day, but in the middle of the night it was treacherous. Of course, roads were never meant to be traveled in the dark. Once he got to the clearing he could pick up the pace and get to this wretched little village that much faster. Mayhap he would bespeak a room for an hour's nap after all and continue in morning's light.

In anticipation, he kicked Pegasus into a more lively trot. He would do the damned deed—he was beginning to regret his impetuous nature, but he believed if a thing was to be done, it was best done immediately—and get back to London before anyone even knew he was gone. Would he tell of Fossey's regrettable behavior? He had not decided. To renege like that would get the cub tossed from all the clubs. But then, after paying his debt to Hardcastle, would he even be able to afford his club dues, especially once word had gone around town that he was beggared?

But that was not his concern. Fossey's future was not his responsibility to fret over.

Yes, finally he could see the clearing, and a little house in the distance down the way, with a walled garden that abutted the road. Maybe he would stop and ask an early rising maid the way to the inn. He was about to kick Pegasus into a gallop now that they were breaking out of the dimness of the wooded lane, when he heard a shout and two men leaped out of the brush into the road. Exhausted and nervous, Pegasus did the unthinkable and reared.

Hardcastle felt himself sliding, sliding, sliding out of the saddle and tumbling backward. Briefly he considered that he had not fallen from a horse since—well, ever.

And then, as he hit the ground, he heard a voice call out in brutal accents, "Stand an' deliver, mate!"

Two

The next thing he knew, before he was even given the chance to respond, a thick-set man raced at him and he felt the first painful blow of a board hard against his back. More footsteps crunching through the gravel, more blows and more pain; Pegasus was whinnying and scuffling on the rutted road, but all Hardcastle could concentrate on was the painful blows, blows that came at such a rate he could not even scramble to his feet to defend himself.

He was shouting hoarse, incoherent demands for the brutes to stop, but nothing, no amount of begging—no, he was not begging, was he?—would make them stop. And then blackness closed in around him, and it seemed the moon was extinguished just like a lantern.

Phaedra Gillian hummed an old Scottish air her nanny used to sing to her, as she gazed, in dawn's first light, out her bedroom window, just under the eaves of her and her father's Oxfordshire cottage. The distant hills beyond the village were misty and the new-green color of the sage that budded and grew in her garden. It promised to be a glorious day, with a hint of early sunshine rising in the pearly eastern sky. She watched a tiny bird battling with a stubborn piece of fluff he was trying to fit into his nest. Wishing him luck, she was just about to continue on her first task of the morning, making herself presentable, when she heard a scream.

What was it now? Sally, her maid of all work, was a dear, but the slightest setback sent her into hysterics. But not this morning! *Please*, not this morning! Her father had been awake all night conning some abstruse point of theological philosophy—she had not heard his footsteps climbing the creaking stairs until almost daybreak—and she would *not* have him disturbed. He needed his sleep; after all, he was not getting any younger. Even as she thought this, clad still in her nightrail, wrap, and slippers, she was racing down the narrow, dim stairs, each step worn in the center with age, to find out what had set Sally off this time, whether a mouse in the cupboard or a particularly pointed remark from the cheeky butcher's lad.

"Miss Gillian. Miss Gillian!"

Phaedra entered the cramped kitchen to find her helper dashing about as though she had run mad. "Hush, Sally. What is it?" Phaedra asked, rescuing a pitcher of water before the maid's erratic movements could send it tumbling off the table. "You know we need to be quiet in the morning so my father can sleep! What is it? Quietly, now."

Sally, young and pink cheeked, her mobcap askew and her eyes glittering, grasped her mistress's hands and, panting, related her tale. "I was a-goin' to milk Bessy, just like every morning, miss, out to yonder barn, and I saw, down the road, a-a-a dark spot—yes, a dark spot. An' I thought to meself, I thought, Sally, what be that dark spot? An' so I, thinkin' mayhap it be old Mr. Brunton what drinks too much sometimes an' falls asleep in the oddest places—I hear'd once as how he fell asleep atop Flo, his old nag whut was just croppin' grass on the village green until his wife—Mr. Brunton's wife, not Flo's, her being a horse and a lady—"

Impatiently, unwilling to hear the whole rambling story,

Phaedra squeezed Sally's hands and released them. "What was the spot, Sally? You did go to investigate, did you not?"

"I did, miss, an', *oh!*" She shrieked and put her hands to her cheeks.

"What is it, Sally?"

"It be a gent, and all bloodylike an' dead, but I thought as how it might be a trick by those dastardly highwaymen whut's bin robbin' folks as travel through these parts, an' I didn't dare get too close, you know, for fear he would leap up an' kidnap me an' take me to his lair an' have his way wiv me, like in the tales Joe Mudge, the butcher's lad, tells—"

"Yes, Sally, like in Joe's overblown and ridiculous tales. Did you not think that the highwaymen are not out after daybreak?" Phaedra did not wait to hear her maid's answer, but flew out the kitchen door, down the walk, out the gate, and toward the road where Sally had seen the "body."

"Oh, Lord," she prayed, under her breath, "please do not let it be a body. Please let it be just old Mr. Brunton, alive and well, but drunken!" But the blood, was that just a part of Sally's overactive imagination?

As she flew down the road, fear making her swift, she could hear Sally running after her. There on the road, up ahead, near the grove of trees that signaled the start of Squire Daintry's land, there was the dark spot of which Sally had spoken. *Please Lord,* she prayed, *let this fellow be alive.*

Shivering from pain and cold, aching in every joint and every limb, Hardcastle opened his eyes, only to be blinded by light—brilliant, glowing light. And out of the light, with an aura of pink and gold around her, was an angel flying toward him, her holy robes fluttering, and she was—was she singing, or was it praying?

He twisted his head farther, trying to see, trying to squint against the blaze of glory from which the beautiful vision wafted—No, not wafted. Floated? Glided? Not quite sure. Hard to tell, with her robes billowing out behind her like that, if her feet ever touched the ground.

Surely, though, surely she could not be an angel; if he were dying—and he felt that he was dying—the last thing he would see was a heavenly messenger. More likely a harbinger of a more southernly persuasion, demons from hell come to torment him. Even approaching death could not persuade him that his destination was anything better than "down."

But it hadn't mattered until that moment, until he had seen this approaching vision, this lovely, glowing seraphim gowned in white, with gorgeous flowing, crinkly golden hair that streamed down over her shoulders, catching the heavenly light from her own aura. Her mouth was opening and closing as she approached, but all he could hear was a strange singing in his brain, a high whine in his ears. Can humans even understand the voices of angels, he wondered? Theological point that, one for the scholars. How many angels can sing while dancing on the head of a pin? Or some such rubbish.

As he shivered and moaned aloud at the agony he was experiencing, a strangely peaceful feeling came over him. If she would only come to him and stay by his side, if she would tarry and give him comfort, he could stand any amount of suffering; he knew he could. In that moment he experienced an ardent desire to be found worthy of her presence. But no doubt the moment she found out who he was, that he was no candidate for heaven, she would recoil in horror and disappear, with one sad look for him, for the life he had wasted— No, not wasted. Surely not that. He had lived fully and completely, loved women, drank wine, gambled, and fornicated but . . . His vision blurred. Oh, if only she would stay! If only he deserved . . . He reached out, reached out to touch that warming glow, for he was so cold, so very cold. He reached one hand out, but then the blackness engulfed him and he felt himself descend into frigid darkness.

"Get Roger and Dick Simondson," Phaedra commanded of Sally. The girl retreated to do as she was bid, and Phaedra crouched by the gentleman on the road.

There was no mistaking he was a gentleman. Even beaten, even stripped as he was of anything of value—his coat, his boots, even the buttons on his shirt—it was clear that he was not some shopkeeper's assistant from Ainstoun, nor a farmhand or dairyman. Her heart pounded as she examined him, remembering that one brief, appealing gesture, that outstretched hand that seemed to be asking, no, *begging* for succor. The look on his battered, bloody face and in his dark eyes had been pain mixed with—with what? Ecstasy? No, surely she was reading strange meaning into what was merely a plea for help.

Well, she would give aid to the extent she was able. At least he was alive; there was that. She glanced around, but it would be some moments before Roger and Dick would gather what a hysterical Sally was asking of them. Tenderly, she brushed the gravel out of his cuts and examined him. The poor gentleman was badly beaten. Blood stained the fine lawn of his open shirt—open because of the stripped shirt buttons. With an experienced eye—Phaedra was the only one in or near Ainstoun with any medical ability at all, as befit the daughter of the local vicar, retired though her father now was—she could see that though badly beaten, the fellow would likely recover, if she could get him off the cold ground soon, that was. It was spring, well into May now, but mornings were still chilly, which she could feel through her drifting, billowing nightrail. Morning dew had settled on the poor gentleman and his clothes and hair were damp. She glanced around, but still Sally was not returning, nor was help on the way.

If the gentleman were conscious she could ask him if he could walk, but she was certainly not able to move a man of such size. Compared to her slim frame he was a behemoth, but there was no fat over his bones. As she ran her hands over his limbs, checking for breaks, she could not help but notice more than adequate muscle and sinew. He was lean but strong, she would guess, and certainly of a class Ainstoun was not accustomed to hosting, so where was he headed in the middle of the night? For she assumed he had been set upon and robbed some time in the darkest hours before dawn. Had he been traveling alone? And where was his horse?

And where, oh *where* were the Simondson brothers? She looked down the road fretfully, then back at her patient. His skin, where it was not bloody or covered in grit, was as pale as marble, and his hair, laying across his high forehead, was raven black and glossy, though road dust clung to it now. He was more still than he had been, was he not? And even more ashen. Was he dying? *Oh, Lord, please,* she prayed. *Not that!* She hesitated, then slipped one hand down under his shirt to his heart and felt the reassuring thud that told her he was still alive, though in very rough condition. Glancing around, she made a quick decision and pulled off her wrap, laying it over his still form, hoping it gave him some small measure of warmth.

At long last, she saw the two young men she had sent Sally for, striding along the road, Dick still carrying his scythe. She colored when she realized she was in only her nightrail now, and on a public road with two young men, no less, but this was no time for missish behavior, and she sternly quelled her shyness and determined to act just as if she were in her proper attire. When there was nothing else one could do, one comported oneself with dignity. "Dick, Roger, carry this fellow to my home. He is badly in need of help."

The two robust young men, unquestioningly obedient, lifted the man by the feet and shoulders.

"Careful. *Careful.* He is badly hurt!"

And so their odd procession made its deliberate way to the small cottage Phaedra and her father called home. Once inside, she only hesitated a moment before asking the two to carry their burden up the narrow stairs to the first room on the right, at the top of the stairs. They did as they were asked, though Phaedra had a worrisome few moments when they came close to dropping their charge as they turned the tight corner at the top of the stairs. But finally the young men lay the gentleman down on the small bed in the tiny, cheerful room and made their way back down the stairs again.

It was not until after she had thanked and dismissed both the Simondson brothers and Sally, that Phaedra realized she should have admonished them not to embellish on this morning's work. There was enough fear in the village already over the behavior of the highwaymen without her fanciful maid retelling this story to the butcher's lad, and the Simondson brothers telling the story over a free pint at the local. However, it was too late for that caution, and it likely would have been wasted breath anyway.

She convinced an uneasy Sally to go back out to the barn and milk Bessy and gather the eggs, telling her briskly—but kindly, she hoped—that she had nothing to fear in the bright light of day. Phaedra then poured hot water from the kettle and carried it in an ewer back upstairs, trying to avoid the stairs that creaked, hoping that her father had not been awoken by the rather clumsy work Roger and Dick had made of getting the gentlemen up to his new, if temporary, quarters. Entering the room, she was struck immediately by how the very dimensions of it seemed to have been shrunk by the presence of the poor beaten gentlemen. It was a small room, with cheerful papered walls, bright woven rugs, and white-painted furniture lining the walls, but somehow, with the gentleman on the bed, it seemed to have reduced to a child's playhouse dimensions. Like a giant in a fairy story, his feet almost hung over the end of the bed, and his shoulders all but spanned the width.

She sat on the edge of the bed, after pouring the hot water into a basin on the small side table, and dipped a cloth into the steaming, fragrant water. She had added a few drops of her precious lavender water, a gift from her aunt in Bath at Christmastime, to the wash water. It had cleansing and soothing qualities, she thought, and never did a gentleman need more soothing than this poor fellow. Where was his horse? she wondered again. Had it been stolen along with his purse and coat and boots? Yes, and rings. She could see the indentations on his long fingers where she guessed rings had sat for many years.

Well, no stalling. She hesitated just briefly, and then, dipping the cloth again in the hot water and squeezing it out, she rubbed it over his dirt-smudged face, along the strong, square jaw bristling darkly with whiskers, and down the thick column of his throat, trying to be gentle, hoping he was in no pain. He was badly bruised and there were a couple of cuts and scrapes on his face—gravel was imbedded and she was grateful he was not awake, for cleansing the wounds would not be a painless operation—but she had a feeling the bulk of the damage had been done to his body. In her brief examination on the road she did not think anything was broken, but she would have to be sure. She had sent a message by way of Sally to the present vicar, who saw the doctor on his travels sometimes. Doctor Deaville would surely pass by Ainstoun sometime within the next couple of days. Phaedra just prayed the gentleman's injuries were not beyond her meager skills.

She pushed back his shirt, briskly quelling the blush that would rise—after all, she had seen a man's chest before, maybe not a man of this quality, but men were men, all equal in God's eyes, were they not?—and applied the cloth to his chest, first checking more thoroughly for broken ribs and listening for any rattle or indication that his lungs had been punctured or any internal damage done. His breathing was reasonably regular, if a little shallow—no gurgling that would have indicated a dangerous internal bleeding—and his heart still beat a firm, regular thud against her fingers. His breathing did not sound wheezy, either, as it would have if he had taken ill from lying on the road, and she nodded, satisfied that he did not seem to be in danger for his life.

Threading her fingers through his dark hair, she felt for any dent in his skull. That was another possible danger, a bad blow to the skull, and there *was* some blood and an abrasion or two, but again, it did not seem too serious. He could have a concussion. Only time would tell some things, she had learned from Doctor Deaville.

So sturdy a specimen as the unknown gentleman could likely take a worse beating and recover. He certainly was . . . sturdy. She felt the blush rise again, and castigated herself severely.

"Phaedra Gillian," she said, out loud, as she rinsed her cloth in the steaming bowl, "you are twenty-seven and a spinster, and a vicar's daughter to boot! And a bookish, learned, *scholarly* vicar's daughter, to add to your other failings! He is a man as far above your touch, as you are above . . . well, above Dick Simondson. So it is missish silliness to blush over his manly perfections of body and looks when he would not think twice about the plain little vicar's daughter." She glanced down at her disarrayed nightrail, now stained with road dirt and blood. Well, it was time to start looking like the vicar's spinster daughter she was, rather than some gothic heroine from a tale by Mrs. Radcliffe.

With a smart nod and a pat for the slumbering gentleman's hand, she rose and gathered some of her things together. She would not weave fanciful dream tales about the man lying so helpless on the bed, not if she was as sensible as she thought she was. And yet, before she exited she glanced back. He was the kind of man females were apt to act foolishly over, she thought, leaning against the doorjamb and watching him slumber. It was written in the tumble of black hair, the breadth of his shoulders, and the length of his strong limbs. No doubt in the drawing rooms and salons of London he was a gentleman the young ladies would swoon over.

But not her. She straightened. She was certainly not the swooning type, for how foolish would that be for the vicar's unwed daughter? She chuckled to herself at the fanciful turn her mind had taken over an injured, sleeping man who would most probably be peevish and whiny and distinctly unlikable when conscious. He would probably awaken from his ordeal moaning and grumbling and whimpering over the level of care he was receiving, and would demand to be carried off to London and the care of a Harley Street physician.

Yes, that would be the end of it, no doubt, and if he was not whiny, then he would likely be sullen or haughty or be encumbered by one of any number of failings that would turn her romantical musings into so much dream-castle fluff. If there was anything she had learned in her twenty-seven years on earth, it was that folks seldom lived up to the impression one gained of them while they kept their mouths shut.

Humming the Scottish air, she left the room and climbed up to the attic room she would be sharing with Sally during their visitor's stay.

Three

His first and most overwhelming desire was never again to move, to stay exactly as he was for the rest of his life, however short it would be; the pain he suffered would seem to indicate he was not long for the world. His second thought was that he had an urgent need to move, for very personal reasons, but didn't know if he ever would be *able* to.

Breathing in hurt; swallowing hurt; flexing his toes hurt; *everything hurt!* Ah, but there was a fresh scent in his nostrils that he could not identify, something sweet and tranquil and quaint, taking him back to a childhood memory of a maiden aunt who had tended him once when he was sick and had to be taken out of school. She had sat by his bedside when he was at his fevered worst and bathed his hot forehead with lavender water. It was the first and last time he had experienced from a woman tenderness that did not demand a return.

But that lavender—could it be that it was he who smelled so . . . so maidenly?

Other scents overtook the lavender; the scent of country air, a mix of horse and flowers and grass and . . . and bread baking somewhere. Hardcastle reluctantly opened his eyes, though he did not feel able to move, and saw above him a papered ceiling, low and slanting, and off to his right a window that jutted out under the eaves. It was open, and a bird sat on the sill and chirped with an air of impatience. It hopped along the sill and with a flutter of downy wings was gone. It was through the window that the varied scents were wafting. Somewhere someone sang, in a sweet if untuneful voice, some Scottish air that he thought he might recognize if the singer were more on key.

He closed his eyes again and drifted for a moment, or an hour, while the scents and the sounds washed over him. In the distance a cow lowed and there was the splash and creak of a bucket in a well. A voice called out something and was answered, and then the humming began again, that Scottish air—

He was not home, but he did not know where he was. Nor did he care. Here there was a measure of comfort in the midst of pain, and the knowledge that at least he was safe and alive. And cared for. Someone cared and would look after him.

Then he could hear a light step in the hall outside the room in which he lay, and the door squeaked on hinges that needed oiling. He opened his eyes again. From his position on a bed he now realized was feathery soft, he saw a feminine bottom push open the door and back into the room, and then a young woman, a maidservant by the look of her clothes, carried in a tray.

If he could have he would have spoken, if just to ask where he was, but he was strangely bereft of curiosity, and voiceless, too. For that moment he was content just to lie in one spot, for any tiny movement seemed to hurt abominably. The girl approached the bed and set the tray on the table. She crouched at the bedside, even with his line of vision, and gazed at him with a crinkled brow.

She was pretty, he thought, and familiar to him in some way, though he could not quite place her. Somewhere, sometime he had seen her before. It was just at the edge of his brain, but the effort hurt too much. He would no doubt remember when his mind was clearer.

She sat down gingerly on the edge of the bed, and his muscles screamed with pain. But he couldn't utter a sound. To his alarm and embarrassment he felt his eyes water, and command it to stop though he would, one tear trickled down out of the corner of his eye into his hair.

"You are no doubt in abominable pain," the young woman said, and he revised his opinion that she was a servant. Her voice was sweet and cultured, touching him with whispery comfort. He tried to nod, which only elicited another tear that made its way down the path of its brother.

"I have something here that will help. But first, you must take a little water. I cannot give you spirits, for we do not know if you have a concussion, but I will not risk you becoming dehydrated, either. I do not expect you to move, but you must help me a little by swallowing what I give you."

She took a cup and a dropper, and gently tugging his chin down with one soft, small hand, eased the glass dropper into his mouth. A few drops of liquid that must surely be elixir of life trickled down his throat. He closed his eyes and felt the parched taste leave his mouth as she gave him more, just a few dropperfuls.

"And now something to take away the pain," she said, and some new liquid slid down his throat.

He opened his eyes again to find her watching him, her lips pursed and her gaze worried. A beam of light found its way into the room and lit up her coiled braid of golden hair. It looked like the aura he had seen in paintings of the Madonna in Italy. For one brief second he thought, *My angel. She is my angel.* But then drowsiness took over and he felt himself sliding into a dark place, not like the cold of the dark on the road, but warm and safe. . . .

The doctor could not come. Sally carried the news up the stairs to Phaedra that there was apparently an outbreak of fever in Fordham Wells some miles distant, and Dr. Deaville did not want to carry it further. The message had come from Joe Mudge, the butcher's lad, who had been told it by Dick Simondson, who had it from his employer, Squire Daintry, who had it from his daughter's friend, Anna Listerton, who had heard it from a shopkeeper in Fordham Wells. And as to Phaedra's other question, the answer was no, no one was expecting a gentleman fitting the description of the mysterious man on the bed. Anna's brother, the young Baron Fossey, had just arrived home the day before and would surely have mentioned if he were expecting company to follow him; he had not said anything of the kind. Nor was the man on the bed of an age to consort with a young man of three-and-twenty, for he must be above thirty, or five-and-thirty himself.

And so his identity would remain a mystery for the moment.

Phaedra smoothed back the glossy wings of dark hair from his brow—she had cleansed the road dirt from his hair as best she could—and felt the scruff of the beginnings of his beard as her hand caressed his cheek. She had been touched deeply by that single tear trickling down his face, one she felt sure he would be ashamed of if he were not in such great agony.

She had sent out the word that the highwaymen were getting more vicious in their attacks, for in the past they had contented themselves with robbery, not stopping to beat their victims so badly. But the local constable was stymied, and no one knew who they were, nor how to apprehend them. Mr. Hodgins felt that this gent had put up a struggle, or the robbers had feared he would, which explained the degree of brutality in the attack. And yet surely that stepping up in the level of their barbarism must signal their growing confidence that no one would apprehend them. They must be caught, and Mr. Hodgins was eager to talk to "the gent," as the injured man would likely be known until a name was forthcoming.

But no one would have access to him until he was able to talk. Standing, Phaedra gave her patient one long look and departed the room. It was time for Father's luncheon, and she had bread to get out of the brick oven in the yard. And she must see if the widow Mrs. Lovett would mind helping her with her patient. There was much work, as always, and not enough hours in the day.

He thought it had been a few days, for he remembered waking twice, or perhaps more times, when it was dark, and then when it was light again. And always his angel—yes, he thought it was the same, the angel from the morning he was beaten—would be there with water, or laudanum, or just a soothing word. There was another woman who came in occasionally. She helped him with more personal duties, her strong arms turning him to allow him to relieve himself, her no-nonsense movements seeing to his intimate cleanliness.

But his angel was there to administer to him in the night and in the morning, bringing him water and washing his face and hands, combing his hair. She hummed in that sweet off-tune tone he recognized as a part of his dreams, and she invariably patted his hand gently just as she was about to leave. He had drifted through those days, not sure what had happened, not remembering nor caring for anything but the relief from pain she brought with her, but now he felt his mind sharpening, coming out of a haze.

It was another brilliant spring—yes, he was almost sure it was spring—morning, and she was about to leave, after which, no doubt, the other woman would come in and see to his personal needs. But he caught her hand as she squeezed his, and she stopped, gazing down at him.

"Are you feeling a little more the thing, then?" she asked, sitting down on the edge of the bed.

He risked nodding, and though his head hurt, it did not feel as though it were going to split like a ripe melon anymore.

She smiled and it was as if a lamp had been illuminated behind her eyes, so light blue and glowing! No wonder he had thought her an angel, for her hair, a golden color and crinkly curly, had been down around her shoulders. How odd that he could remember not only the sight of her, but what he had thought and felt. He had thought she was an angel, and that he was dying. And he had wanted . . . He had wanted to be good enough that she would stay by him, had actually regretted some of his debauched and devilish life.

The delusions of a severely injured man. He had never regretted indulging himself in any and all pleasures of the body, and he was not going to start at four-and-thirty. He had had a rich and rewarding life of earthly delights.

She was gazing at him with a question in her eyes. "What do you want? Do you want to know where you are?"

Ah, she had guessed. She seemed to read his eyes.

"I am Miss Phaedra Gillian, and this is the home of my father, Mr. Phineas Gillian, retired vicar of this parish, and myself. I know it is odd for a vicar to retire, but my father is a gentleman and a scholar, and the rigors of preparing a weekly sermon were most detrimental to his health. You are in Oxfordshire." She paused and cocked her head, an appealing birdlike movement. "That meant something to you, did it not? There is something about Oxfordshire. Do you have family here? Friends?"

He shook his head slowly, painfully. What was he doing in

Oxfordshire? There was something . . . But taxing his brain was hurting too much. He let go of her hand and lifted his own hand to his brow.

"And now you need to rest some more. Mrs. Lovett will be in to see to your needs, sir, and I will bring in some broth for your lunch after you have had a nap."

In the hallway Phaedra accosted the woman coming toward her. "Mrs. Lovett, our patient is awake and on the mend, I most fervently pray. Do you have any idea who he is yet? Has anyone said anything about someone expecting a visitor? Or a family member?"

"No, Miss Gillian, not a soul, though all the village is agog, I must say. Such a handsome man, and so very . . . well, so very manly!" She hefted the water jug on her hip. "And now, if he is awake I should tend to his needs. Must say he is a cut above my usual patient in most ways," she said with a wink. "The personal business is not the drudgery it usually is. Rather like getting my hands on him." She chuckled and moved off toward the bedroom.

Phaedra flushed at the good woman's broad references to the stranger's physique. If Mrs. Lovett had a failing, it was a sometimes too-earthy sense of humor and an overly vigorous appreciation of male beauty. But then the woman was a widow and more was allowed of women of that class who were more experienced. But still! She really should think of whom she was talking to. Phaedra determinedly set her mind to thinking of other things, and went to see about the candle making Sally was attempting in the yard.

He was in a hot, dry place, parched and black, and yet he could not get away, could not move, it seemed. And then there was the scent of lavender, and he felt a small hand on his chin and a trickle of cool, delicious water wet his mouth.

Blessed relief! He opened his eyes to find his angel sitting on the edge of his bed in her white nightrail, with her hair down around her shoulders. There was a candle sputtering on the table beside his bed. "More," he whispered, and she gave him more, caressing his cheek with the palm of her hand after she had given him some.

She picked up the bottle of laudanum from the side table. "Would you like some of this? Would it help?" Her voice was a soft whisper in the darkness.

He shook his head. He didn't want the fuzziness that the medicine induced anymore. He wanted to see and feel and heal without it.

"That's all right, then. We won't give you any more unless you want it. You need only ask, sir, and it will be yours."

He nodded. She squeezed his hand and was about to stand, but he grasped her hand in his. "Stay," he managed, his voice a croak.

She sat back down. "All right. Would you like me to read to you? No? Sing? No? Talk? Ah, talk. Hmm. About what, I wonder." She gazed into his eyes, searching for some clues, perhaps, and then nodded. "All right. I will tell you about myself and my life, though there isn't a lot to tell. I expect you to reciprocate, sir, when you are able, for I am quite eaten up with curiosity about who you are and what you were doing on the road in the night. By the by, the robbers who did this to you have not yet been apprehended."

He shrugged. For some reason it did not matter. He closed his eyes and listened to her soothing voice as she told him about herself.

Phaedra thought for a second. She had suggested telling him about herself because in his position, she would want to know with whom she was staying. But now she wondered what to say. Her life, to someone of his class, would likely be dreary. However . . . "I have lived here all my life, near Ainstoun. It is a dear place, with good people, for the most part, and I have been fortunate. My father was the vicar during my growing-up years, and my mother an exemplary vicar's wife. We lived in the vicarage, then, a rather larger house, and my father had two livings, so we did not do badly. I had a nanny, a formidable Scots lady with whom I still correspond, though she has gone back to her little seaside village on the Firth of Lorne." She gazed at her patient and saw the subtle changes that indicated he was relaxing, hopefully to sleep, for sleep was the best healing agent she could think of for his battered body. She reached out and smoothed his hair back and touched his cheek.

"My mother was a good vicar's wife, as I said," she continued, quieting her voice as his breathing took on an even rhythm. "She had a garden that I loved, and grew lavender and hollyhocks and herbs that she used to tend to the sick. I remember once when I was ill, she brought me in a broth of herbs and made me drink the whole cup, though I protested. I was well by morning, and ever after I always thought of her as 'the doctor.' My mother died when I was fourteen, and I still miss her every day. I miss having her here to talk to, and to ask advice of, and just to laugh with. My father misses her, too, and was never able to do his work so well after she passed away. 'Tis why he retired." Phaedra felt the tears well up in her eyes and dashed them away impatiently, then glanced at her patient. He was asleep; she could tell by the slow rhythmic rising and falling of the bedcovers over his chest. She leaned over, tucked them up around him closer, and kissed his cheek, the familiar brush of whiskers like her father's face in the morning.

"Sleep well," she whispered. "Sleep well, and may God have his hand in your healing, and may I help just a little."

Hardcastle awoke to the knowledge that sometime in the night he had passed some milestone in his healing, some point past which his body would begin to respond to his commands. It was small things at first. He could turn his head without pain, and move his legs—his bare legs, for he realized he was clad in a nightshirt considerably shorter than one made for him would be—under the covers, which he had not been able to do before without shafts of pain shooting through him. And though his first experiment with turning over onto his side elicited an involuntary groan from him, he did it.

Mrs. Lovett's help was still required, but now he was conscious enough to be embarrassed at the intimacy of her ministrations.

She gave him a wry smile, noting, perhaps, the reddening of his cheeks. "You'll not be needing my help much longer, I'm thinking," she said. "Pity. I could get used to nursing the likes of you. It's a fair change from tending to old Mr. Fogerty and his piddlin' in his pants if you don't watch him." She laughed at the expression on his face. "Don't be going shy, sir, for I have the feeling there's been many a woman handling what I've been handling. Mayhap not for the same reasons, but it's all the same in the end, I say. Women there at your birthing, women there in between, and women there to help when yer getting old."

Mortified by the indignity of being an invalid, Hardcastle had still not recovered his equanimity when Phaedra came in laden with a tray. She set it down on the side table, and gazed at him, head cocked to one side. Relief flooded her blue eyes. "You are getting better, aren't you?"

"I believe I am," he croaked. "Thanks to you."

Her face flushed, but she beamed a happy smile. "I am so

relieved. Doctor Deaville was not able to come but gave me some advice by letter, and I was so praying and hoping and . . . Well, you are getting better. Now, perhaps, you will be better able to answer some questions, for I have been terribly concerned about your family, and how they must be worried about you. I will get word to them now, if you tell me your name, and who to send to."

He cleared his throat, but the hoarseness would not go away. "I am—" A sudden reluctance to tell her his name, notorious as it was, overcame him. He had no way to know if a young woman of such limited experience would recognize it, but he did not want to take that chance. And yet he must. She had been so good to him. Exhausted, he croaked, "Lawrence—Lawrence—" But he couldn't say another word. He closed his eyes against the pain that was clogging his throat.

"Well, Mr. Lawrence, pleased to make your acquaintance. For now, I think you should have your breakfast; then you can dictate a letter to your family to tell them you are all right."

Drowsily, knowing he should correct her impression of his name but reluctant to do so, he muttered hoarsely, "I-I have no family. None."

He opened his eyes to find her gazing down at him with pity in her lovely eyes, and he caught his breath. What was it about her that even pity, an emotion he had rarely experienced and could not bear toward himself, was acceptable from her? Was it a sign that he was still very badly hurt that he did not mind her feeling sorry for him? It must be. He closed his eyes again, the effort of talking exhausting him.

"I am sorry, Mr. Lawrence."

He felt the bed depress where she sat at his side and he wanted to curl himself around her and feel her hands on his face, as had happened in the night. He remembered a few

36

times waking to her hands on his hair, or his face, and once he thought she had kissed his cheek. It was merely the comfort she brought him that he sought. Nothing wrong or weak in that, was there?

Her touch, when it came, jolted him with an unexpected streak of warmth through his battered body. She rubbed his shoulders, and he almost groaned aloud at how good it felt even as it hurt, how her small hands were kneading just the right spot, how she seemed to heal with her touch. But too soon, she stopped.

"I-I will come back shortly and give you your breakfast," she said, her voice a little higher than normal, and breathless. Her steps were quick as she left the room.

Four

"Miss Gillian, are you all right?"

Phaedra pulled herself up and took a deep breath, closing her patient's door behind her. She had just experienced a strange new feeling and did not know what to make of it, but she did not feel comfortable sharing it, especially with Mrs. Lovett, one of the village's most inveterate gossips. She was a good woman and invaluable in this instance, but still, the interpretation she was likely to make of it if Phaedra told her the truth! She must not reveal her susceptibility. "I am just fine, Mrs. Lovett. Are you still—I mean, should you not be getting back to little Susan soon?"

"Oh, my daughter will be just fine with old Mrs. Jones. The good lady is teaching her to knit, an' Susan is afire with her new skill."

"I'm so glad." Phaedra felt the unaccustomed flush leave her face and body, and relaxed. She felt a momentary urge to giggle, for if Mrs. Lovett knew of Mrs. Jones's past as the valued mistress of a duke, the good woman would have had second thoughts about the placement of her daughter there, but Phaedra had no qualms. It was ancient history, in relative terms, for "Mrs. Jones," as she had designated herself, had taken her generous settlement and retired more than twenty years before. Since then she had led an exemplary life and was even a valued supporter of the local church. "I will start Susan's cooking lessons anytime you want."

"There's no one with a hand for bread like you, Miss Gillian," the widow said. "Wife or servant, my Susan will have all the skills to be useful and happy."

"I so appreciate your help with Mr. Lawrence," Phaedra said, speaking obliquely of the trade of favors they had arranged, her baking skills passed on to little Susan in exchange for Mrs. Lovett's no-nonsense and extremely personal nursing. "I don't know what I would do without you."

"Speaking of which," the woman said, patting the pile of linens she had in her hands. "I was just on my way in to change Mr.—Lawrence, did you say?—Mr. Lawrence's bedsheets. Will you lend me a hand, or"—she stared into Phaedra's eyes—"or are you just going somewhere else?"

Under the older woman's shrewd gaze, Phaedra felt compelled to buck up and leave behind her ridiculous panic over the odd feelings she had experienced rubbing Mr. Lawrence's poor bruised shoulders. "Certainly I can help." She took a deep, bracing breath. She would not let unaccustomed feelings alarm her.

Phaedra's day had always been full, but now, with a patient lying helpless upstairs, she had no time to think, and maybe that was a good thing. Lunch for her father was one of her most important duties, though, for he would forget to eat at all if she did not carry it in to the library and sit down to eat with him.

"Father, lunch!"

"Eh, what?"

"Lunch," she repeated patiently.

"Impossible. We just had breakfast." The elderly man looked up from his book and frowned. His glasses sat down on the tip of his nose, and he looked absurdly lovable to his only child.

Phaedra set the tray down on the desk and pulled back the curtains to let in the spring sunshine. Her father's tendency to shut himself up in the gloomy closet that passed for a library in this tiny cottage worried her, but she did her best to bring him out and keep him connected to the day-to-day world. She threw open the window to let in some of the sweet spring air.

"It is past one, Papa. Time to eat. I have brought mutton and bread and a beef broth."

As always when forced to come back from his deep thoughts and research, Mr. Gillian was cheerful enough. "How is our patient, Phaedra, my pet? Up and about yet?"

"It will be a while before he is able to walk, I think. Mrs. Lovett agrees. The bruises on his back and legs are especially bad, and he needs some time to heal. No bones were broken, though, and that is a miracle. Mrs. Lovett and I just changed his sheets this morning, and he tolerated it all pretty well for one so damaged and is now sleeping comfortably. I just hope he is going to recover."

"Eh, young men are tough creatures. Not easily killed. I shall visit him this afternoon, if you will remind me, my dear. Do you think that is wise?"

Phaedra encircled her father's shoulders with her slim arms and laid a kiss on his wrinkle-soft cheek. "I think that would be a marvelous idea. By the way, he was able to tell us his name. He is a 'Mr. Lawrence,' but he says he has no family. Is that not sad?"

"Every man should have a family," Mr. Gillian agreed, patting his daughter's hand. "Without you, my pet, I would be lost. After Constance went to the Lord—" He broke off and shook his head.

Determined to bring a more cheerful tone to the luncheon, Phaedra sat down opposite him at the desk and turned

40

the topic to some of the villagers. "I took some of my new ointment down to Mr. Ferguson; he has that infectious toe, and I am worried about him. I hope Mr. Deaville will soon pass through, for I want to consult with him about the case."

"Perhaps the apothecary at Thame could send something?"

"Mr. Ferguson would barely even accept *my* help. I was lucky he did not toss me from the door."

With an affectionate look, Mr. Gillian said, "Not a single man nor woman in this village would toss you out, my dear child."

"And I saw Mrs. Boyer this morning," Phaedra said of the vicar's wife. Mr. Boyer was still referred to as the "new vicar," even though he had taken over when Mr. Gillian had retired more than ten years before. "She will be having her child anytime, I think. Old Mary, in the village, wants to help, but I think Mr. Boyer has religious scruples."

"He will put aside those scruples quickly enough when his wife is screaming in her labor and there is no one but him in the house," Mr. Gillian said with a chuckle. "How foolish it is to reject Old Mary's aid just because of her reputation. I happen to know her belief in God is as firm as her faith in herbal remedies."

Phaedra nodded in agreement, buttering a morsel of bread. "It is those silly Druidical airs she puts on. Scares the Evangelist in him."

Frowning, Mr. Gillian said, "Do not dismiss our ancient ancestors, my dear. 'Silly Druidical airs'? Faith in a higher power was theirs, even if it does not agree with our Christian faith."

"I did not mean to dismiss Old Mary's ways, Father," Phaedra said with mild tones. "Now, eat your bread and mutton." They ate in silence for a moment. "I have been wondering," she said, finally, "if Mr. Lawrence can describe the items he lost to the robbers, perhaps it will help in their recovery, for if anyone local has seen them, it will surely lead to the highwaymen."

"Could be, my pet. Could be. Speak to Squire Daintry about it."

At that moment, Sally came to the door of the library twisting her hands in her apron. "Miss Gillian, I didn't know what to say to—Miss Peckenham was at the door, an' I told her you was havin' lunch with your pa, but she said as how she would come in an' wait, and now she's a-snoopin' an' I didn't know how to tell her . . . I didn't know—" The girl broke off with a wail of consternation.

"It was just a matter of time," Phaedra muttered under her breath, putting down her bread and gazing in dismay past Sally into the hallway. She could hear the sounds of Miss Peckenham in the parlor. It was amazing, perhaps, that the woman had not come before this, considering how Mrs. Lovett had been asking around the village about her houseguest's identity. "I'll come, Sally. Go back to your chores."

With a pat on the shoulder for her father, who had absentmindedly returned to his book even while still eating his bread and mutton, she "girded her loins," much as Boadicea must have many centuries before, to do battle with the foe. Not that Miss Peckenham was the foe, she reminded herself; she was a good Christian woman. However . . .

With a determined smile on her face Phaedra sailed into the parlor, catching Miss Peckenham in the very act of mounting the stairs. "How nice of you to visit us, Miss Peckenham," she said.

The woman started and whirled, and Phaedra was forced to conceal a smile.

"Miss Gillian! Has that naughty maid of yours disturbed your midday meal? I told her I would await your convenience." Miss Peckenham, short, rotund, and with a tiny upturned nose and small currantlike eyes, had recovered her equanimity and seemed not at all fazed by being caught in the act of intolerable snooping. She had made an art of the time-hallowed position of village gossip. Once, many years before, she had been governess in one of the most illustrious houses in the nation, and she had been trading on it ever since.

She crossed the room and took Phaedra's hands in her own. Peering shortsightedly up into her hostess's eyes, she said, "I heard, you know, that you had rescued a gentleman from those dreadful highwaymen, and I just wanted to congratulate you, my dear, on your hardiness." She shuddered. "So intrepid! So brave!"

Phaedra sighed. "Miss Peckenham, please sit down and have some tea." She signaled to Sally, who stood at the door watching uncertainly, and then led the woman over to a settee. "I did not 'rescue' him, ma'am. Indeed, the robbers were long gone, for it was daylight." Phaedra bit her lip, wondering if the lady had pictured her dueling with a swarthy opponent over the fallen body of her patient.

Leaning forward, the older woman, glancing around the room as if the chairs had ears, whispered, "I hear he is—ahem—a very well set-up young man. Quite one of the gentry, according to Lucy Lovett."

Mildly shocked, Phaedra was speechless.

"I hear that he is—" Again, Miss Peckenham glanced around the room. "I hear that he is exceedingly well knit, so to speak. Lucy Lovett says that he is the finest specimen of—er—manhood, she has ever seen."

Good Lord, Phaedra thought. *Was Mrs. Lovett bragging? Or—or gloating?* "I-I really have not noticed."

"I was just concerned for you, my dear. A young man of the gentry, in this house, with you *alone?*" She raised her eyebrows and waggled them.

"I am not alone! There is Sally, and if you remember, my father is present at all times to offer me countenance." The maid, just as her name was mentioned, brought in a tray with tea and scones, and Phaedra poured for herself and her guest as the maid retreated hastily.

Miss Peckenham's expression, speaking, as always, told a tale of how little her father was thought of in the village as protection for Phaedra. Her little currant eyes were hard and bright, and she looked away from Phaedra's steady gaze after a moment and cleared her throat. She took a sip of tea and then set the cup back down in its saucer.

She turned her inquisitive stare back to Phaedra's face. "I came to offer my assistance, my dear. If, at any time—once the gentleman has gained consciousness, you know—if you feel the need for adult female companionship, I place myself at your service. I can move into a spare room and be your chaperon day and night, you see."

Phaedra bit back a hasty reply, framed as a sarcastic inquiry as to where Miss Peckenham thought the Gillians had tucked away an extra room in the tiny cottage, since the stranger had her room and she was sharing Sally's, up under the eaves. Did the inquisitive lady suggest bedding down in Mr. Gillian's chamber? But Phaedra's better nature surfaced. Miss Peckenham, for all of her gossiping ways, was a good woman, just lonely. Also, she subsisted on a very small pension and so her encroaching manners were often a way to survive, to cushion and extend her meager allowance.

"Thank you for your kind offer, Miss Peckenham, but I don't think—"

"The least I can do right now," that lady said, gulping

down the last hot swallow of tea, "is to see if I can identify the mystery gentleman." She rose and headed for the stairs. "After all, I did spend many years among the gentry, you know, and have not lost all of my faculties, yet."

"Ma'am," Phaedra said, setting down her own cup. "He is sleeping, and I would not have him disturbed—"

The older lady had already started her ascent, though, and Phaedra understood that to deny her was wasted breath. This was what she had come for, and she would not leave until she had accomplished her mission.

"Ancient saints preserve us," Phaedra muttered under her breath, but she followed in the tiny woman's footsteps.

Miss Peckenham found Phaedra's bedroom and opened the door, quietly, at least, Phaedra was glad to see. She tiptoed into the room and stood at the slumbering man's bedside, gazing down at him. Phaedra watched her curiously, and noted the flickering of expressions across her round face.

She knit her furrowed brow and gazed up at Phaedra. "What did Lucy Lovett say his name was?"

"She wouldn't have said," Phaedra whispered. "We just found out today that his name is Mr. Lawrence."

"Yes," Miss Peckenham said absently, staring fixedly at the sleeping gentleman. "But she did say. I spoke to Lucy as she was leaving your cottage to go to Mrs. Jones for Susan. She did say you had discovered his name to be Mr. Lawrence."

They both stood gazing down at the man. Phaedra watched him sleep and found she was smiling. His black hair was silky and clean, and the harsh lines of his face were softened. There had been times when pain had twisted his handsome face, but for the moment he appeared to be at peace.

Miss Peckenham grasped Phaedra's arm and drew her away from the bed. "But you see, my dear, he looks so very much like . . . Well, I shouldn't say, I am sure, but he is the very likeness of the third Earl of Hardcastle, you know, that terribly angry gentleman who was killed in a duel about the time I was governess in the home of the fifth Earl of Mannering's second son, Mr. Worth. I saw the man once, when he visited, and this gentleman is the very *image* of the third earl, down to the black hair and . . . and . . . well, his stature."

Phaedra pulled her arm from the woman's grasp. "Miss Peckenham," she said with clipped accents, "he is Mr. Lawrence, not some nasty Earl of Hardcastle; you can be sure of that. Really, what would an *earl* be doing on the road to Ainstoun in the middle of the night? And alone!" She shook her head, trying to bite back her impatience. Miss Peckenham was an elderly lady, she reminded herself, and liked to make herself important by her long-ago tenuous connection to the houses of the nobility. If she had ever caught a glimpse of this Earl of Hardcastle, Phaedra would be amazed. In softer tones, she said, "It is likely just a chance resemblance, ma'am. Nothing to trouble yourself over."

Miss Peckenham stared at the figure on the bed. Her hard little eyes held a troubled expression and her lips pursed. "I hope so, my dear. I truly hope so. The Hardcastle line is full of bad associations. I have heard . . . Well, I have heard from my London connection that the present earl is even worse than his father: wilder, more dissipated, a fornicator and a gambler."

And they said that wild imaginings were the province of the young, Phaedra thought. She barely restrained herself from rolling her eyes. Miss Peckenham's "London connection" was a niece who was governess to the children of a baron who rented a London house for the season every other year. "Do not concern yourself, Miss Peckenham, please," she said firmly. "This is no Earl of Hardcastle, and he is surely no danger to any of us."

As she exited the room, the lady murmured, "I hope so, my dear. I truly hope so."

It was dark. Why was it so cursed dark? For one wild moment Hardcastle feared he had lost his sight, but then he realized it was just that it was night, and his candle was burned low, just a guttering, flickering flame to give relief to the absolute darkness.

"You are awake." The voice was soft and velvety, like the gloom. Out of the murky depths of the room the young woman came and sat down on the bedside. "Are you feeling any better?"

He was, he thought. Somewhat. He nodded.

"Good. Will you take some of this broth?" She picked up a cup from the side table and held it to his lips.

Who would have thought beef broth could taste so delicious? He licked his lips in appreciation and drank some more. "Enough," he whispered, after about half the cup. She looked pleased, he thought, her lovely face alight with a soft glow. What a breathtaking young woman she was; he had not truly noticed it until now. Before this he had just thought her angelic, but now he saw that she was ravishing. There was a subtlety to her beauty, an evanescence that no painter would ever be able to capture. She was springtime and flowers blooming and fresh, sweet country air. She was untainted and—He stretched out one hand and touched her hair. It was soft, not at all what he had expected from the crinkly texture.

"Soft," he whispered. "Pretty."

Her face alight with a shy smile, she said, "Thank you, sir. Now go back to sleep. I hope you are feeling better." She rose, but he grasped her hand. "What is it?"

"Don't go," he whispered.

"All right," she said and she pulled a chair close to the bedside. "But you have to close your eyes."

He did. His mind drifted once more to the sweet maiden aunt—his mother's sister?—who had nursed him through that long-ago childhood fever. Had she been young or old? Pretty or plain? He could not remember. It would not have mattered to a nine-year-old boy. What he did remember was that she had smelled of lavender and had stayed by his bedside day and night. She had kept a cool cloth handy and had wiped his hot brow all through the night.

She had, he rather thought, saved his life, for in the school infirmary many boys had died of the fever that awful autumn. Had he ever thanked her? Was she still alive, perhaps? He did not think he had seen any of his family for an age, not even— Did he not have a sister somewhere? He drifted off to sleep wondering about that, and yet soothed by a gentle hand smoothing back his hair and a low, sweet, off-tune voice singing a Scottish air.

Five

"So this is our houseguest," Mr. Gillian said.

"Yes, Papa. I think he is feeling a little better this morning. He passed a better night, anyway, and took more broth than he has been able to so far. Mrs. Lovett remarked on his improved color." Phaedra smiled down at her patient. "Mr. Lawrence, this is my father, Mr. Phineas Gillian."

The rueful expression on her patient's face made Phaedra smile. "Yes, we realize you cannot stand and shake hands," she said, as if she understood him. "I will leave you two gentlemen alone, as I have a multitude of household chores to take care of and a lady 'with child' to visit."

Hardcastle watched her leave the room and then shifted his gaze to his pretty savior's father. Her teasing had hit far from the mark. Rather than wishing he could stand and greet his host properly, he had in that moment realized that, now with his recovering senses, he really should correct her mistaken impression of his name. But he found himself not wanting to and that had puzzled him until he thought that perhaps, dependent on her as he was, he did not want her knowing his past just yet. That had to be the explanation, for it could not be that he truly cared about how she felt.

Mr. Gillian dragged a white painted chair close to the bed and sat, sweeping the skirt of his outmoded frock coat out of the way. "Can you speak, young man?"

"Some," Hardcastle croaked, examining his inquisitor. Mr. Gillian's face looked a little like a wax doll that had been put too close to a candle flame and had melted into soft, sagging folds. But his expression had an unexpected sweetness about it and his eyes were bright and focused. His eyes. He really did not resemble his daughter at all—she must have gotten her ethereal beauty from her mother—but her eyes were from her father. His were just the same sky blue, if a trifle bloodshot.

"That is good. Phaedra surmised that perhaps when the villains accosted you, they managed a hit to your throat, for there is a bruise there, and it could be that which impedes your speaking. By the by, our good neighbor Squire Daintry has been informed of the robbers' villainous treatment of you. As has the constable, Mr. Hodgins. They both wish to speak to you when you are able."

"Was it—" Hardcastle tried to clear his throat, but found it would not clear. "Was it close to this house? How . . . How did it happen?"

"Ah, yes, it did happen quite near our home. I cannot believe how bold these fellows are getting, but it must be explained by the copse of trees that encroaches the road near our cottage; it is the only sheltered spot for several miles and the robbers would have used it to hide from view. We are a little lonely here, apart from the village. You were lying unconscious on the road, which is how our maid found you, and she fetched Phaedra, who had the Simondson boys carry you in here. Is that what you are asking?"

Hardcastle nodded and struggled to sit up against the pillows. He examined Phaedra's father with interest. A retired cleric. There could not be a gentleman in the width and breadth of England with whom he had less in common. And yet there was something about Mr. Gillian . . . "I am grateful, sir," Hardcastle croaked, not recognizing his own voice, so altered was it, "that you and Miss Gillian—" He could not speak more. It was getting too difficult.

"Think nothing of it," Mr. Gillian said, airily, waving one hand in the air. "Made us the center of attention in our village. Not our intention, but there you have it; not much to talk about in Ainstoun. Quite a page from Luke, eh? I must say, my daughter does practice what I preach." He chuckled at his own gentle witticism.

Hardcastle had to concentrate fiercely before he remembered back to his youth and the story from Luke of the Good Samaritan. He supposed he should be ashamed it took him so long to remember the reference, but a blow to the head made an easy excuse.

"So, sir, are you an Oxford or a Cambridge man?"

"Oxford," Hardcastle croaked.

His eyes wide, the vicar leaned over. "Balliol?"

"Magdalen."

The elderly man shrugged. "Good enough, I suppose. At least you are Oxford."

Hardcastle frowned. What the hell did it matter? And then he saw the twinkle of laughter in the man's eyes. There was some private joke there, some humor that he did not quite get.

"I say, do you play chess?" Mr. Gillian asked, his sagging face still lit with a beatific smile.

Hardcastle nodded. Of course he played chess. Every gentleman did.

"Marvelous. I will bring in my board and we shall rig up a way for you to play. Phaedra beats me regularly, but she is so busy lately that we seldom have the opportunity to match our wits."

Phaedra was turning out to be quite the little Jill of all

trades, it seemed. Hardcastle felt his eyes drift closed and couldn't seem to do anything about it. When next he opened them, Mr. Gillian was gone. And sleep beckoned.

Again nighttime, and he was awake. Lord, but the nights were long when one slept through the day. The door to his room opened and the familiar figure of his pretty protectress was outlined by the dim light of the candle she carried.

"I thought you might be awake," she whispered.

He watched her, an unexpected sentiment oddly like gratitude warming his heart. She was always there, just as he was bored or lonely or in pain; she seemed to know, and come to him. It was how his days and nights were broken up, with the visits and company of his angel.

"I have brought you a tisane. Old Mary in the village sent this over. It is a mixture of herbs, and is said to be good for the throat. Drink it."

She held it to his lips and he drank the repulsive mixture, palatable only because it was Phaedra who gave it to him. She set aside the empty cup with a pleased look on her pretty face. Her flaxen hair, lit into sparkling golden light by the candle, hung like a curtain as she bent over him, and he inhaled that faint lavender fragrance that clung to her.

"Now, sir, it is imperative that when you are ready to move about, your muscles have not atrophied from lack of use. Mrs. Lovett says that massage is efficacious for that purpose, and so I will massage at least your shoulders, though I do not think . . . That is . . ."

She trailed off in adorable abashment, and Hardcastle thought he had never seen a sight so sweet and lovely. He should find maidenly confusion revolting—no self-respecting rake would admit to finding an innocent alluring—but instead found it entrancing. He gazed at her steadily, but she

52

avoided his eyes at first, as she sat by his bedside, leaned over him, and set her slender fingers to work manipulating his muscles.

"This will improve the blood flow and that, apparently, is why it works," she explained.

Her face was growing pink from exertion. Or from something. He preferred to imagine the "or something." Blood flow, eh? Astounded, he realized that the blood was definitely flowing through his body, for her touch was doing strange things to his nether regions. He gazed up at her and finally caught her eyes. Ah, so she felt it, too; he could see it in the pink of her cheeks and the wide startled look of her gorgeous blue eyes. The intimacy of her actions, and especially since they were alone and it was the middle of the night, was arousing him with an unexpected rush of desire. Unexpected, but not unwelcome, first as a sign of his body's revivification, and then as an object for him to concentrate his mind on.

He wanted her. Or at least his body wanted her. But no, it was not a purely physical response, for he found the idea of making love to the pretty vicar's daughter appealing, as outrageous as it was. He was not one for virgins, nor for pretty but poor spinsters. But Phaedra Gillian, he suspected, was not in the usual run of vicar's daughters. Or perhaps he had just never spent the time to get to know one.

Oddly, dressed in her simple white nightrail and wrap, smelling only of lavender water, she appealed to him as no woman in recent months had—he who was accustomed to women wrapped in ermine, their limbs scented by costly sandalwood, jewels clinging to their exquisite throats! He had been without a woman for some time, by choice. One society widow and a couple of birds of paradise were casting out their lures for him, but he had not, as yet, succumbed. Had it been boredom? The knowledge that the affair would take on a certain numbing sameness? Perhaps.

But Phaedra Gillian—she was deliciously different. He could teach her things about her own body . . . Her small hands stopped, and she straightened. Still pink cheeked, she said, "I think th-that is enough."

"Thank you," he croaked. In the normal run of things it would be anathema to be beholden to someone, especially a woman, but this was different. He owed her, quite possibly, his life, and yet the burden did not weigh heavily. An obligation was there and he would find some way to make it up to her, but it could wait. It could wait. As his eyes drifted closed he felt her small hand caress his cheek and he turned his head so that his lips brushed her palm.

"Damn and blast," he muttered. "When the devil did they start putting sleeves in such awkward places?"

"I see you are feeling better." Phaedra stifled the smile that came to her lips as she caught her patient in the act of trying to pull on a robe that would be much too small, since it was her father's. She had brought it in and laid it on the bed while her patient was still asleep, but only with the idea of getting some notion of his size and whether it could accommodate his larger frame.

"I—" He had the grace to look mildly embarrassed.

"It is all right. Even my father—a vicar and generally the most patient of men—has been known to use the same words when recovering from a bad bout of the gout that plagues him. I find it interesting that gentlemen always get testier as they get *better* rather than more ill."

"It is the curse of men to be impatient. Ladies are much more serene."

"Your voice is sounding better too; that is good. The tisane I gave you in the night is said to have restorative qualitics for the larynx. As for your comment, I believe that women are just as impatient, but we have learned that impatience is a waste of energy."

"How philosophical," he replied.

Ignoring his bad humor, she said, "I truly am delighted to see you feeling better. Mrs. Lovett says you barked at her twice while she was shaving you."

"Damned woman doesn't know how to handle a razor. Only men should be entrusted with that task."

"Which brings me, circuitously, to my next point. Now that you are feeling better, I must ask who I may contact. There must be people looking for you, alarmed for you. Family? Friends? Even servants? I assume the man who usually shaves you is your valet."

Hardcastle shifted uneasily under her bright stare. This was a point concerning which he could not feel comfortable. He abhorred any kind of subterfuge or underhandedness, and yet he was engaged in deceiving this young lady, and for no good reason other than—well, other than the fact that he did not want to see her warm blue eyes turn glacial when she learned his true name and the reputation that went with it.

It was a new and unwelcome feeling, this regret over his past, but it was just that even a village spinster like Phaedra Gillian would have heard of the infamous Earl of Hardcastle, for he had drunk and gambled and womanized his way across England and half of Europe, and when she found out who he was, and remembered all the stories she must have heard—or was he being conceited? Maybe she had never heard of anything outside of her village.

He watched her rearrange his side table, her small, neat figure tidy in an old blue sprigged muslin. What was it he wanted from her? In the night when she had come to his bedside, a new sensation had coursed through him at the gentle touch of her hands as she massaged his shoulders. Spontaneous arousal from the merest touch of a female had not happened to him for some time. It usually took some skill and concerted effort for his light o' loves to ready him for lovemaking—an effort they willingly expended given his generosity—and yet Phaedra's lightest touch had sent his temperature up into the fevered range, and caused him to have erotic dreams of making love to her in a field of lavender.

However, the moment she learned of his true identity her sweet expression would freeze into disdain and he would be treated with frigid courtesy from then on, if he was not thrown from the Gillians' home as an unworthy tenant. It was a strange feeling to regret portions of his life, but he would give much if he could erase some of his blackest moments, his darkest dissipation. It would certainly ease the road to seduction if she did not hold him in contempt. Did he really mean to seduce her? He was mightily tempted, but if that was his aim, it would have to be approached with utmost discretion and surpassing skill. She must never discern his intentions.

And none of this woolgathering solved his current dilemma—how to avoid telling her his identity without causing her to become suspicious of him. She stood eyeing him with barely concealed impatience, waiting for him to name some family member or friend she could contact with the news of his whereabouts. But there truly was no one, besides his household staff, who should be told. And they knew not to expect him for some time, for he had gone off before on a whim, occasionally with some new light o' love, to disappear for weeks at a time.

"There is no one," he said, and watched pity sadden her eyes.

"I am sorry," she said. "No family?"

He shook his head mutely.

"Well then, what about staff? You must have servants, someone . . ."

He shook his head again. "I . . . They knew I was leaving for some time. To tell them my situation would only distress them. But . . . But if I am become burdensome to you—" He tried to move to get up, but she quickly put out a staying hand, just as he knew she would.

"No, Mr. Lawrence, no. You are no trouble, I assure you. If there is no one worrying over you, then my mind is at ease and you may rest and recover here as long as you need to."

He relaxed back. Ah, yes, just the invitation he sought. Why did he feel uneasy rather than complacent, then? He should tell her his real name. Never before had he engaged in subterfuge or misled anyone. It went against his character and made him uncomfortable.

On an entirely different track, it occurred to him to wonder what would he be thinking if he were a different man. He was in bed, tended intimately by a lovely young lady who attracted him as no woman lately had done. She was so many good things: lovely, intelligent, compassionate, good-humored. He had lately been wondering what it was that caused a man—a sensible man—to fall in "love," whatever that vague word really meant. He had watched an acquaintance, the now-infamous Lord Byron, court and eventually win a girl much like Miss Gillian. The former Annabella Milbanke, now Lady Byron, was pretty, good, and intelligent—at least so he had been told—but she was also unrelievedly humorless. And yet Byron had gone to some lengths to woo and win her, her first rejection of him only spurring him on to greater attempts to win her love.

What made a man of Byron's brilliance and disposition as a rake and a gambler fall in love with a woman of Annabella's character? And why had he, Hardcastle, never been similarly tempted?

Of course it was a misalliance from the start and had ended badly. She had attempted to "redeem" Byron, which just drove him to greater lengths and deeper depths. Redemption, it seemed, was a treacherous path. Just a month before Hardcastle had seen Byron off, accompanied by a party of his friends, to Dover, from which the author and bon vivant took a boat to the Continent to escape the encroaching gossip and soul-destroying rumors that haunted him—justified or not, Hardcastle was not willing to judge. A fatal and ill-conceived desire to be "redeemed" had destroyed the man's life. He was no longer welcome in polite society, when once he had been revered and lionized. It was a depressing, wearisome business, and Hardcastle turned his thoughts away from Byron and toward Miss Phaedra Gillian.

As he watched her, she finished her tidying and bent over the end of his bed, tucking in the covers more securely. He admired the curve of her bosom and the arch of her neck as any connoisseur of feminine beauty would. Would another man in his position—a man of less rakish leanings, perhaps—instead of just admiring her form and thinking of seduction, be falling in love with Miss Phaedra Gillian? She was the spinster daughter of a retired vicar; a marital alliance between them would be outrageous to many in society, but not outside the pale. She was undoubtedly cultured and of good family; her father was poor, but intelligent and well educated. A man could do worse in a father-in-law.

". . . and Old Mary, in the village, she is a real character. Some of the children are frightened of her, and I have always wondered . . ."

She bustled around, talking to him as she brought some books to within his reach. She was trying, he could tell, to take his mind off of his "lonely" life by telling him of some of the village characters. Her idle chatter left his mind free for these unusual musings.

Like, what would it feel like to be falling in love with her rather than just desiring her? He had no idea, and yet better, wiser men than he had fancied themselves in love.

He drew back from the idea as from a scorching fire. He had never intended to marry, never wanted to marry, not even for the succession. He was not applying to himself those wild musings on love, it was some other unnamed, unimagined gentleman he was thinking of. For himself, he would be content with *making* love to her just once. It would be like sampling a wine one had never tasted before, a country wine distilled in a private cellar. One taste would likely be enough for him to acknowledge that his palate was too jaded, that he needed the fine skills of a London courtesan to entice him.

But he did relish the thought of that one taste. He followed her progress as she chatted and tidied and made everything neat. She was attracted to him, he thought, remembering her blush the night before, and the certain softness when she gazed at him. He would use that, play upon it. But it must be the most delicate dance of seduction he had ever embarked upon. One false move, one misstep, and she would comprehend his intentions and the dance would be over.

With a touch of shame at the depths to which he was willing to sink to further his plan, he gave a stifled moan of pain. Phaedra rushed to his side. "Mr. Lawrence, you poor man! Here I have been chattering away insensible to your pain. What can I do to make you feel better?"

Hardcastle looked up into her heavenly blue eyes and thought that if he was truthful, she would run from the room—no, she would slap him and *then* run from the room. The truth would get him nowhere, and he realized that he was quite willing to use subterfuge instead. He had not thought himself so low, but there it was. His desires, it seemed, were stronger than his conscience.

And yet he had always prided himself on his honor. It was the one point upon which he was inflexible. Where would this strange interlude take him?

Six

"Deborah!" Phaedra welcomed her guest with warmth. She had known Deborah Daintry from that young lady's birth, and had been amazed at the transformation in the last year, from boyish hoyden to delicate young lady of beauty and flawless dress. Today's outfit was a springtime confection in pink percale over a white muslin chemise with small bunches of silk roses and green ribbon leaves gathering the skirt up into deep swoops of fabric. Her bonnet was a masterpiece that no local milliner had created, a sweet turban that perched over Deborah's dusky curls. Two pink-dyed ostrich feathers nodded jauntily at Phaedra. It was a creation clearly direct from London. Which reminded her—"What are you doing back in Ainstoun? I had thought you in London for the season."

The young lady's brow furrowed. Absentmindedly, as she entered the hallway and followed Phaedra into the parlor, she tapped her parasol against her leg as if it were a riding crop. "Charles left London suddenly, and I have come home to find out why. His closest friends are not talking to me; they would not tell me why he left. It is most annoying."

She spoke of her childhood sweetheart, Charles Fossey, now Baron Fossey since his father's death the previous spring. Her green eyes darkening with annoyance, she went on, "I cannot imagine what is wrong. He was to escort me to

Almack's—Almack's, Phaedra; can you believe I received tickets?—but sent me a note saying he was going home immediately. So after trying to worm out of his friends what prompted his sudden departure, I came home, too. I rode over there yesterday afternoon, but if you can believe it, I was turned away! Some nonsense about fever in the house!"

"I am sorry, Deborah. Come and sit. Let us have a chat." Phaedra rang for Sally and ordered tea. She was not quite sure why, but with Deborah, one of her oldest friends, even though there were some years between them, she could not bring herself to bustle around like a housewife making their tea as she normally did when it was any other guest. It galled her to always wonder if the girl was looking down her charmingly retroussé nose at the "poor vicar's daughter." Even more galling, though, was that she could be so shallow. Deborah had truly never given her reason to feel the difference in their stations. The girl was kindness itself. Before going off to London she had brought over a trunk full of her old dresses, telling Phaedra that she had far too many, and since they were of a size she thought someone might as well get use out of them. Phaedra was grateful—she really was— and did not mind *too* much the remarks some made about recognizing the dresses from Miss Daintry's previous season.

But the girl had been chattering away and she had not been attending. Sometime in the intervening minutes the subject of Deborah's chatter had changed to the stranger in their midst.

"—and so I told Mrs. Lovett that such a grand gentleman could not possibly be simply Mr. Lawrence, and that I wondered if he had received a blow to the head and did not know who he was."

"Our patient is quite coherent, Deborah, I assure you." She chuckled to herself at the girl's romantic imagination. "I suppose, like Miss Peckenham, you are imagining him to be the dastardly Earl of Hardcastle, even though that man has been dead these long years."

Green eyes snapping with curiosity, Deborah said, "Miss Peckenham has seen him and fancied some resemblance to the old Earl of Hardcastle? What she cannot know is that the new earl—not so new; it has been twelve years or more, I suppose—is accounted to be the very image of his father, only even more wicked!" Her voice hushed and she leaned over. "It is said that he has never seen a woman he will not bed!" She shrieked with laughter and covered her mouth. "Is that not delicious?"

"No, that is scandalous," Phaedra said, deliberately squelching Deborah's high spirits. It was one of the things she found reprehensible in the girl, her willingness to listen to gossip. She would be as bad as Mrs. Lovett and Miss Peckenham given time.

"Do you not love a rogue? I thought every woman did," Deborah said, with a sly smile on her pretty face. "If I were not devoted to Charlie, I would be susceptible. The earl is very, *very* handsome, I assure you. He is said to be able to seduce a maiden with the merest look of his black eyes."

"Black—" Phaedra paused. Black eyes. Well, many men no doubt had black eyes. "Where is Sally?" she said, glancing impatiently toward the partially open door. How long did it take to make tea? "Excuse me, Deborah, but I must go see what is keeping that girl."

She bustled back to the kitchen to find Sally leaning against the doorjamb, giggling at some witticism the butcher's lad was making. "Sally, we are expecting our tea!"

With a guilty blush, the young maid skittered back into the kitchen with just one flirtatious glance back at jaunty Joe, who went whistling about his business, which was certainly not delivering anything to the Gillian household! It was only Monday and they did not get their Sunday joint of mutton delivered until Friday. It was surprising, though, how many times Joe Mudge just happened to be "passing by" on his way somewhere.

Feeling ashamed of her shrewish behavior toward Sally, Phaedra made it up to her by staying for a moment and preparing the tea tray, laying out some of her best linen napkins and china teacups, and filling a platter with a pretty spread of scones, thick-sliced bread and butter, and blackberry jam. She directed Sally to bring it to the parlor. But when she returned to announce that their tea would be there momentarily, it was to an empty room. Where had Deborah gone? She waited a moment, but at a sound from above she gathered her skirts and raced up the stairs in unladylike haste.

There, at the door to her room, was a wide-eyed Deborah just ready to enter.

"Deborah Daintry," Phaedra hissed, "don't you *dare* bother my patient." She pulled the girl away and headed with her back down the stairs. "You did not awaken him, did you?"

"No, Phaedra, but, oh!" Deborah hopped as they reached the bottom of the dim stairs and clapped her hands together. "How can you not know? Your patient is no Mr. Lawrence! It is the Earl of Hardcastle himself—'Hard-hearted Hardcastle' as he is known to all! I know, for I happened to see him once. He must have had a blow to the head and lost his memory to tell you he is mere 'Mr. Lawrence,' for it is the earl himself, I assure you."

Hardcastle awoke to the crash of a tray on his side table. "Wha—?" It was Miss Gillian at his bedside and, dazed, he smiled up at her. "Is it time for my midday meal, already?"

"It is."

Watching her for a moment, Hardcastle thought something had occurred; she was not acting herself. Her movements were jerky and awkward, with none of the grace she had always shown. What was wrong?

"Smells wonderful," he said, watching her, noting the little glances she cast his way as she moved the unused laudanum bottle to the washstand. He was adept at reading women, he had always thought, and if he did not know better he would think that she was longing to give him a scathing tongue-lashing. But that did not accord with what he knew, so far, of Miss Phaedra Gillian's mild temperament.

"It is merely beef broth with bread and some cheese and pickle," she said stiffly, laying a napkin out over the quilt. "Homely fare, not worthy of much notice." Her cheeks pinked as she said that, and she glanced at him with a fulminating look.

"Miss Gillian, have I offended you in some way?" He shifted uneasily on the bed and groaned at the twinge of pain that shot down his back.

She immediately crouched at his side and gazed into his eyes. "Are you uncomfortable, sir? Do you need to move?"

Now *that* was better. She was back to being solicitous. He gazed over at her, thinking how pretty she looked with her cheeks still pink and her blue eyes full of worry. She was adorable, but not in any childlike way.

"I am still in pain, of course, but do not worry about me, please, Miss Gillian." He had not meant it to, but it did sound rather plaintive.

She bit her lip and looked away, then directed a more open gaze into his eyes. She took a deep breath, and said, "What is your name, sir? Your true and complete name?"

Damn and blast. So that was it. Someone had twigged to his true identity. He frowned. "I am Hardcastle. Have I never told you that? Lawrence Jamison, Earl of Hardcastle."

Her eyes widened. "Earl of—" She stopped. "Oh, Lord." She sat down abruptly on the bed and stared out the window, where a small bird—the same constant visitor—hopped on the ledge and twittered. "Y-your first name is Lawrence?"

"Yes," he said, watching the play of emotions over her face. Would she accept that he really had not meant to mislead her—or had he?—or would it require an explanation?

"But you let me continue calling you 'Mr. Lawrence.' What a fool I have been!"

"How a fool, my dear?" he said, finding himself unexpectedly chagrined that his deception had caused her such consternation. "You did not know. I . . . To be truthful, it was an honest mistake at first. I was groggy. But then I did not want you to feel—I was concerned—" He shifted uneasily, and her hands automatically went out to fluff his pillow and help him settle more comfortably under the hand-sewn quilt. He caught her hand in his own and she gazed down at their twined fingers. "I did not want to distress you. This ridiculous title—I worried that it might hinder y-your sweet, unaffected generosity. It tends to make people stiff and formal, and I did not want that." He found that some of that, at least, was true. He did not want her to put him at a distance.

She smiled. He sighed with relief, finding himself unexpectedly concerned that she not toss him from the house. It was not his physical condition that worried him. With the help of his serving staff and a London physician, he was sure he could be removed to his London house with little suffering, but he did not want to leave. Not yet.

"I thought—" She stared back down at their entwined hands, and her cheeks flushed a deeper crimson. He watched her face, entranced by the flicker of emotions that twitched her lips and fluttered her eyelashes.

"I worried," she continued, "that you were secretly laughing at us—at our simplicity, at our . . . oh, our country ways and country food." She pulled her hand from his grasp.

"I would never laugh at honest goodness such as yours. How could you think it?" And that was true, too. He was not one of those so puffed up with London manners that they found country ways ridiculous. No one with her dignity, composure, and perfectly elegant, if relaxed, manner should worry about being an object of laughter.

"It was just a shock, I suppose. I had no idea . . ." She trailed off and left unsaid what she had no idea of.

"How did you recognize me?" he asked. In a curious way it was a relief to have the truth out.

"Miss Deborah Daintry, a young neighbor and a friend, recognized you immediately. You made quite an impression on her in London, though she seems only to have seen you from a distance, never having been introduced to you."

No, she wouldn't have been. London mamas and chaperons closely guarded their chicks when he was around, not for fear that he would debauch them, for he had never been in the habit of seducing little misses in their first season. It was his reputation that preceded him, and London matrons looked at him with a skeptical and knowledgeable eye. They knew that even to be asked to dance by such as him threw into question a young lady's character. Not that he often asked the young girls to dance. He was more likely to be prowling a ballroom looking for a willing widow or wanton wife. And how much of this had the precious Miss Daintry offered to her friend?

"I see," he said. "Though I am at a loss to know what Miss Daintry was doing up here in this room."

"She is an enterprising girl, and you must know the whole village has a curiosity about the Gillian household's mystery man. We-we did not know who you were, you see; we were trying to find out who you were as we were concerned about family, friends—"

"And instead you find I have none to worry about me."

She frowned. "How is that? Surely you have *some* family, somewhere?"

Hardcastle thought about his family, such as it was. Living, there was only his sister, and she was older, married, and ensconced in comfortable middle age on an estate near the border with Scotland. He had not seen her in ten years, though she faithfully sent a package every Christmas with a letter asking the same question; when was he going to marry and carry on the family name? "I have a sister," he replied. "But we have not spoken in years."

"I see." She stood and gazed down at him. There was indecision on her face, but her next words were merely, "Your lunch is quite cold by now, I imagine."

"I do not mind it cold, Miss Gillian. I-I suppose now that you know I could easily order my serving staff to come get me, I should unburden your household—"

She shook her head. "No. Do not worry, Mr.—uh, Lord Hardcastle—"

"Just 'Hardcastle,' please, Miss Gillian."

She laid one hand on the blanket over his stomach, and he felt his muscles contract involuntarily at her touch. "I feel . . . You will laugh, but I cannot help it. I truly feel you will recover best if you do not attempt the move back to London, but . . . but also—" She broke off and searched his eyes. "I feel as if you have been sent here for some reason."

"You think brigands and robbers were sent to accost me?" he said, laughing. "Oh," he groaned, holding his ribs. "That hurt. I am not well enough even to laugh yet."

She grinned, and Hardcastle caught his breath. It was like sunshine poured from her when she smiled so brightly. "No, sir, I do not think God uses brigands and robbers to do his work. Or do I?" She cocked her head to one side. "I shall have to think about that."

It occurred to Hardcastle in that moment that the robbers *had* affected one thing; he had not made his way to that reneging whelp Fossey's estate, yet, to demand his due. Somehow, with the pain reviving in his back he could not care about it overmuch, but he would. He knew with a certainty borne of experience that he would. Dishonor always angered him. A small quiet voice asked if there was no dishonor in the pack of lies he had told Miss Gillian lately, and if it was not equally dishonorable to stay in the Gillian household under false pretenses, as he had been, draining their likely meager budget. Surely it was *not* the same thing. And it was all aboveboard now; the deception was over. He would make it up to them somehow.

Phaedra turned and picked up the tray. "I should get you some fresh broth. This will be cold by now." She rubbed her thumb against the tray handle and gazed down at her patient. "Y-you really are an earl?" she asked.

"I am."

Sighing, Phaedra turned back and gazed down at the man lying in her narrow bed. She should have known; there was always something about him. But those stories Deborah had told about him! "Lord—uh, Hardcastle—Deborah Daintry said . . . Well, she said—"

She caught the look in the depths of his black eyes; it was expressive of good humor, patience in the face of adversity, and oddly enough, *humility*. Yes, humility; he was not got up with his own conceit, nor was he the pompous prig she had always assumed the nobility would be. Surely his reputation could not be so very black. She had seen no sign of the vice that must be an innate part of so very hardened a rake, but she could think of no reason her friend would lie. However, Deborah *had* been known to exaggerate. That must be it, blessed thought! Deborah was retailing secondhand gossip and innuendo. She nodded.

"What is it, Miss Gillian?"

"Nothing. Nothing at all. I will be back in a moment."

Brooding, Hardcastle watched the door, thinking that lying as a helpless patient had made him a different man. In London, a simple country girl, a vicar's spinster daughter, for God's sake, would not have interested him. He had always preferred a knowing look in the eyes of his conquests, a signal that they knew what they wanted and they knew what *he* wanted, and were willing. In a London ballroom would her sky blue eyes and sweet, artless smile have him captivated as he was now?

Perhaps, but more likely not. More's the pity, he thought. Maybe if he had spent a little more time with the unaffected goodness of someone like Miss Gillian, and with men of Mr. Gillian's intelligence and good nature, he would not have so much in his history to hide from someone like his hosts. Wretched thought! There he was back at pure females and their redeeming qualities. And the knowledge that he had concealed so much from the Gillians. But he was not *hiding* anything; he just was not burdening them with the darker side of his exploits. That would be idiotic and pointless. And they might shun him; that would matter to him. Why, he still did not know, but it would.

He turned his mind from such thoughts. It disturbed him to think he was changing, that he was somehow a different man than the one who had rashly galloped down a country road in the dark. It had to be merely a temporary effect of his invalidism. Instead, he turned his thoughts to Fossey. Lord, how had he forgotten, over the last few days, his anger toward the young man? He supposed most of his forgetfulness could be put down to the pain and the laudanum. Even now that young dog was probably making plans to leave the country. One just did not renege on a deal, and a gambling bet was a deal. He moved uneasily in his bed and groaned aloud at the pain that now centered in his back.

A few more days. With luck, he would be up and able to ride—Good Lord, Pegasus! What had happened to Pegasus?

The door opened and he blurted out, "Miss Gillian, has anyone found my horse? He is black with a white blaze down his nose and two front socks; has anyone found him?"

"Don't know, young man. I should think Phaedra would be the one to ask." Mr. Gillian, carrying a board under one arm and holding a velvet sack in his free hand, entered.

Hardcastle, who had half raised himself, slumped back on the pillow. "Mr. Gillian, sir, how are you?"

"I am fine, Mr. Lawrence. You see, I remembered," the man said, proudly. "I remembered that you play chess, and that I promised you—or you promised me, I don't remember which—a match. I always keep my promises, though I don't often expect others to keep theirs—though most people generally do, quite surprisingly—but if you don't feel up to this, you must tell me to go straight to the devil."

Hardcastle blinked, speechless in the face of such a muddled discourse. "I would be honored to play you, sir, but I was asking—"

Phaedra reentered with the luncheon tray at the same moment. "Papa, his name is Hardcastle not Lawrence; it was my misunderstanding of his unconscious murmurings that led to the confusion."

"Oh. All right, Mr. Hardcastle. Any relation to the Earl of Hardcastle?"

"Papa, he *is* the Earl of Hardcastle."

"Oh. My, that was quite the monumental misunderstanding, eh, Phaedra, my dear? A real live earl in our home. How novel. Anyway, chess?"

And with that simple exchange the confusion was handled. What admirable people, Hardcastle thought, as Phaedra gave him his lunch and Mr. Gillian set up the chess board on the side table. The father and daughter kept up a constant conversation, their relationship relaxed and cordial, affectionate, even. What a difference from his own with his long-deceased father. The third earl was a miserly curmudgeon who begrudged every shilling spent on his heir's education and maintenance. And he was a dastardly cheat, besides. It did not bear thinking about.

As he ate, relishing the full flavor of the beef broth and the sharp cheese and fragrant bread, Hardcastle listened. The father and daughter had moved from talk of some village folk who required their aid and were now talking, oddly enough, about a theological point of some contention. Finally, Miss Gillian said, "Papa, we have spoken of this before. I defer, of course, to your greater knowledge, though it seems to me that Mr. Proctor is wrong in this case. If you feel you must consult the *Codex* to settle your difference of opinion, then of course you must go to London."

"Pet, I cannot go to London." The retired vicar cocked his head to one side and eyed his daughter. "You may think me abysmally ignorant of our finances, but I do know we have not the wherewithal to afford that luxury. We could not even pay the stage, much less a hotel and meals."

"Papa!" Phaedra threw her patient an agonized look.

"What?" He looked over at Hardcastle, then back at his

daughter. "You are chary of discussing financial matters in front of our guest?" He peered at the earl. "My lord, does this disturb you in the slightest?"

Trying to stifle a grin, Hardcastle confessed that it did not bother him at all.

"There, you see?" Mr. Gillian said in triumph. "He does not care that we are poor. Or at least, it does not affect his opinion of us."

"Papa!" Phaedra groaned and put her hands over her eyes.

"Pet! May I remind you that pride is one of the deadly sins. Humility in the face of God and others is essential."

Hardcastle caught the gleam of a wicked twinkle in the older man's eyes and realized he was roasting his daughter, quite deliberately teasing her. Knowledge dawned in him that the father and daughter could never do anything that would make the other not love him or her. Their bond was close and fast, stronger than the foundation of the Tower of London. It would survive even the grave, he had no doubt. It humbled him and entranced him and saddened him. What must that be like? How would it feel to know you were loved so greatly, so *adamantly,* that you could never fall from grace?

Avoiding Hardcastle's eyes, Phaedra said, "Papa, it is not pride, but not everyone must know of our . . . our finances."

"My dear," he rejoined mildly, "anyone looking around our abode would know in a moment of our circumstances. Many would be able to reckon down to a farthing our worth, and some have; no doubt, the worthy Miss Peckenham is among them. Being poor is not a sin."

"I know, Father," she said. "I know it is not."

But she did *mind,* Hardcastle thought, watching her go about her business, folding some clean but shabby towels by the washbasin. She would like pretty things, maybe, and to not have to work so hard. For she did work. Her days seemed to be taken up constantly with duties, large and small. She baked. The bread he ate was made with her own small but strong hands. He had gathered from Mrs. Lovett, who was garrulous even with a patient who could not speak much, that Miss Gillian cooked and sewed and superintended the maid in her duties; she made candles and soap and wine and preserves, prepared baskets for the poor, visited the elderly and sick, grew herbs in a small garden outside of the garden. In other words she was unrelievedly good and kind and perfect. *Irritatingly* perfect.

He bit back his irritation, which seemed to arise from some small pit of shame within himself that he was adding to her burden of daily duties, without even offering his own staff to relieve her. Somehow, some way, he would make it up to her. He never *ever* stayed indebted to anyone, even paying his tailor on time, much to the poor man's chagrin. It would have been a badge of honor to be able to say that the impeccably clad Earl of Hardcastle owed Taylor & Sons for the clothes upon his back.

To change the direction of his thoughts, he went back to his original concern. As Phaedra cleared away the remains of the lunch he had just eaten and helped her father move a low, small table from the hallway to the bedside for chess, he remembered his earlier concern and said, "I have just realized no one has said anything about my horse. It has been some days—four, is it?—since I was beaten. Has anyone seen Pegasus? He is a black stallion with a white blaze and two white front socks."

"I wondered about that," Phaedra said, straightening. "The Simondson boys, who work for Squire Daintry, say that a beautiful stallion has been sighted roaming free. For a reward I think they could be persuaded to capture it."

Groaning inwardly as he imagined two country bumpkins

trying to capture his spirited and willful stallion, he said, "I suppose, if they will be careful. Pegasus is used to only the best care. He is stubborn and strong, and will not stand for rough treatment. I will give a reward *and* pay generously for the care and treatment of him while I am laid low."

"I will relay the message exactly. Dick Simondson is a wonder with horses, and with the word 'generously' involved, I think I can assure you Pegasus will have all but a featherbed to sleep on at night." Phaedra chuckled, glanced at the two men, and shook her head as Mr. Gillian moved the chess board to the low table. "I will see you two gentlemen later. Enjoy your game; Mrs. Lovett and I have laundry to see to."

Seven

Rakehell.
  Rogue.
  Debaucher.
  Libertine.
  Rake.
  Standing near the old apple tree in the laundry yard beside
the cottage, Phaedra bent over a washtub and scrubbed,
feeling a slow flush that only had a little to do with the manual
labor of laundry mount her neck and face. Deborah Daintry's
words, after her shocking disclosure, floated through
Phaedra's mind: "able to seduce a girl with just a glance," "a
shockingly loose-fish," "famous as a rake of the highest
order." Pausing to swipe at a loose curl that insisted on dan-
gling down on her sweaty neck, Phaedra gazed up at the bedroom window where the object of her thoughts was
ensconced.
  The Earl of Hardcastle. Lord above, what was an earl
doing in her bedroom? In her *bedroom!* And not only an earl,
but an earl with a reputation, if Deborah could be believed, as
an infamous gamester and shocking libertine.
  The afternoon sun, warm on a spring day, beat down on
her and she wiped her hands on her apron, deciding to take a
break for a moment under the gnarled apple tree in the cottage yard. Mrs. Lovett had had to leave; Susan had some sort

of accident at Mrs. Jones's and needed her mother, and so the laundry was left entirely to Phaedra, Sally being engaged in butter churning at that moment. Phaedra slumped down on the seat under the tree and gazed down at her wrinkled, puckered hands with a frown. They were becoming quite callused, no matter how much mutton grease she used on them. Deborah Daintry's were white and soft, and her complexion was as pale and pretty as a lily. It was not fair.

And that kind of thinking made her an ungrateful wretch. She had so much when others had so little. Not fair? How could she think that, while she had a home and a father who loved her, and food to eat and decent clothes to wear? And more, she had her health, and her mind, and unshakable faith. What else could a woman want?

Love?

It had occurred to her over the years that even beyond society's expectation of a lady in her class, she would *like* to marry. It would suit her disposition to have a husband and family. She would have liked Deborah's opportunity to gaze about her and choose a gentleman she could love, a man who would share her burdens and with whom she could have children. But wishing for what was never to be was an exercise in futility and would only lead to dissatisfaction with her lot in life.

She leaned back with her head against the gnarled trunk and gazed up into the green leafy heights, admiring how the midday sun sparkled through as leaves and the last faded petals of the apple blossoms danced in the breeze. Her father had always said that destiny was a higher power at work in one's life, but she had never truly felt a higher power at work. She did what she did—helped others, was industrious in her home—because it was her life; the gratitude of others did not motivate her. She wanted to make a difference. She wanted, after she was gone, for people to say that Miss Phaedra Gillian, village spinster of Ainstoun, lived a quiet life, but she had made a *difference*.

"Hssst!"

Phaedra glanced around at the hiss to find Miss Peckenham crouched low by the old stone wall that enclosed the cottage yard. "What are you doing, Miss Peck—"

"Shhh!" Miss Peckenham, her eye on the house, bustled through the ancient gate and scrambled over to where Phaedra sat. She grasped Phaedra's hands and said, "My dear, it is not too late, I hope and pray. You must leave at once. Come stay with me. I will protect you."

Caught between laughter and alarm, Phaedra pulled Miss Peckenham to a seat beside her and said, "What is wrong? Why must I leave?"

"I have just heard from my girl, Flossie, who had it from Miss Daintry's maid, Ellen, that your, er—houseguest is *the* Earl of Hardcastle, the present one!"

Perplexed, Phaedra waited for more. When it didn't come from Miss Peckenham, who was casting shifty glances at the cottage, she said, "Why should I leave?"

Miss Peckenham, her beady eyes wide, pulled herself upright. "My dear, you are in danger! He is a libertine, a gambler, a-a-a fornicator!"

The last word was said with revulsion, but Phaedra thought she detected more than a hint of excitement in the quivering woman's demeanor. "He is my patient, at present," she said, firmly. She looked down at her faded blue gown and work-worn hands and pushed back a strand of hair that had strayed from her severe bun. "And really, Miss Peckenham, even if he were healthy and able to move on his own—which he is not, I assure you—what danger am I in? Look at me!" She held her hands up and away from her body. "I am the spinster daughter of a vicar, and I do much of my own scrubbing and cooking and . . . and . . . well, really! What temptation do I present to an earl? An earl who is no doubt sought by the most beautiful women in England, women much more accomplished and intelligent and . . ." Cataloging her various failings was depressing and Phaedra faded to a halt and folded her hands in her lap. She cast a glance up at the bedroom window and sighed. What she said was too true.

But Miss Peckenham gave her a dark look and said, "My dear, it only proves that you know nothing of the ways of the nobility that you should think that being plain or poor offers some protection. Why even I—" She stopped and swallowed, visibly shuddering.

"What is it, ma'am? Please, tell me. Are you all right? Shall I get you some water?" Phaedra took the woman's gloved hands in her own and felt them trembling. Whatever the cause, Miss Peckenham was moved by some powerful emotion.

"I have never told a soul this, my dear, and I must ask you to promise—no, to swear on your poor mother's *grave,* that you will never tell a soul!"

"Ma'am, you must know I would never make such an oath," Phaedra said quietly, truly concerned for the older lady's well-being now. "My mother's grave is sacred and I will not sully it with oaths. But you have known me from my cradle, and know I do not gossip. There is much a vicar's daughter learns that is not for general conversation."

"I know I can trust you, child." Miss Peckenham, tears in her eyes, reached up and patted Phaedra's cheek, the first time she had ever indulged in such a gesture. "So much like your mother!" she murmured. "She was so very good to me. I will tell you a story. It is a tale of a young and very plain girl, a governess in a good household. She was naive, yes, but intelligent and modest. There came a visitor, a very great man, an earl. He was a drunkard and a gambler, and a lout, but the governess did not know that, and . . . Well, she became entangled in a very awkward position with the rakish earl. When they were d-d-discovered, she was let go." The last words were said in a rush with a great woosh of air.

Her mind struggling to grasp the concept of a young Miss Peckenham in the lascivious grasp of an ardent aristocrat, Phaedra said, "I-I had no idea! I am so sorry."

The lady struggled to regain her composure and then said, "And that is why you must leave right now, this minute, with me!"

Phaedra shook her head and stared, puzzled, at the woman. "What? Why?"

"The acorn doesn't fall far from the tree, you know," she said in a whisper. She waggled her eyebrows and motioned with her eyes toward the upstairs room where Hardcastle was ensconced.

"Oh, you mean—Miss Peckenham, please do not concern yourself. The situations are so different! To begin, the earl is not his—I assume you speak of his father?" When the other woman nodded, she went on. "And I am not a girl friendless and alone among the nobility, as you must have been. I am in the home of my father, and he will protect me. And, too, the earl is injured, barely able to move. Until he is well again, he has a place here. He offered to have himself removed, but I do not think it is in his best interest."

Phaedra wondered if that last was quite honest. Why did she not want him to summon his staff and remove himself from the Gillian cottage? What she had told Hardcastle was quite accurate; she did feel that he was there for some reason, and had felt that from the first moment she had seen him on the roadway, helpless and bloody. But still . . . She gave Miss

Peckenham's gloved hands a squeeze and released them.
"And you were blameless in your dismissal. Even if folks in
Ainstoun were to find out, no one would hold you to blame, I
am sure." Nor care about something that had happened in
the last century, for goodness' sake, Phaedra thought but did
not say. Looking at the woman today it was hard to imagine
the former Earl of Hardcastle overcome with lust for Miss
Peckenham, but who understood the nobility? She did not in
the least doubt the veracity of Miss Peckenham's story. The
older woman had been reluctant to tell it and so fearful of it
getting out.

Miss Peckenham looked doubtful and still extracted a
promise from Phaedra to come to her if she needed advice.
Phaedra was touched by the sign from a woman many dismissed as a busybody, that she cared for a girl wholly uncon-
nected to her by birth. It was a lesson not to dismiss anyone in
life, for a fast friend was a valuable commodity; who knew
when she might need Miss Peckenham's help?

The former governess stood, composed herself, and with
one last, long glare at the cottage, bade Phaedra farewell.
There was no avoiding it. She had to go back to her labor. As
she scrubbed linens and wrung them out, she thought about
Miss Peckenham's story. How clear and unfaded it still remained in her memory, though it must have happened at least
twenty or even more years before. Though she had not elabo-
rated on her story, it seemed to Phaedra that there was an ele-
ment of force involved in the earl's violation of the young
Miss Peckenham. How frightened she must have been, and
then to have been let go! For a girl alone in the world and with
no one else to care for her, with only her own hard work as her
saving grace, it must have seemed like the end of everything
for her.

Was the present earl like his father, or even worse, as

Deborah had intimated? Was he a debauched reveler, a seducer, Satan in human form, as Miss Peckenham would no doubt name him? Or was he what he seemed—well-intentioned, gentle, good-natured? She was used to judging people by their actions, not by what others thought of them, but how much did she really know of his actions? She had only seen him in his present state, injured, unconscious most of the time, weak as a lamb.

Looking up at the window, Phaedra shivered at the light breeze that danced over her bare, wet arms. Was he a different man than the one he appeared to be to her? What was he, really?

Expecting to beat the vicar easily, Hardcastle had been puzzled and a little peeved to find himself checkmate within a couple dozen moves. It must be the pain fogging his brain, he thought. Or the distraction of thinking about a fair-haired angel who was in his thoughts far too much.

He moved his bishop, intent on positioning to capture the queen, and was startled when Mr. Gillian crowed, "Got you again, young fella! Check and mate."

"Damn and blast—uh, pardon, sir. How did that happen?"

"You are not yourself, no doubt, my lord," the older man said kindly. He cocked his head to one side, a mannerism common to both father and daughter, Hardcastle noticed. "Are you generally a better player than this?"

Hardcastle thought about it a moment. Chess was not his game of choice. He preferred something he could wager on. "To be honest, I don't think I am a much better player than I am this moment." He laid back against the pillow and regarded the gentleman in front of him for a moment. How did an ethereal beauty like Phaedra Gillian spring from the loins of such a foggy, frumpy gent as this? "Sir, if it is not too painful, would you tell me what your wife was like? Phaedra's—er, Miss Gillian's mother?"

The vicar glanced up in the act of scooping the carved wooden chessmen into the velvet sack. "What? Ah, Constance. You are asking about my Connie." He tightened the drawstring on the sack and stared at the wall with a fond smile on his face. "She was a gem, was Constance Leonora Allen—m'wife's name b'fore I married her, you know. I was a curate—poor, young, foolishly idealistic. Constance was better than me in every way. Family connections, wealth, opportunity. But we fell in love."

Hardcastle moved irritably on the bed. He wanted to know about Mrs. Gillian as it related to Phaedra, not about how the vicar and she met. He opened his mouth to speak, but Mr. Gillian was already talking again.

" 'Twas summer, and I was lucky enough to get the curacy of a Mr. Franklin Arbuthnot, in Shropshire. And there was Constance—daughter of Baron Darden—like some kind of angel; great bell-like skirts, walking through the long swaying grass, the brilliant sun making her hair like some kind of halo."

Hardcastle closed his eyes. Phaedra—he could see *her* walking through the long swaying grass, her skirts fluttering in the breeze, the afternoon sun making her crinkly golden hair like a halo.

Mr. Gillian's gentle voice continued. "I fell in love that first moment I saw her, coming through the meadow toward the church. I knew in that instant that everything had changed; my *life* had changed. I had not intended to marry. I received a fellowship—took first in Greek at Balliol, y'know—and it was almost my sole subsistence beyond the small wage promised a curate. And I sincerely felt my first duty was to God, but oh, how I wanted to believe that Constance would only enhance that duty, not distract. And yet it was four long years before we were able to marry."

Hardcastle opened his eyes. Despite himself, he was interested. "Why? Did she not love you back?"

Mr. Gillian smiled. "Oh, yes, she did. I did not know it for quite a while—a maiden will not make it obvious, y'know, if she is the right sort of girl—but she did love me. I will never understand why. No, we could not marry as there were family objections and financial barriers. She was sent away when it became clear to her father that she would marry no one but me. Those were different times, none of this modern notion of children arranging their own marriages, falling in love. She was promised already to another man, a powerful man. She could have had wealth, but she wanted me."

Silence fell in the tiny room as Mr. Gillian, swept back in time, smiled a gentle smile that radiated from his eyes as much as his lips. Hardcastle frowned and stared at the wall. This was the sort of romantical nonsense he had never believed in. "Falling in love." Ugh. When his friends spouted such nonsense he generally left the room, for there was nothing so idiotic as a man in love. And look what it did to them—what it had done to Byron, poor chap. And yet . . . He gazed again at Mr. Gillian's rapt expression. Here was a man of sense, of intelligence, and logic, judging by the way he played chess, and he believed in love.

"Sir," Hardcastle said, loath to break into the man's reverie but overwhelmed by curiosity, "you said it changed your life, your plans. How so?"

Mr. Gillian smiled. "I had great plans. I distinguished myself at Oxford, you know; took first in Greek, as I said, and in classical studies, too. I was going to be the one to definitively translate the Greek texts—if you are not familiar with the

Book, you may not be aware that there is some controversy surrounding the translation of the Book from Greek into English. I was the one who was going to solve that. I would have been content to live on my fellowship for the rest of my days so long as I could study the Book and work."

"The book? What book?"

The smile broadened. "Young man, you really should not display your ignorance quite so profoundly. Think to whom you are speaking. A vicar. To what Book would I be referring?"

Chagrined, Hardcastle thought maybe he ought to apologize, but the twinkle in the older man's eyes showed him there was no need. "Miss Gillian is a very lucky girl to have a father like you," he said without thinking. "I would have given much—" He broke off, confused that he had spoken his thoughts aloud. That was unlike him. And even those thoughts were unlike him. He moved restlessly, trying to find a comfortable position.

Mr. Gillian assessed him shrewdly. "Father not all he should have been, eh? But now you are the master of your own life. Your father does not control you anymore, and you can be whomever or whatever you please."

"And I am. I do what I want and go where I please."

"Do you?" Mr. Gillian cocked his head to one side. "Do you, indeed? Or do you do what you do, live how you live, to spite the old man, eh? Or to prove something to others?" He stood and picked up the board, tucking it under his free arm. "I forget you are still an injured man and my daughter will never forgive me if I tire you overmuch. By the way, as to what you said, I am the lucky one, m'boy. She is a rare one, is my Phaedra, a shining credit to her mother's upbringing. I am not perfect. I am one to try her sorely, I am afraid. But she bears it well. Good girl."

Mr. Gillian nodded and then headed toward the door. He turned, as he opened it, and regarded Hardcastle for a long moment. "Live your own life, young man. Make your own choices and live your own life, not your father's, not your friends', not your betters' nor your inferiors'. It is your life and the only one given you in this time and place. Choose wisely. Not my place to say of course, but it is what I would say to you. Choose wisely, your actions, your companions, your path. Get some sleep now. You're looking frightfully ragged."

Eight

Phaedra poked her head into the bedroom. Good. Lord Hardcastle was asleep and she could do a few things in the room without having to talk to him or feel his eyes on her. She tiptoed in and started tidying by moving away the table her father and the earl had used to play chess.

And inevitably she snuck glances at the man sleeping under her pristine white counterpane in her low, narrow bed.

He was handsome, more so now that the bruises were fading and the cuts healing. His black hair lay in careless waves across his broad forehead. He moved restlessly, and her gaze was riveted by the image of his powerful frame outlined by the covers as he twisted and turned in some kind of unsettled dream. His hands clutched and grabbed at the cover. She had never quite noticed before the strength in those hands, callused likely from hours holding the reins.

". . . kill you, you dogs—" he shouted hoarsely and flailed.

"Lord Hardcastle," Phaedra said, flying to his side and grasping his shoulders. "Sir, you are dreaming!"

"Wha—" His black eyes open now, he glared at her for a moment, and then his body relaxed, all the tension easing as his gaze sharpened.

"You were having a nightmare, my lord. Was it of those villains who attacked you?"

"Yes, only this time I gave as good as I got. I fear I shall never be satisfied until I do."

Phaedra kneaded his shoulders, feeling his muscles loosen. "Squire Daintry has hired extra men to patrol the roads, but with so many roads and so few men, I fear it is a lost cause. There have been no more attacks since yours four nights ago, though."

"They are probably still lying in a drunken stupor from the proceeds of that robbery."

"Did you have a lot of gold with you?"

"No, not much, but enough for them to get drunk on. Not more than a hundred guineas or so."

"A hun—oh, Lord, to be rich enough that I could speak so casually of a year's income."

Hardcastle stared up at her, and she suddenly felt self-conscious massaging his shoulders. She stopped and folded her hands together. Blood flow. She had just been helping him maintain the blood flow to his muscles. His splendidly *bulky* muscles. Mrs. Lovett had intimated that he was thus all over, a "right prime specimen of manhood," she had called him. And who would know better than a married, or formerly married, woman? Her face felt warm of a sudden.

"Do you long to be rich?" he asked.

His quiet regard was flustering her. Debaucher. He was a rake and a roué. How that knowledge had changed how she regarded him, even though she didn't want it to! She couldn't help it, though. It was as if she examined everything he said now, every glance, every gesture, through the lens of that knowledge.

But he had asked her a question. She considered it. "No," she said slowly. "No, I don't think I long to be rich." She must be honest, must answer truthfully. "Well, maybe sometimes. I would like to be able to help people more. There is so much good that money can do, and there is so much need. And I would like—"

"Some pretty new dresses," Hardcastle said with a smile.

Stung, Phaedra stood and patted down the old blue print. "I . . . No . . ." Confused, she turned away.

"No new dress could make you prettier than you are this moment, you know."

His voice was low toned and gentle and felt almost like a physical caress. Taking a deep and shaking breath, Phaedra stared at the floor, at the faded pattern of the ancient carpet. Seducer. Rakehell. He was practiced at using his words and voice to tempt women.

And then in the next second she chastised herself for being so utterly foolish. He was being kind, not flirting. Vanity. She was prey to it and it vexed her sorely. It was a besetting sin and she would not let it make her absurd. Stiffening her spine she turned back to him and smiled. "Thank you, sir. You are very kind."

He gave her a surprised look. "Do you think so?"

She chuckled. "Yes, I do. Why do you sound so . . . disbelieving?"

"Maybe it is because nobody has ever called me kind before."

"And nobody besides my father has ever called me pretty before," she responded, tartly.

"Then you reside in a village of idiots."

She could almost believe him when he spoke so fervently. Gazing steadily at him, she saw only honesty in his eyes, and yet, how could she believe that he was genuine? He was a practiced flirt, a rake, and if his words were not inspired by that side of his character, then he was merely kind. And it was easy to say a few words. Were not rakes insincere flatterers by nature? Or was it unfair to judge him based on the gossip that had been relayed to her by Deborah Daintry? She turned at a light tap at the door.

"Miss Gillian," Sally said, her eyes straying to Lord

Hardcastle, "Miss Daintry has arrived for a visit, and says—"

Phaedra waited. "Says what, Sally?"

The maid's gaze snapped back to her mistress's face. "Oh—" Her cheeks flushed. "She says she will wait for you in the parlor."

"All right. Thank you, Sally."

Sally was staring back at the man on the bed.

"That will be all, Sally," Phaedra said somewhat louder.

The maid, who had only been in the earl's room when he was sleeping, and then only to remove the slops, flushed an even deeper cherry and hustled from the room with a flip of her skirts. Phaedra wondered how much of Sally's fascination with the earl was with his personal attractions, which were considerable, and how much had to do with the rumors of his reputation, which had been circulated among the serving staff of the village by Deborah's verbose maid. What was it about the distaff half of society that was attracted, utterly and completely, to a rogue? She had seen the enchantment on Deborah's face when she discovered the identity of the Gillians's patient. And Deborah, more than Sally or even herself, had seen enough of society to know the heartache a rake could cause.

She turned back to the bed in time to catch a grin on Hardcastle's face. He must be used to conquering the hearts of maid and mistress alike, she thought sourly. "I must see to my guest, sir, and leave you to your own devices for a while."

"Miss Daintry is the young lady who flushed me from my covert, is she not?"

"She is. I will return with Mrs. Lovett later, Lord Hardcastle. It is time you were up and about, Mrs. Lovett thinks, and I concur."

"I look forward to it."

"You won't when it happens," Phaedra said darkly. "It

will hurt abominably, my lord, but we must get you moving."

"Anything for you, Miss Gillian."

Deborah Daintry was turning a small china bird over and over in her hands when Phaedra joined her, and her expression was troubled.

"Deborah, how nice of you to visit again. I am surprised that you have not yet returned to London."

"I'm not going back until I talk to Charlie," she said sullenly. "And I cannot even get a message to him right now because he has some of his fellows turning people away, saying there is fever and no one must approach. It is ridiculous."

"There has been fever locally. Dr. Deaville has been away for a while for just that reason."

"But that is at Fordham Wells. Thwicke House is far enough away that they are not in danger; it is just an excuse," Deborah said, setting the bird down with unnecessary force.

Phaedra picked up the little bird, one of her mother's cherished possessions, put it away from the girl, and said, "Why would you say that?"

"I just know something is wrong. When you love someone, you know when they need you. I know you wouldn't understand that, having never had a . . . er, well . . ." She trailed off, flustered.

Never having had a beau, Phaedra thought, finishing Deborah's thoughtless statement. She brushed it aside in her mind, put her arm around the girl's shoulders, and pushed her over to a chair. "Sit. We will have tea and you can tell me why you think something is wrong."

An hour later it still didn't seem to Phaedra to be much more than an ill-defined "feeling" on Deborah's part. But the girl had cheered up considerably and was flitting around the room restlessly, chattering about her London experiences.

Finally, she settled back on her chair and gazed at Phaedra with an innocent expression. "So, Phaedra, what is it like living with a rake?"

Sighing, Phaedra looked back into the girl's green eyes. "I wouldn't know. Mr.—er, Lord Hardcastle does not detail his amorous conquests to me and I have not asked."

Deborah giggled and sprang to her feet again. "Perhaps he would like a visitor," she said, dashing to the foot of the stairs and looking up toward the second floor. "I could read to him, or cool his fevered brow."

"Deborah Daintry, don't you dare! I will tell your papa, and he will lock you in your room until you behave. Besides, he is not fevered, just injured."

With a sly look, the girl returned to her seat. "So, you are keeping him all to yourself. Well, he is handsome, I will give you that. And his physique! Mrs. Lovett says he has the most muscular legs—"

"Deborah!" Phaedra felt the flush well up in her face as her cheeks turned hot.

"Phaedra!" the girl echoed saucily. "Do not tell me you have not even noticed how very good-looking he is. Mrs. Lovett says you come out of his room looking just as flushed as you are this moment."

"I do not!"

"And she says that Sally told her you visit his room every night!"

"I check to make sure there is nothing he needs! Deborah Daintry, I cannot believe you would stoop to common gossip with the servants!"

"Where else does one get gossip from? They notice *everything,* you know."

Her face burning, Phaedra wondered how far the gossip was going, and how to stop it. But there was nothing wrong with having a visitor under their roof when her own father was present at all times. Was there? So far the gossips had said nothing that was not strictly true, but it was how it sounded! Visiting his room every night, coming away looking flushed? It sounded positively as if there were some wickedness going on. But he was an injured man! *Badly* injured!

"I suppose I should be going," Deborah said, standing and glancing over at the stairs again. "Unless you really would like me to entertain your guest for a while?" she said, a hopeful note in her voice. "You are so busy. I could keep him company while you go about your duties."

"He is not my 'guest.' He is badly hurt, barely able to move."

"So Mrs. Lovett says. She says she hopes he stays hurt, for she rather likes looking after him. Especially his daily bath!" She giggled and raised her eyebrows significantly.

"He is getting better," Phaedra said with a quelling tone in her voice.

"So, what reason did he give you for not telling you he was the Earl of Hardcastle?"

"It was the merest misunderstanding," Phaedra replied as airily as she was able.

"Ah, I see."

"You see, he said 'Lawrence,' and I thought it was his last name, but it is his *first* name, and—"

A thud interrupted her, and a loud groan. Phaedra, alarmed, paused only a moment before racing up the stairs and into her erstwhile room. Hardcastle lay on the floor, his bare legs exposed.

"My lord!" Phaedra cried, racing into the room. "What are you doing? I told you Mrs. Lovett and I would help you get up for the first time!"

"Can't have you—ow! Can't have you run off your feet for

me every time I need something," he gasped.

Deborah had followed her upstairs, and between them they helped him back onto the bed.

"You will do me no good by hurting yourself worse," Phaedra scolded, fussing over him and tucking him back under the light covers.

"No," Deborah agreed, a furtive smile fleeting across her pretty face. "After all, you may have to stay here indefinitely if you hurt yourself again, and Phaedra would not like that at *all!*"

Hardcastle grimaced. "I hate being helpless. Damnation, but this hurts!"

"I will get you a tisane Old Mary sent for the pain."

Deborah pulled a chair to the bedside. "And I will keep his lordship company until you come back," she said with a determinedly bright smile. "Run along, Phaedra. I will talk about London with Lord Hardcastle."

Fuming, Phaedra retreated to the kitchen where she threw around a couple of pans until she felt ashamed of her outburst and heated some water to infuse the herbs. What was wrong with her? Even now, she was worried about what was going on in the room upstairs. Was Hardcastle being enchanted by Deborah's indubitably pretty face and bubbly charm? Was she falling under the spell of his dark eyes and husky voice? Were they even now finding small ways to touch each other, the brush of a hand, the eloquent glance—

Stop! What rubbish! She must stop this foolishness. Lord Hardcastle was her patient, and nothing more. Deborah Daintry, for all her silliness over the presence of a real live rake in their midst, was as in love with Charles Fossey as ever, and it would end in marriage, no doubt. That was Deborah's plan and dearest wish. Though entranced by Hardcastle's charms, she was not so foolish as to throw away the love of her life for a, in her own words, "debauched rake."

She carried the cup of herbal pain remedy up the stairs in time to hear Deborah's charming voice retailing a story of London life, ending with, "And so in the end, Lord Jeffrey lost both his horse *and* his fiancée to Mr. Battleston!"

Gripping the mug tightly, Phaedra entered the room to find Hardcastle with a frozen look of dismay on his handsome face. He cast her a look of such pleading that her heart was touched. And pleased. For she understood him in that second.

"Deborah," she said gently, "I think Lord Hardcastle needs to rest after his ill-fated effort to get up." Gratitude flooded his expressive, dark eyes.

A little huffily, Deborah stood. Phaedra handed the earl the cup, bade him drink it, and said, "I will return in a moment, after I have seen my guest out."

At the door, Deborah, having regained her equanimity, said, "Do be careful of him, Phaedra, for he does have a reputation."

"Don't worry about me, Deborah. I am a sensible woman. I am not one to have my head turned by Spanish coin, not after all these years."

With a flash of her occasional insight, Deborah said, "However, it is not as if you have been flooded with honeyed words. And do we ladies ever grow out of our love of flattery? We are frail creatures in some regards, Phaedra, and yet so very strong in others." A sad expression crossed over her face and she took Phaedra's hands in her own. "You will tell me if you hear anything about Charlie, will you not? I am starting to get worried. This is so unlike him."

Phaedra squeezed her hands. "I will let you know if I hear anything." She closed the door behind Deborah and mounted the stairs, to find her patient asleep with the empty mug in his strong hands. She gently took it from him, covered him, and tiptoed out of the room.

Nine

Morning prayers with her father, a habit left over from his days as the vicar of Ainstoun, were done and he had retreated to his library. Phaedra sat by the open window in the parlor watching the barn swallows swoop and glide over the field by the old barn behind the cottage. As always, she had been moved gently into a quiet, contemplative mood by the reassuring rhythms of morning prayer, and she went to that calm, still place within her soul to ask herself a few questions, questions she had been avoiding.

Was she jealous of her friend, Deborah Daintry, and that girl's glowing future as a wife and mother? Perhaps. It was something Phaedra had hoped for as a girl. And she could have married, if she was brutally honest with herself. There had been young men who showed an interest in her, but she had always frozen their advances with an aloof manner, for various reasons. She worried about her father and felt an obligation toward him that time would never erase. Always she would be there to look after him.

But that was not all. Ultimately, it was just that not one of the young men who showed an interest in her had engaged her own interest, nor stimulated her mind or imagination, nor come close to the dream she had once had of marrying a man whose intelligence, wit, and gentility matched her own. It was not that she felt herself above others in Ainstoun, it was just that she dreaded an unequal marriage. She had seen the results of that, and it was a sad vision of dwindling hopes and dreams, and that was so much worse than staying a respectable spinster. Unlike some poverty-plagued spinsters, she felt confident that in her own village she would never be a spectacle of ridicule, even after her father passed on and she subsisted on whatever was left of their savings from her mother's modest inheritance, and what she could earn taking in young girls to teach, perhaps.

Was she a fool? Some would say yes. Some would say a respectable marriage to a good man, even if he was not of her class, would be the answer to her lifelong quest to find what her destiny was. A husband, children, a home of her own; were those not the concerns and occupations that were ordained as her lot in life, as a woman? Phaedra sighed and folded her hands over her prayer book. Yes, that was what she had been taught all her life. She gazed blankly out the window, but her eyes no longer took in the blue of the sky, nor the pleasing symmetry of their old barn.

Instead, the doubts that had plagued her throughout her adult life came back; was there not more to marriage than a respectable settlement, a mild tolerance for one another, as husband and wife? Was there not a fire that burned between a man and woman who loved each other, a fire that was not extinguished with time and all the cares and worries that came with life and family? With her mother gone, there was no one of whom she could ask such intimate questions.

Her thoughts inevitably turned to Lord Hardcastle and how she felt in his presence. A frisson raced through her, a thread of excitement when she looked at him and touched him and spoke with him. But that was merely the agitation of the flesh, nothing to do with her soul. It was, perhaps, just the animal reaction of male and female in close contact. Or was it the womanly weakness that seemed to be prevalent, the fatal fascination with a rogue? Was it the challenge to reform or "tame" a man that women seemed to seek in a rake? Was it the feminine version of hunting wild prey, the thrill of the chase, the bloodlust of the kill?

She jumped up and laid her prayer book aside. There was too much to do in a day to spend time idly pondering unanswerable questions. It was pointless in the end anyway, for there would never be anything more between her and Lord Hardcastle than the relationship between patient and nurse. The moment he was able, he would leap onto his horse and leave Ainstoun behind in a cloud of road dust.

With renewed determination to not let the enigmatic man upstairs disturb her equilibrium, Phaedra headed to the kitchen and set about putting together a breakfast tray for him.

The sun stole across the bed coverlet and onto his face, and Hardcastle felt the warmth as he crept toward awareness. He stretched, groaned a little at the tightness of sore muscles, but then awoke more fully to the realization that he felt better than he had yet upon awakening, since the assault. He opened his eyes to the now-familiar sight of the papered ceiling and homely furnishings, the tatted covers on the washstand and dresser, the hand-sewn curtains that dressed the window.

What was he doing here? Why had he not summoned his valet from London and traveled back there, to his Mayfair house, to recuperate? He should be resting between covers of Irish linen, and awakening to his butler's customary opening of the grand red velvet curtains in his own huge bedchamber. His head would be aching from too much wine, and his lungs from the foul air of London.

At that moment his door swung open and a small, rounded bottom pushed in, followed by Miss Phaedra Gillian bearing a tray with a teapot, scones, jam, and eggs. Ah, yes, he thought. That was why. Like spring water to a jaded palate, she had awakened him to the likely fleeting charm of simpler tastes. Her fresh prettiness contrasted favorably with the painted faces of London doxies and even the practiced expressions of society belles. She was like the bracing breeze of the Lakes when contrasted with the stuffy miasma of London.

"Good morning, my lord. I trust you slept well?" she said cheerily.

"I must have. I remember nothing after that ridiculous fall yesterday. Whatever was in that foul potion of Old Mary's must have knocked me out. I should take that foul decoction to London with me and have it analyzed and bottled. Many would pay much for that kind of sleep."

She eyed him critically as she set the tray on a table. "You do look better. Or is that just my imagination?"

"No. You are right. I certainly feel better. I should take that awful brew every night if it has this effect."

Phaedra shook her head as she poured a cup of tea for him. "No, Mary was very specific on that point. A person should only take that particular potion once in their life. Do not ask me what is in it, for I do not know and she will not tell me, but she says it would be dangerous and foolish to take it more than once."

He shivered melodramatically, and quoted, "What, no friendly drop left to help me after?"

"Wrong play," Phaedra retorted, laughing. "But right author. I have always wondered if Old Mary is one of the original three weird sisters from MacBeth, living still, through the ages!"

Hardcastle caught his breath as her laughter knifed through him down to his very soul. What was there in her simplest expression that twisted his insides until it hurt? She was just a country girl, a parson's daughter! And yet there was something magical about her beyond the angelic looks and sweet voice. Something in her lack of pretension, the honesty that came from her very soul.

Her cheeks were staining with a soft rose; she had caught his expression. He must be gazing at her like a mooncalf!

"So," he said quickly, shifting up in the bed and wincing at the slicing pain that shot through him at the movement. "Do you think I will be able to get up today?"

"After that experience yesterday? We shall see," Phaedra said.

Their conversation turned to prosaic things, her duties for the day, which included a trip into the village to help out an elderly Mr. Ferguson. But when he could, as he ate and drank with more appetite than he had yet summoned, he stole glances at her. She was pretty and sweet natured and clever. How had a girl of such sterling quality failed to marry? Were the men such dolts in Ainstoun that they could not see a bright gem in their midst? Even her poverty should not have turned away the ardent affections of at least a few of the village gallants. Was there no suitable young man nearby, no squire's son or handsome vicar?

Not that he was complaining. He would have her for himself, if not in honorable marriage—perish the thought; he was not and never would be the marrying kind—at least in his arms for a few minutes of stolen bliss. He had been called a great many things—rake, rogue, seducer among them—but he always persuaded, never demanded, and he never, ever left a lady unsatisfied. Lately, in fact, he had not been earning his reputation. He had been circumspect and boring in his love life, not able to summon up the energy or enthusiasm to pursue a new lovely, for they all looked monotonously alike after a while, painted and perfumed, cosseted and corseted. And yet now, in his invalid's bed, he had found a new object. Phaedra Gillian, vicar's daughter. His juices were flowing, his interest was high, and his body already anticipating the warm closeness of little Miss Gillian's sweet, soft form.

She turned back from the window where she had been drawing back the curtains and opening the sash, and brightly said, with just a hint of high color, "It is time you had your wash-up now, my lord."

"Hardcastle. Just Hardcastle."

"Yes, well, Hardcastle, then. Mrs. Lovett is not able to come until this afternoon, and I think that with a little help from me you should be able to take care of your own, hmm—needs, now."

Warring within him was his innate honesty, and yet his desire to have her close, and to further the intimate contact in which they had been in the last few days. Until now he had been in too much pain, or in a laudanum fog, to enjoy the closeness, but now he was feeling more himself, just as she would back away from him.

"I-I suppose I could try," he said. He shifted up in bed and was almost happy to feel a twinge of pain shoot through his back. An unfeigned groan issued from his lips.

"I will help you," Phaedra said hurriedly. "B-but only so far."

Her confusion was adorable and a hunger built within him for her touch, for her glance, for her nearness. She disappeared for a few minutes and reappeared with an ewer of steaming water. Her hands were shaking, he saw, and misgivings welled up in his heart. She was a maiden, after all, and an innocent.

"Miss Gillian," he said gently. "I will do what I can for myself, but why do you not call your father? He can—er— help me with things of a more personal, masculine nature. I would not for the world have you troubled."

"I cannot disturb my father," she said, with a shocked expression. "He is engaged in research of a most important and deep nature. He needs undisturbed peace to work."

"I honor your filial respect, but I am sure he would not mind shielding you from the kind of intimate contact with a male that my needs would necessitate." Even as he argued against her having any kind of personal contact with him, he was finding the idea unbearably exciting. Would he disgrace himself, he wondered, with his reaction to her touch? Would he be able to conceal from her the way she was beginning to affect him? And ultimately, would it further or hinder his cause if she found out how her touch stirred him?

She visibly braced herself and said, "Sir, I have nursed many gentlemen in my time. I am seven-and-twenty, not seventeen, and there have been times when I was the only one in the village with adequate medical knowledge. I can certainly give you the aid you require."

He relaxed. What would be would be. But in the end he could not bear to have her see his vulnerability. He did what he could for himself, even though the back pain started up again as he looked after his personal needs and cleanliness. What was wrong with him he would not venture to guess, but he could not accept her help without some measure of guilt. He could hire a servant to help her. He was rich enough to purchase the help of a dozen servants, and yet he let this girl toil for him, do laundry for him, *feed* him, even. And she did it all, knowing him to be an earl, indubitably knowing he had money, without a hint of reproach or any suggestion of asperity.

What did it matter that he intended that she would not suffer for helping him? What did future aid mean to one who labored now?

"Miss Gillian," he said, watching her as she rinsed out the cloths she had given him to wash himself with. When her back was turned he had slipped on the clean nightshirt she had provided for him, and noticed that it was bigger and longer than the one he had been wearing.

"Yes?" she said, wiping her hands on her apron and turning toward him.

"I-I should leave. I am a burden to you, and I truly do have the wherewithal to leave."

"Do you want to go?"

"No," he said. "No, I don't. There is something so healing in this household." He would be honest. "In your presence. I do not think a raft of servants and a dozen Harley Street physicians could help me recover faster than you and your painfully horrid herbal decoctions."

She chuckled. "Then don't leave until you feel well enough to," she said with an open expression and a shy smile. "You truly are no burden to me. I-I like your company."

Hardcastle settled back against the newly fluffed pillows and sighed. Had any confession so simple acted in such a way on him? A warmth budding within him, he said drowsily, "And I like yours, Miss Gillian. I like your company, and your laughter, and your sweet, sweet smile—"

Phaedra stood staring down at him long after sleep had claimed him. Without thought she reached out and ran her fingers through the silky, coal-black hair, pushing it off his brow. Was this what all London rakes were like? What an entrancing breed, then, and how understandable was female infatuation with them. He was by turns boyish and manly, helpless and indomitable, harmless and seductive.

"Is our patient sleeping, my dear?"

Phaedra jumped back from Hardcastle as if she had been singed and whirled to see her father standing in the doorway. "Papa! Yes, he is just now asleep."

"And is he getting better?" Mr. Gillian moved into the bedroom. He had the chess board with him but laid it aside.

"I think so. But the morning routine exhausted him. Mrs. Lovett says that he is a well-knit man, though, and should recover from the beating in time."

Mr. Gillian put his arm around his daughter's shoulders. "You are not tiring yourself out, my dear, are you?"

Phaedra threaded her arm around her father's waist and leaned her head on his shoulder. "No, Papa. This is not tiring to me."

"You are like your mama. You like helping people as much as she did. He is a handsome young man, is he not? I am no follower of feminine tastes, but I would say he is a gentleman to appeal to ladies."

"He is very handsome, Papa. Almost as handsome as you."

He chuckled and laid a kiss on her hair, squeezing her shoulder. "Do you like him?"

Phaedra pulled away from her father and gazed into his innocent blue eyes. "Whether I like him is neither here nor there, Papa. He will heal and then he will be on his way, wherever that may be."

"You do like him. He is an intelligent lad, that I will say. And he has the good taste to think you as lovely as I do."

"Papa!" Phaedra turned away in confusion and poured the soapy water into the slops basin under the washstand. But she straightened and turned back to her father with a serious and determined expression on her face. "I will not pretend to misunderstand you, Father. Please, if you have any thoughts of a match between me and Lord Hardcastle . . . Oh, it sounds ludicrous to even say it out loud! He is an earl! And a rake!"

"Is he now? That I did not know," Mr. Gillian said, his gaze straying to the slumbering earl. "Do you know that as a fact?"

"No—yes—I am not sure." Phaedra hesitated. "But there is nothing to worry about, so do not concern yourself. He has been very respectful toward me, as much as any lady could want."

"I would expect as much." Mr. Gillian frowned. "A rake, eh? I had not thought it of him. I had thought there was too much intelligence in the lad for mindless sensuality."

Phaedra regretted her hasty words. If only she could take them back! Now there was another who would be looking at the earl through the lens of his supposed reputation. But she must trust her father's good sense. Never had he let reputation or gossip change the way he treated a body. As a vicar he had shocked many a good church-going lady of the parish by going into the homes of the fallen woman or drunken man.

No, if there was anyone she could trust, it was her father. She gazed at him with affection. She returned to his side and put her arms around his rotund waist. "I am going downstairs to start the bread. It has been proofing quite long enough."

"I am going to stay here for a while, my dear. I shall set up the chess board and see if his lordship will play me a game when he awakens."

"I will leave you to it, then, and bring your luncheon up here."

"Do that, m'dear," Mr. Gillian said, absently. "Do that."

Ten

Hardcastle awoke to the knowledge that he was not alone and opened his eyes expecting to see Phaedra close by. That it was her father instead did not surprise him, for some reason.

"Listen to this, Hardcastle," Mr. Gillian said, without looking up. He peered down at a book on his lap through his spectacles. *"Where both deliberate, the love is slight; Who ever loved that loved not at first sight?"*

"Marlowe?"

"Mhmm. *Hero and Leander.* Nice piece, that."

The ridiculous aspect of a plump, bespectacled Church of England vicar quoting love poetry from the rebellious and disturbing—to most prudish minds—Marlowe, merely illustrated what Hardcastle had come to suspect; Mr. Phineas Gillian was no ordinary parson. Hardcastle pushed himself up in the bed and wiped the sleep from his eyes. "Love at first sight, eh? Don't believe in it, sir. Sorry."

"Don't you, then? Too bad, that. I should think a rake of some renown would; though on second thought, what has being a rake got to do with love, eh?"

Hardcastle frowned but did not reply. The vicar, his eyes on the book again, was silent for a moment, but then looked up. "Offended you?" he asked, gazing over the top rim of his glasses with a gleam in his blue eyes.

"What? No, of course not," Hardcastle said. Was he offended? He wasn't sure. No one had ever called him a rake to his face.

"Sorry if I did. Not my intention, to be sure. No point in beating about the bush, though, is there? It is what I have heard of you, but if it is a lie, tell me so now. I shall believe you, you know. Frightfully naive, I am. So you don't believe in love at first sight. Do you believe in love at all?"

Peevishly, Hardcastle looked around for something to drink, but there was nothing on the side table. His mouth was parched and tasted bad. But his host was waiting for a reply, and he focused on the older man for a moment and thought about it. "I don't think I believe in the kind of love the poets would have us believe in, hearts and flowers and love everlasting, all that rot. So, no. I suppose that love exists, though I have had no experience of it, but if there is true love in the world, I think the poets know precious little about it."

Gillian leaned forward and gazed at Hardcastle seriously. "Where, then, do you think the poets got their inspiration from, eh?"

"Infatuation," Hardcastle said. "The silly devils generally see some woman from afar and prefer to worship them with words without getting to know the real woman. When they do, they find out that women are every bit as fallible and corrupt as men." Even to his own ears he sounded bitter and jaded, but it was merest truth, and the vicar seemed to want his true opinion, so he would have it, unvarnished. If he was offended, so be it.

"Right you are, young man," the elderly vicar said, stabbing the air with his forefinger. "At least you are sensible. Glad to see it."

Of all the possible reactions, this was the one he would have least expected. Hardcastle gazed silently at the man who sat with one leg crossed over the other, a book of poetry cradled on his lap. Not the bible—*poetry*. What a very odd parson!

Gillian took a deep breath and blew it out slowly. "Young people, young gentlemen, especially, so very often expect the ladies to be perfect, and I often think how disturbing that must be for the feminine folk. What a burden, to be expected to be morally perfect, impeccably behaved, untainted, pure, with no thoughts that God Himself might not eavesdrop on."

"B-but are not women more . . . innocent? Do they not need to be protected?" Hardcastle, against his own intentions, was becoming intrigued with this gentleman's original ideas. He did not necessarily believe the latest theory that women were more innocent and pure than men and needed to be sheltered, just as he did not accept the older notion that women were the bearers of the burden of original sin, but he thought he would just throw it out for discussion, so to speak.

"Women, my lord, are every bit as strong, and perhaps stronger, than men. And they understand evil instinctively, not like men, who struggle against the knowledge."

"But that oversets common wisdom, sir, if you do not mind me saying so."

"I do not mind you saying anything you think, as long as it is honest."

Hardcastle shook his head to clear it. In such a short time they had traversed from love at first sight to the frailty of women and then the strength of women, and now to evil. "Are not women, sir, meant to redeem us morally wayward male creatures? Is that not their purpose? It seems to me lately that that is all anyone speaks of, in polite company, anyway. Men moan on and on about what angels their women are and how they simply have no desire to be wild any longer. How their lady wives have wrestled them onto the straight and narrow road to salvation." He thought about

Byron and his marital woes. "Or they fail utterly at being redeemed and make their ladies miserable and themselves in the process."

Gillian snorted. "Don't believe in redemption, myself."

"What?" Hardcastle frowned. A vicar who did not believe in redemption?

"Not in redemption prompted externally, I mean." He frowned and pursed his lips. "I think the only redemption comes from within. No man changes unless he wants to, after all. And no woman can make him. He may *want* to change for her sake, but unless there is a true inner resolution, unless he really wants to change for his own reasons, it will not stick. It will fade along with his love for his wife."

The vicar was reading another poetry passage, and there was silence for a few minutes while Hardcastle digested the older man's words. He supposed it made some sense. In that light Byron's marital failure was a foregone conclusion, for the poet did not want truly to change his life. He had wanted both Annabella *and* his cronies and wayward ways. His mind went back to one of the first things the vicar had said to him. They had started the conversation by speaking of love. "You wondered out loud what a rake would know of love. I am not claiming the title yet, sir, but is not a rake a specialist in love?"

Mr. Gillian tossed the book aside and knit his brow. "No, not at all. He is a specialist in *seduction*." He drew out the word, pronouncing every syllable with ringing resonance.

"Is that not the dance of love?"

"No, that is the mating dance. Every grouse in the field does that, putting on a display for his lady, drawing her in with his fine feathers and wonderful voice. Have you never seen a peacock's display? All for the peahen, to bring her to his nest that night."

Grumpily, Hardcastle considered how ridiculous the elegant ballet of seduction seemed when reduced to a bird's mating habits. "But it is different for humans!"

"Certainly, but only because we have been given the capacity to love. It is a unique and precious gift."

"Have you ever—" Hardcastle caught himself before asking. This was none of his business, after all.

"Have I ever been in love?" Mr. Gillian's smile became beatific. "Yes. Yes, and in fact I fell in love at first sight, just like Marlowe said."

"With—"

"With Phaedra's mother, to be sure."

"Ah, yes, I remember you telling me about her, about seeing her in a field."

Mr. Gillian nodded. "My Connie. But love at first sight, tricky thing, you know."

"How so?"

The soft folds of Mr. Gillian's face sagged even more, and his face set in a serious expression. He pulled off his spectacles and leaned forward. "Gets tricky when you find out the love of your life can be a bit of a shrew." He sat back and laughed.

Hardcastle blinked. "A-a shrew?"

"Yes. Women find men exasperating most of the time, don't you know? And the first time my Connie told me to get my head out of the clouds and start living in the real world, we had a set-to, didn't we just! We were wanting to get married by then, but we didn't have enough money, for as I have said, the moment I married I lost my fellowship annuity. I had spouted some nonsense about living on love, and she told me only poets live on love, that humans must live on bread. 'Course, that did not sit well with me. I was a bit of a romantic in my youth."

The door swung open at that minute and Phaedra came

through holding a pile of linens. "Papa, you did not tell me Lord Hardcastle was awake! The poor man is probably parched with thirst! How could you not call me the moment he was awake?"

Mr. Gillian winked at Hardcastle. "See what I mean? Bit of a shrew."

Phaedra laid the linens down and planted her fists on her hips. "What are you two giggling about? Never mind. I don't want to know. I shall get you some water, my lord, and then bring our luncheon up."

Mr. Gillian stood and shook out the folds of his frock coat. "I have sincerely enjoyed our discussion, my lord, but work beckons. I have been working on a most fascinating theory on the biblical interpretations of the original Greek texts, and I must get back to it. I shall leave the book of poetry for you, my lord. Even if you don't believe in poetical love."

And with that, he bowed and left the room.

The room had gotten darker as twilight descended. It was late, possibly even near midnight by now. Hardcastle was intolerably bored and feeling just a little sorry for himself, for Phaedra had been busy all day with her various chores and a trip to the village to help some old man who would allow no one else near him. She had taken luncheon with him, but had merely sent his dinner up with Sally as she had some errands to run, she said. Mrs. Lovett had been in to help change his bed, but left soon after, laughing gaily about some broad jokes she had made at his expense. After she went, Hardcastle made one experimental attempt to get out of bed. It was a little easier than the last time he had tried it, and he didn't topple over this time, but he was still as weak as a day-old kitten.

And so all evening he had been left with his thoughts.

Should he be staying? He thought seriously about his purpose in staying when he could easily leave. He had been bored for a long time now in London, even when well. If he went back to London in his current invalid shape he would be stuck in his town house with only his rakish friends for company. Somehow, in his present state, that did not seem tolerable. Phaedra Gillian, on the other hand, was the tonic he needed. He liked her, he was attracted to her, but more than that, she was good for him.

Only because he was injured, of course. When mended he would take his vengeance on the insufferable Baron Fossey and return to his home.

But back to the problem at hand. He was mightily tempted to seduce the vulnerable Miss Gillian. She was twenty-seven and had little experience of men, if he was not mistaken. She exposed her preference for him in little ways, in the pinkening of her cheeks and the trembling of her hands, her breathlessness and wide-open gaze. Whether she knew it or not, she was a ripe little plum ready for the plucking, and he had not sampled such a tasty, fresh morsel for an age. Seducing her would be a sweet reward for the hours of pain and necessary patience while his body mended.

And yet—

How could he? She had been so good to him; both father and daughter had been. Would making love with Phaedra be a treachery? Or would the rewards he was willing to heap on her and her father—monetary rewards that would help them attain a better style of living—be worth it to her? She would only be giving him, after all, that which no other man had apparently sought.

But how could he equate monetary rewards to the Gillians with the sweetness of herself, with the lovely gift of her innocence, if he should be so fortunate? It was a disturbing thought, and not one he had ever had before. When giving a lady little gifts of jewelry or gold, tokens of his appreciation, he never ever felt like he was purchasing her favors. But he had the feeling Phaedra Gillian would not see things that way, and he would never want to shame or hurt her. It would have to be delicately done.

At that moment the object of his thoughts crept into the room, candle held high. She always seemed to know when he was awake and lonely. "Hello," he whispered.

"You are awake." She came into the room and set the candle on the side table. "How are you feeling?"

"Better," he said. He watched her move toward him, the curves of her body outlined by the unexpectedly erotic, soft white muslin of her nightrail. She sat on the bed beside him and he was almost suffocated by his awareness of her, her scent, her warmth, her sweet breath fanning his face.

"I'm glad. Tomorrow we shall have you up and about, I think; there was no time today, what with one thing and another. But we will wait until Mrs. Lovett comes before we attempt it. She is stronger than I if you start to take a tumble."

Unwilling to confess that he had already tried that, he stayed silent. Without consciously willing it, his hand went up and he touched her hair. She sighed, and her lovely eyes glowed in the flickering candlelight. So sweet. What would making love with her be like? It would be her first time, he thought, and her untutored responses would be as fresh and lovely as she was.

"Phaedra, I . . . Has anyone ever told you how lovely you are?"

Mutely, she shook her head.

"Has any man ever kissed you?" he whispered. In the almost dark of the room, he found the outrageous things he wanted to say came naturally.

She nodded.

"And did you like it?"

"No," she whispered. "He-he was young and so was I, and he . . . It was wet and—"

He didn't need to hear any more. He put his hand behind her head and pulled her down until she was hovering just over his mouth, her lips just inches from his. Her blue eyes were closing, closing, closing. Her lashes fanned down and touched her cheek. She was waiting, not pulling away, not moving forward, just waiting.

A first real kiss. When was the last time he had ever given a woman her first *real* kiss? Their lips touched and he was lost in the velvet darkness, lost to thought or sense. Instinct taught him not to push too hard, not to take her breath away. He paused, let her regain her equilibrium, and then took her lips again in a kiss, moist but not wet, soft, not hard; he felt her surrender to feeling, felt her muscles relax and her body sag against him on the bed.

His fingers itched with longing to touch her, to explore her lithe, lovely body, but she was not ready, not yet. He released her and she sat upright again and raised one hand to her lips. That simple, innocent gesture fed his hunger for her, and he had to clench his fists at his sides to keep from taking her in his arms—damn the pain—and making love to her. He battled his physical lust and won, though the intensity of his desire surprised and alarmed him.

"Why did you do that?" she asked.

He shrugged. He could not let her see how affected he was. It might frighten or worry her, and the last thing he wanted to do was give her any hint of his intentions. "Every girl should experience a real kiss at least once," he said, keeping his tone neutral and his manner nonchalant.

"Oh." She blinked and straightened. "Well, is there any thing you want, my lord?"

Only you, my sweeting. He shook his head, not trusting his mouth to form a negative response.

"I-I should go back to bed then," she said.

"And where is your bed?" he said.

"I am sleeping with Sally right now. I should get back before she misses me. She has been—" She didn't finish her sentence.

It suddenly occurred to him that this was a very small cottage. "Please tell me, Miss Gillian, that this is not your room I have been taking up."

She shrugged and smiled. "It does not matter, sir."

"But it does! Lord, you should have told me."

"No," she said earnestly, placing her hand on his chest as he raised himself up. "No, my lord, please! Do not trouble yourself. I still feel that you were sent here for a purpose. Do you know, my father rarely comes out of his library voluntarily? And yet thrice he has come up to visit you with no reminder from me. Even if there were no other reason, the difference you have made to my father would be enough. He has so little intelligent male companionship. H-he finds you interesting, I think," she finished, with her head cocked to one side exactly like her father.

He let out a roar of laughter and then stifled it. "If I am of some service to you, Miss Gillian—may I call you Phaedra? Please?"

Shyly, she nodded.

"If I am of some service to you, Phaedra, then I will learn to be glad I was assaulted and robbed by roadside bandits." He gazed up at her in the dim candlelight. She was not some London siren casting out her lures for him; neither was she a lusty widow, nor a voluptuous courtesan, and yet she piqued his curiosity and sharpened his appetite as no woman had in a year. Even if Fossey were long gone by the time he made his way to the estate, he would be glad of this interruption. Without it, he would never have met Phaedra.

"I must leave you now, sir. But I will be back at first light with tea."

As she left, taking the light with her, Hardcastle turned onto his side, noting that there was definitely less discomfort than even that morning, and drifted to sleep with the memory of that first delicate taste of Phaedra. He must have her, but it would take a subtle seduction indeed to win her with no reservations on her side.

But it would be worth it. Ah, how it would be worth it.

Eleven

She must be wicked. Or was she? The most amazing sensations had raced through her the night before when Hardcastle had taken her in his arms and kissed her. To him it might have been in the nature of a light relief from boredom, but to her it was a revelation. Never had she experienced a longing to just lay herself down next to a man and be swallowed up in his arms. But then, never had she been kissed since she was ten and young Albert Deaville, the doctor's son, had told her he knew a secret and she would have to kiss him to learn it. His secret had turned out to be that he knew a way to get girls to kiss him.

Phaedra was taking a turn in the garden just as the pearly dawn began to creep over the horizon. A shawl covered her shoulders, because despite the budding warmth of spring—May would soon give way to June—mornings were still a little chilly and dewy. And she wore a newer dress, a buttercup yellow dimity gown she had just altered, one of the ones that Deborah had given her. Vanity. So much to do in the world, so many troubled people, so many with little to eat and illness to plague them, and she had spent a few hours the night before making over a dress, so she would appear prettier to an idle peer of the realm. It was foolishness and vanity, and she would stifle it, if she could.

But still, there was no sense in changing out of the pretty yellow gown, was there?

★ ★ ★ ★ ★

"You look like sunshine this morning, Phaedra," Hardcastle said, following her about the room with his eyes only. It had seemed a long and dreary morning until she had come in, the sunshine of her smile more radiant than the comely yellow dress.

She seemed pleased, but merely turned and smiled at him, and said, "As soon as we can get you up and about, you may experience a little of the real thing, sir, and then my false radiance will seem a little dimmer."

"Why do you do that?"

Puzzled, she gazed steadily at him as though trying to read his eyes. "What? Do what?"

"Turn a compliment away. You shun it like a bold stranger at your door."

"I do not do that, do I?"

"Often, yes. I have never met a woman who did so. You are pretty; own up to that, at least."

Phaedra shook her head and laughed. She finished tidying the room and sat down next to him in a chair by the bed. "You must be bored. I will leave the chess playing to my father—he enjoys the game, but I do not much like it—but would you like a game of cards?"

Hardcastle brightened and said, "I did not know you would play cards. I had always thought parsons objected to cardplaying on moral grounds."

"Not all parsons are so stiff and righteous, you know. You must have guessed by now that my father is no ordinary vicar." Phaedra hopped up and retrieved a pack of cards from the drawer of a small table by the window.

They played, her sitting in the little chair and he propped up in the bed on pillows. She was good, Hardcastle found, though why that should surprise him he did not know. They played a few hands of piquet, but changed to euchre at Hardcastle's request. She was good at that, too, and won as many games as she lost, but as the stream of sunlight moved across the covers of the bed, Hardcastle found the challenge waning with no incentive. He glanced up at Phaedra speculatively and said, "Why do we not play for penny stakes? It will add a little excitement to the game."

"Gamble?" She paused in midshuffle and lost a card.

Hardcastle found the shock in her voice amusing. So, she had a little of the Puritan in her after all. "Penny stakes, my dear, the merest tiny wager to add a little fun to the game."

"I don't think I could gamble," she said, retrieving the fallen card and adding it back to the pack.

"Don't prim up on me, Phaedra. Is it the money you don't like? All right, how about instead of penny stakes, we play for little favors?"

Phaedra frowned. "Favors? What do you mean?"

A devilish idea entered Hardcastle's brain and would not go away. Since the kiss the previous night, he had felt an increasing hunger for the sweetness of her lips, but instinctively he knew that in the light of day, she would shy from such contact like a nervous filly. "I mean small favors, little things, inconsequential deeds."

"I still do not follow you, my lord. What can you do for me from your bed, and what do you need that I have not already done for you?"

He shifted impatiently, glancing down at the hand she had just dealt him. She was far too reasonable and far too unlikely to flirt. Another woman would be playing the coquette at that moment, and would have guessed what "favors" he had in mind. But then, was that not one of the things he liked about Phaedra, her refreshing lack of coquetry? "Perhaps there is nothing I may do for you at this moment, but"—he had a sudden brainstorm and glanced up—"I am sure there are those in your parish who could use a few favors. Are there no young men who could use an apprenticeship at England's best stable? Are there no youthful scholars who could use a patron to further their schooling? Could the village poor box not stand to be enriched?"

She shook her head in dismay. "Do not tell me you would gamble for such things? It is too bad of you. The poor box is meant to be charity, and good for your soul, not the object of a gambling wager."

He chuckled. "My dear, you must know that after all you have done for me, I will do some of this anyway—I am not ungrateful, after all—but humor me and let me name these boons as gambling wagers. It will hurt no one and would add to the enjoyment of the game for me. And you can see that I lose just as often as I win."

Sighing, she said, "Very well. But what may I do for you if I lose?"

He waved his hand and said airily, "I will think of something, my dear, never fear."

He was almost tempted to deliberately lose, just to soften her and lull her into overconfidence. But it went against his every instinct and every notion of honor to cheat, even to lose. There was no point to a game of chance if the participants did not play fairly and pay up honorably if they lost. As luck had it, he did not have to *try* to lose. She was good and she was lucky and she won. Before long, in a string of winning games, she had gained a generous contribution to the new roof for the church, two apprenticeships, one in his stable and one in his estate house, and a goodly tithe to the local almshouse. But finally, he bent all his effort to winning. He had never in his life failed to win when he put all of his effort and skill into it. To his surprise, he still lost one more game before finally winning one. It was very close, but he did *finally* win.

Flushed and pretty, enjoying the gambling far more than she would likely admit to him, she said brightly, "And now, sir, what may I do for you?"

He pretended to think hard, knitting his brows and pondering the question with gravity. "I will not be hard, I think. I would ask as my boon, one kiss."

Her face paled. "You would wager for something like that? Th-that is not what I thought we were playing for!"

She was flustered. This was not good. Or was it? It mattered to her, if she should be so flustered. Had the kiss the night before meant as much to her as it did to him? He could hope.

"Come, Phaedra. It is not so much. Nothing more than a little brotherly salute, if that is what you wish to make of it."

Stiffly, she put aside the deck of cards and said, "I have made a wager and I will keep to it, sir, never doubt that." She moved closer to him and sat on the edge of the bed. "Shall it be a kiss on the ch-cheek, then, or-or . . ."

He watched her for a moment. In her present state of mind he would likely get a cold and formal peck, and that was not at all what he had in mind. She sat primly, her hands folded on her lap, looking the very picture of a prudish vicar's spinster daughter, not at all the warm, tender bundle of the previous night.

"I think, miss, that I shall defer my prize until a later point."

"What? Why?" Startled, her lips formed a small O. She shook her head. "I will not ask your reasons, my lord. No doubt you have your own. Very well." She stood. "I must see if Mrs. Lovett is here yet, and we shall see if we can get you up and about. I am sure by now you would like a change of scene."

"I must confess," he said, "I have made the attempt and find I can stand well enough, if with some pain. I shall need a little help to manage the staircase, but I think I can do it."

"Good. Then it is past time you got some exercise."

Phaedra bustled around and found a robe for the earl. She brought it to him and then shyly handed him a pair of carpet slippers.

He glanced up at her. "Surely your father and I do not have the same size foot."

"No, I-I made them for you. You have no footwear and I—" She shrugged.

"You made them for me?" Hardcastle felt a twinge of embarrassment, but that was quickly overwhelmed by the awe he felt on finding that someone had thought of him enough to take so much time over his needs. He had often laughed at his married friends and their pride in their wives' accomplishments, but at that moment he would gladly have boasted in any London salon of Phaedra's neat stitches and professional handiwork. More than that, it left him feeling ashamed of the trickery he was indulging in just to gain a kiss. Not ashamed enough to forgo his prize, just enough to feel uneasy over his method of obtaining it.

An hour later, robed and slippered and with Mrs. Lovett's strong shoulder to lean on, he had made it down to the neat parlor that overlooked the walled garden and the barn beyond. It was a curiously powerful delight, after five days, to be in a different room with different surroundings.

"Just give me a call when you need to get 'im back up the stairs," Mrs. Lovett said as she exited the parlor to go about her business.

Hardcastle looked about himself. Phaedra followed his gaze and wondered if he found the room unbearably shabby. To her it was comfortable and familiar, but he was used to

such grandeur, such elegance, no doubt. She noted with chagrin the tattered upholstery and faded curtains, the worn rug
and small dimensions.

"This is marvelous," he said. "You cannot imagine how
wonderful it is to see a fresh view when one has been in the
same room for almost a week."

"I do know," Phaedra said, relieved by his honest enjoyment of his surrounding. She should have expected it of him.
She knew by now that he was not ungrateful, nor was he a
snob. "I remember when I was afflicted with one of the usual
childhood diseases and spent the week in my room. When I
recovered somewhat, my mother let me come down to the
breakfast parlor in the vicarage. It was as if I had never seen
the room before." It was odd, she thought, that though
Hardcastle was indubitably used to more elaborate surroundings, he seemed to be fitting himself to the room in some way;
he was absurdly at his leisure in a wing chair by the parlor
window, with a cup of tea at his elbow, like some genial
country squire. Or a comfortable husband wearing his wife's
handiwork on his feet.

He looked down at his slippers, holding one foot out and
admiring how it was shod. "You have an elegant stitch, my
de . . . uh, Phaedra. I have never had such a perfect pair of
slippers since I was a lad of nine or so, when a maiden aunt
made me a pair while I was ill."

"Don't be absurd, my lord. You undoubtedly have most
elegant slippers in your London home, made by the best of
cobblers."

"Ah, but while cobblers understand very well the art of
making the perfect Hessians, they know nothing about the
comfort a man needs in his slippers. I am convinced only a
woman's touch can do that."

He was being preposterous, and she was tempted to laugh,

though she was trying to maintain a cool demeanor in the light of his outrageous behavior in claiming a kiss as the result of winning a wager. She still didn't know what to make of that, whether to be offended or flattered or to feel trepidation. And she never knew what to make of *him,* for one moment he was the frosty, collected aristocrat, and made her feel unsure and shy, and the next minute he was making absurd jokes and putting her very much at her ease. At that moment there was a rap at the door, and Sally poked her head in. "Miss Gillian, Dick Simondson was just at the back door, and 'e says as 'ow 'e an' Roger found that there fine 'orse of 'is lordship's. They was wanting 'im to know as 'ow they was lookin' arter 'im fine."

"What marvelous news," Phaedra said, glancing over at Hardcastle. "They actually have Pegasus?"

"Aye, miss. They say as 'ow t'were a bit o' a struggle, but the 'orse gentled some once they fed 'im some oats. 'E's in the squire's barn now, they say." She curtsied with an alarmed glance toward the earl, and left, letting the door close behind her.

Phaedra pointedly opened the parlor door, and left it open. She was not going to let Sally get any more ideas as to what was going on in the cottage. It had been annoying in the extreme to find that the girl had the soul of a gossip, and she had been taken to task for talking to the other neighborhood serving staff. From now on, the door would always be open, Phaedra had vowed, when she was with Lord Hardcastle alone, even in his bedchamber.

Brightly, she turned to Hardcastle, willing to let bygones be bygones—she would think about that infernal wager later—and said, "You have never yet told me, sir, what you were doing riding to Ainstoun in the middle of the night."

Hardcastle stretched and folded his arms behind his head,

crossing his legs at the ankle. He winced a bit but then said, "I was not riding *to* Ainstoun, except in the most indirect sense. Tell me, do you know all of the gentry of these parts?"

Phaedra sat back down in the other wing chair and admired the way a ray of sunlight caused blue-black light to blaze in the earl's hair. She shook herself out of her thoughts though, and said, in answer to his question, "I do. I have lived here my whole life, after all. Were you set to visit someone? Should I have notified someone of your trouble? I would be glad to do so even now, and could have a message—"

A devilish grin twisted Hardcastle's lips. "Oh, no, my dear. This was to be a surprise visit. I only hope I am not too late and the rascal has not fled to the Continent."

"What do you mean?" A thrill of presentiment passed through Phaedra, but she could not understand the meaning. What had this to do with her? Nothing, she presumed, and yet she felt sure that something was about to happen.

"Do you know of a young man, a Baron Fossey? Does he live nearby, do you know?"

"Well, yes, I know Charles. He lives about ten miles from here, a very pretty estate called Thwicke House. He is several years younger than I, and so I do not know him so very well. He has been away at school and in London, you know. But I know his sis . . ." She trailed off as she watched the earl's expression harden.

"He is the reason I am here. We made a bet and he lost, and the scoundrel fled without paying me my due."

"Charles? I have never heard him to be a gambler. What did he gamble?" Phaedra felt her heart thumping in her chest as she remembered Deborah's desperation and her assertion that only the most dreadful calamity could keep Charlie from speaking to her. She jumped up nervously and went to a side table to pour herself another cup of tea from the china pot.

"We played a friendly game of euchre. I put up my stable and he put up his estate, and he lost. I have come to claim my winnings."

Her legs quivered unsteadily, but she refused to collapse. Carefully, carefully, she put the pot back down and turned to look at the earl. "He put up his estate, you say. What part? The farm? The orchard? The stable?"

"Please give me some credit, my dear," the earl said with a sardonic lift to his eyebrow. "My stables are renowned throughout the country. He put up his entire estate against my stables, and he lost."

"He lost his entire estate? On a game of euchre?" The sunlight dimmed and Hardcastle was shrouded temporarily in the gloom of shadow cast by the draperies. She moved to stand in front of him and stared down at him.

Frowning, he said, "Such a wager is not unusual. But most losers are man enough to own up to their debt and settle it in an honest manner."

"But Charles is the sole support of his mother—she is almost sixty—and his sister. Poor Anna is a widow, just my age or a little older, and has no other means of support. Surely Charles would not—*you* would not—" She was shocked beyond speech, but willing to find that she was mistaken. Charles Fossey would not gamble his whole estate on a turn of the cards, and merely for some dilettante's stable! He had always been a reasonably sensible young man, though his head had been turned in the last year by his sudden ascension to his baronial title. Hardcastle was joking. It was a jest. In a moment he would quietly say, "You do not think I really would, do you, my dear?" Wouldn't he? *Please,* she prayed, *let it be an ill-timed joke on his part.* She watched his face, noting the hard jaw, the tight mouth, the bright gleam of his black eyes.

"Fossey did and I certainly will! He will not rob me of my just winnings."

Phaedra examined his face. A bright ray of spring sunlight found its way through the gathering clouds and streamed in the window. "You don't understand," she said, kneeling in front of him and laying her hands over his. "It is all they have, the estate. It is how they support themselves. Anna has no pension from her late husband, and had to come home to her mother and brother after his death. Lady Fossey is in poor health and afflicted with a nervous disorder since the death of *her* husband."

Hardcastle gave a mirthless chuckle. "Do you know how prevalent are tales of woe in London? Every other person has an ailing mother or a sickly child, especially if they have just lost at cards."

Phaedra was taken aback at the callous tone in his voice. She sat back on her heels and gazed up at him, searching for signs of clemency, looking for pity or mercy—something! Some tender emotion. "But this is true! This is not Charles telling you, it is I, and—"

"It does not matter," he said, putting up his hand. "He lost the estate. It is legally mine, and yet the whelp reneged and slunk back here to Oxfordshire. That is why I was riding in the middle of the night along this road. I intended to be at his estate at first light to confront him with his dastardly flight."

This was it, Phaedra thought. This was the reason he had been waylaid and stripped and beaten; it was to keep him from impoverishing poor Charles Fossey and his blameless sister and mother. It would be up to her to convince Hardcastle that he must not claim his debt. She had come to know the earl over the last few days. He did not seem the despicable kind of creature who would toss an elderly woman and a widow from their only home. Surely not! She would appeal to his better nature.

"My lord," she said carefully, glancing over his dark eyes and drawn-down eyebrows, the hard glint and obstinate jaw, "I do not think you understand. Anna Listerton, Charles's sister, is a widow. She has nothing, no means to live apart from what Charles allows her. And the dowager baroness, she is sickly. The poor thing is barely able to stand the sunlight on her face! To be . . . to be ejected from her *home* . . ." Words failed Phaedra. Simplicity was best, she thought. "It would kill her, without exaggeration."

"My dear," Hardcastle said, his eyes kinder. "Please, do not distress yourself over this." He took up her hands and caressed them, rubbing his thumbs over them.

Phaedra watched him, gratitude in her heart. She sagged against his knees, relieved. Thank a benevolent Lord for causing Hardcastle to pause in his way—even if he had to suffer, it would be worth it in the end for all concerned—and for showing her the way to him. He would let Charles Fossey free from his debt. He would say that, of course, he never would cast a widow—*two* widows—out into the cruel world.

"My dear," he said gently, squeezing her hands and raising one to his lips, "it is none of your concern, so please, do not distress yourself. Charles Fossey should have thought of that before he wagered his estate. I am heartily sorry for the widowed Mrs. Listerton and the dowager baroness, but they are not my concern. I made a wager in good faith, and the very fabric of our great nation would crumble around us if wagers were not seen as a sacred trust. What of honor? What of honesty? I cannot and *will* not let that young whelp cheat me, for he would be cheating himself and every other gentleman by reneging on his debt. No, Charles Fossey must pay up, and the moment I am able, I will be on Pegasus and on my way to Thwicke House to demand my rightful due."

Twelve

"Is there anything you want before I retire, my lord?"

Hardcastle lay on the narrow bed and brooded. Phaedra's demeanor toward him had frozen into abhorrence since the new information, that he was set on beggaring her neighbor and friend. And yet that was not true! He was *not* set on beggaring them, just on claiming what was rightfully his. He was doing nothing wrong, and he would not let a little snippet of a country parson's daughter make him feel otherwise.

"Come here, Phaedra," he said. The room was dark, and she glowed like a phantom in her virginal white nightrail. She moved toward him, her candle held in front of her so he could not quite see her face. She put it on the table and looked down at him. "Yes, my lord?"

Damn and blast! Against all of his intentions, against every instinct, he heard his voice, harsh in the quiet room, grind out, "I wish to claim my wager from you."

"Yes, you always do claim your wager, don't you? No matter what." Her voice was thick with unshed tears.

"I do," he said, quelling a sensation akin to pain. "I claim what is *mine,* by rights. And you owe me one kiss. I demand it now."

She sat stiffly on the side of the bed, and he thought miserably that this would be the death of any hope of enticing her into his bed. She would never put herself in any position of vulnerability again, for she would be cautious next time. And this kiss would be a cold, hard little peck on the cheek, no doubt.

But not if he could help it.

He sat up on the bed, thankful that now his limbs were beginning to respond to his will. She closed her eyes as he took her slim shoulders in his hands and pulled her toward him. He studied her face up close in the candlelight for a moment, memorizing the soft slopes and downy texture, the pale pink blush that sat like two circlets of felt on her cheekbones. Then he claimed her lips and was entranced at the soft, moist, dewiness against his mouth. Hungrily, he suckled the soft flesh of her lip, feeling a mad desire to nip at her like a hungry wolf nips at a tender lamb. His body throbbed to life, a heavy, hot pulse in his nether regions urging him to lay her down and pin her to the bed and kiss her until she admitted what was between them, admitted that she was hungry for his love, as he was for hers.

He released her lips so he could ask her to stay, the madness in his soul making him forget everything but his need for her.

"Is the wager satisfied, my lord?" Her voice was cool and calm in the dimness.

Damnation. "It is," he said, his voice hoarse. She was untouched. How demeaning to find that the kiss that had so moved him had left her cold. He released her shoulders with an effort.

"Then I have maintained my honor. Is that right, my lord?" Her voice trembled on the edge of tears.

His heart thudded. "Phaedra," he said gently. "My dear, did I . . . did I hurt you in any way, or was I too rough?"

"Not on me," she said. She would not meet his eyes. "How could you be so hard, so cruel to poor Anna and Lady

Fossey and Charles? What have they ever done to hurt you?"
She caught back a sob.

Tears. By God there were tears in her voice. Hardcastle
swallowed. She had begun to like him, he thought, had
warmed toward him and was vulnerable to him, and now that
was in danger of being forfeit because of that damned wager.
"They have done nothing to hurt me, my dear little one." He
reached out for her hand, but she pulled it away from him.
"Phaedra, I am not doing this to punish them." He tried to ignore the soft, still voice in his soul that reminded him that
punishment had been very much on his mind where Charles
Fossey was concerned. "But I cannot and will not let that
young man renege on his wager. There would be no honor
left in this world if we did not enforce our bargains. Surely
you see that?"

"Honor? You speak of honor? You would force an old lady
and a widow into the poorhouse, and yet you speak of
honor?"

"Stop being so melodramatic, Phaedra," Hardcastle said,
pushing himself up against his pillows. "Act me no
Cheltenham tragedies, if you please. You know damned well
they will not go to the poorhouse. There will be some relative
willing to take them in for the dignity of the family name, and
the young man may have to work for his living. It will do him
good. He may be more cautious next time he challenges a
man to a card game."

"How hard you are."

"I have learned to be hard. Do you not think that young
Baron Fossey should have thought of his dependent family
before he wagered all for my stables? I would have paid him
that moment if he had won, and he would have expected it!
He would have had the deed and the keys before the sun came
up the next morning. Do you think he would have told me to

keep my stables? Why should I not expect the same compliance from him? Should he not have thought of the possibility of losing before he bet with me?"

"Yes," Phaedra said, her voice as soft as the dusky darkness of the room.

Taken aback, Hardcastle said, "What?"

"Yes, he should have thought of the consequences before he wagered with you. But he is young; now he will have learned his lesson. And you have the chance to do something truly noble. You have the opportunity to give him and his family a second chance." She clasped her small hands together in an expression of supplication and leaned toward him so that he could feel the warmth of her, could smell her intoxicating scent. "Oh, please, my lord, be noble. Be good. Be the man that I believe you to be."

Her words and her tone were bewitching. How grateful would she be if he did as she asked? Grateful enough that all of her resolve would melt and she would come into his arms? *Be the man that I believe you to be.* Oh, to hear her whisper her thank-yous in his ear as they made love. But then his heart hardened against her entreaties. She did not know what she asked. He was once young, too, and if he had learned anything from his father, it was that there *was* no second chance. Life was hard. The sooner Charles Fossey learned that, the better for him.

"You do not understand," he said. "It is not noble to just let someone free from a wager they made in good faith. What is the point in wagering if one does not pay up an honest loss? Did you refuse to honor your wager? No. You kissed me just now, though I am sure you did not want to."

She gave a little gasp, but then shook her head. "Surely common compassion—"

"Why do you think I have any compassion at all?" he said

132

hoarsely, driven to bald honesty by the bewitching force of her tear-filled eyes and trembling voice. If he was not blunt and forceful this moment he would promise her anything, only to regret it in the daylight hours. "Even if I were weak enough to think of letting that young man off the hook, I would not. Not for him. He reneged. He is a cheat, and there is nothing more filthy in this world than a cheat. A cheat tears at the very fabric of our society. How many things and people and principles depend on all of us keeping our word? I have an estate, and the people I employ depend upon me keeping my word that I will pay them what I say I will. I do not gamble more than I can afford to lose. I *always* keep my word. No, my dear, I am sorry, but honor must be satisfied."

Phaedra stood. "Very well." There were no tears in her voice now, only fury. "I hope you will be happy with your honor, knowing that you have cost decent folk any hope of comfort or independence with your talk of honor." With that she whirled and left the room.

Long into the dark night Hardcastle tussled with the dilemma. He could afford to let the young man go. Phaedra would be grateful; he would be a hero to her. He might even win in his effort to seduce her. He recoiled from that thought. If he won her, he wanted her because she wanted *him*, not out of some mistaken gratitude or misunderstanding of who he was. No woman had ever succumbed to him out of *gratitude*.

No, he couldn't do it. Fossey had lost and then had reneged on his debt by running away, and that was unthinkable and unforgivable. The sooner he regained his strength and went after the young man the better. And he had best do it before he weakened in the face of Phaedra's soft entreaties. As he drifted off to sleep he remembered her submission, the way she offered herself to him, paying her debt in full when she could have only given him a peck on the cheek. The memory flooded his body with heat and desire. Wouldn't his friends laugh to see Hardhearted Hardcastle in thrall to a pretty little country vicar's daughter? Perhaps not, though. More likely, given this particular vicar's daughter's soft curves and winsome expression, they would all be entering the competition to seduce her and make her their mistress.

He turned over and stared through the dimness at the ceiling. Was that all he was doing? Was she the ultimate challenge, a virtuous maiden to be led down a dark trail of seduction and lust until she betrayed her moral upbringing? He shifted uncomfortably onto his side and pummeled his pillow. *Don't be ridiculous,* he told himself crossly. He was not going to set her up as some Haymarket doxy. He just wanted her to offer him her lovely body. He wanted to sample her charms, to make love to her in a mutual giving and taking of pleasure. She was a woman. Very much a woman, he thought, remembering how perfectly she fit into his arms, and the sensation of small, perfectly shaped breasts brushing against his chest—

Augh! He turned over onto his stomach and buried his face in the pillow. If he entertained any more thoughts like that he would toss and turn all night. Willing his body to behave in a more appropriate fashion, Hardcastle finally won sleep in a close battle with a clutch-fisted Morpheus.

But Phaedra did *not* sleep. After tossing and turning, giving poor Sally a restless night at the same time, she finally got up before daybreak and made the dough for bread, punching it down with angry vigor, shaping it into loaves, and setting it aside to let it proof for later. She stood in the doorway and drank a glass of buttermilk while she watched the morning sun rise over the horizon. She was gazing off to the east. In that direction was Baron Fossey's estate, and poor Anna Listerton. What was she going to do? The new knowledge that the whole family was about to lose its home left her distraught and overwhelmed.

And how could she justify, in the light of her new knowledge, that she still felt a tenderness and desire for Lord Hardcastle that was completely out of keeping with the coldness of his own heart?

He had thought she acquiesced to the kiss the night before because of the wager, and that had been how she rationalized it to herself. But she was ever honest, and she knew that what she wanted from him had nothing to do with their wager. She wanted him in the way a woman wanted a man. Perhaps she was innocent in the ways of the flesh, but she was a country woman. Male and female mating habits were no mystery. And one could not listen to the women of the village without learning that human male and female habits were not so very different, except that occasionally, if one was very lucky, one received love, God's gift to humanity.

No, her response to him had nothing to do with paying off a debt, and everything to do with the mesmerizing force of his black eyes and the thrilling feel of his arms around her, caressing her. She had entered the kiss eagerly, and she had had to will her voice into a cool, collected calmness after, when she asked him if she had satisfied her wager, because with the touch of his lips and his arms he had changed her from a rational woman into a trembling, quivering girl experiencing desire for the first time and helpless in the face of it. It had been all she could do to gaze at him icily when she wanted to throw herself back into his arms and kiss him again. And yet, that was over. He was a cold, cold man, and she had no desire to lose herself in the black pit of his soul. That way lay madness. She pushed away from the door frame and set about her morning tasks with a saddened heart.

"Well, me lord, seems to me that you've got something—or should I say someone—on yer mind," Mrs. Lovett said, lifting the covers and peering under them. She snickered and winked.

"I can take care of my own personal needs, now, Mrs. Lovett," Hardcastle said, snatching the covers away from her. She had come upon him unexpectedly, awakening him from a tender dream of Phaedra, a dream of sweet surrender, soft skin, murmured words of love.

"I'll bet you just can, me lord," the woman said with a salacious grin. "But if I can help you in any way . . ." She let the words trail off, leaving it to the imagination what kind of help she meant.

"I shall be all right, Mrs. Lovett. Is Miss Gillian about?"

"Aye, she is. She and her da are at morning prayers in the library."

"Morning pra—oh, yes. Tell me, Mrs. Lovett, why has Miss Gillian never married?"

The woman paused in the act of emptying his chamber pot into the slops basin and frowned. "I've always wondered that meself. Don't think she's ever been asked. Mayhap it's just that there's no one suitable in these parts. There's been those who have fallen for her—there is not a soul in Ainstoun that has an unkind word to say about Miss Gillian, and she's a pretty gel, no mistake about that—but not a one would have dared court her."

"Why? She's not—she doesn't seem cold-natured to me." Hardcastle grimaced at the depths to which he had plunged, interrogating the serving staff to learn more about Phaedra. How he would have derided such actions a mere week before!

Mrs. Lovett did not seem to find it strange, though. She rinsed the chamber pot and tucked it away, then sat down on the end of the bed. "No, she's not cold, just . . . ah, what's the word I'm lookin' for? She knows how to keep the fellas from makin' a cake of themselves before they even start."

"She is aloof?"

The woman looked doubtful. "Mayhap that be the word. If you say so, me lord. Not much material in the way of beaux around these parts for a young lady like Miss Gillian."

Phaedra came in at that moment, carrying a pile of clothing in her hands. "Mrs. Lovett, are you done here?"

"Just now," Mrs. Lovett said, jumping up from her relaxed seat on the end of the bed.

"Good." Phaedra turned toward Hardcastle but did not meet his eyes. "I have mended and laundered your clothing, my lord. And the Simondsons have sent over the bag they found with Pegasus. It was somewhat mangled—they think the horse spent some time in the woods—but there are still your own nightshirt and a few other things that I will launder, as they seem a bit the worse for wear. After your venture yesterday, I thought you might like to go outside today, into the garden. It promises to be the warmest day we have had yet."

"I would like that immensely," he replied. Her voice, her presence was enough to send his mind tumbling back to his dream, and further, to their kiss the night before.

"We do not have a jacket that will fit you, though; those dreadful robbers took yours and there was not another one in your bag." She bit her lip and glanced up. "But I think it will be warm enough that you will not need one, and if you do not mind going without—"

"I don't need a jacket, Phaedra. And thank you for mending and laundering my clothing." He held her gaze with his own, trying to express without words how sorry he was that they had quarreled. He was rewarded by a thawing of her blue eyes and a softening of her expression.

"It is nothing, really. I was glad to do it."

There was silence for a moment. Hardcastle could not tear his gaze from her and she seemed uncertain, almost. Mrs. Lovett cleared her throat. "Yes, well, if yer well enough to dress yerself, me lord, then we may as well leave you to it." She took the stack of clothes from Phaedra and dumped them on the bed. "But if you need my help to get into yer breeches, you just give a holler," she added, winking.

"I don't think I will need any help," Hardcastle said dryly, noting Phaedra's quick turn away and the mantling of pink on her cheeks. Maybe there was still hope. That one long look between them had shown him she was still susceptible to him, so perhaps there was still a chance for them.

Phaedra knelt by the edge of her herb garden and pulled out a couple of vigorous weeds that had taken root just within days, it seemed. She had been spending far too much time alone with Lord Hardcastle and not nearly enough time tending her duties, and her garden was becoming neglected. She dusted off her hands and sat back on her heels, surveying her work with satisfaction. It was only May, but already the borage cutting she had planted the previous summer was showing encouraging signs of vigorous growth and the savory and thyme were well on their way. Bay and oregano, mint and sage, all were doing well thanks to her careful preparation of the soil and Bessy's invaluable contribution.

"What a lovely spot."

Phaedra whirled and plunked down on her bottom, startled by the voice behind her. "My lord," she gasped. "I did not expect you."

Hardcastle was leaning on a chair on the flagstone terrace, and though his face was white and his dark eyes shadowed, he was smiling. "I delight in surprising you, Phaedra, especially if it causes you to land in such a pretty confusion."

Phaedra jumped up and dusted off her bottom. Somehow he always managed to make her blush. In his room earlier, she had been surprised by the warmth still evident in his eyes, even after their quarrel the night before. Now was the time to test her theory. She had begun to wonder if he was hard by nature, or if there really was a warm, compassionate man lurking underneath the aristocratic facade. His main objection to releasing Baron Fossey from the results of his disastrous wager seemed to lie in the young man's supposed intention to cheat the earl. But if he truly did not mean to renege—

"Will you sit down, my lord, and let me bring you breakfast out here? I have some fresh scones and honey laid out and ready." She smiled at him sweetly. One did not catch flies with vinegar. If honey would soften the earl and regain the Fossey estate, then she would drown him in it.

Thirteen

A day like this really did show off her Oxfordshire home to its best advantage, Phaedra thought, taking in the radiant scene of blue skies, birds chirping in the hawthorne and the mellow golden stone of the garden wall lit by the morning sun climbing higher. She glanced over at her companion, who appeared to be watching a wren stealing pieces of straw from her flowerbed for his nest. She crumbled a bit of her breakfast, the last of one of her own scones, and tossed it onto the flagstones that made up the terrace. The bird hopped over and stole the crumb, flying off with it.

"This is a much different scene from that of London, I imagine," she ventured at last.

"Much," he agreed, as they watched the bird return and hop over to another crumb. It gazed up at them for a second and chirped a thank-you, before stealing the last crumb and fluttering off to the wall to consume his breakfast. "In London, even the birds are quarrelsome and demanding, shrieking at one like a fishwife instead of chirping in tune like they do here. I have not spent a spring in the country for . . . well, for more years than I can count. I had forgotten how peaceful it is."

Hope welled like a new spring in Phaedra's heart. No man who spoke thus could be entirely without feeling, without ruth. "My friend, Anna, says the same. When her husband was alive she spent all of her time in London, and she told me that coming back to Oxfordshire, even though it was in tragic circumstances— her husband was a lieutenant in the light dragoons and lost his life at Quatre Bras—was like a reawakening. She cannot imagine now going back to her old life." She glanced over at the earl, but there was no sign on his face that he remembered who Anna was.

"But there is much to distract one in London," Hardcastle said, stretching out his long legs and grimacing. "Ow. There is still pain in my muscles. Will this never go away?"

"Be patient, my lord. You must learn patience." Phaedra pondered how to introduce the subject she had in mind. She had intended to work up from the mention of Anna, Charles Fossey's widowed sister, but that had not gone quite as planned. "You mentioned last night that you had a country estate. Where would it be?"

"Northampton," he said.

"That is just north of us. Is it very big?"

"Fair. I have another in Dorset and a hunting box in Exmoor."

Phaedra clenched her hands in her skirts. Hearing him enumerate his holdings was only making her grow more angry that with all he had, he would still take away poor Charles's estate. It was shameful! How could he not . . . She forced herself to calm. He likely did not see things her way. To him this was a matter of principle. How principle could make him steal the only home the aging dowager baroness and a poverty-stricken widow had, she could not reconcile, but if she was to win this battle, she must remain clear-sighted.

"And I believe I own a small estate in Yorkshire, as well, of course, as the house in London."

Too *much!* Phaedra leaped to her feet and stood in front of Hardcastle. "How can you even think about taking away

Charles Fossey's home when you have four? No, *five!* I cannot believe how arrogant and unfeeling you are. Why can you not just let the poor idiot off the hook instead of making him pay for an idiotic wager, and not just him, but his whole family must suffer. It is unconscionable." Phaedra clamped her lips together to stop her vitriolic tirade. Lord preserve her! It was exactly what she had not intended to do, but that last little addition, that estate in Yorkshire that he could not even recall! She wanted to scream at him. She slumped back down in her seat, turned her face away and stared off into the distance, biting her lip. *Blessed are the meek, for they shall inherit the earth.* Not bloody likely! The meek, it seemed, were destined to be turned out of their homes and inherit nothing.

"Phaedra," Hardcastle said, sitting up and gazing over at her with a mild look on his face, "you must see that this has nothing to do with how many estates I own. That Charles Fossey had only the one should have made him more careful of it. Especially if, as you say, that is the home of his mother and sister, too."

The calm reasonableness of his voice only made her want to throw something at his head, preferably something heavy and rotten. No one else had ever affected her this way, making her by turns amused, passionate, and furious. And no one had *ever* made her want to throw something at them! But that would do Charles and his family no good, and she had made a promise to herself to put their interests above everything else. She would do anything and everything she could to keep them from losing their home. This was not just for Charles, but for Anna, her friend, and for Deborah, who had hopes of marrying Charles before too many more months passed. This spring was to see her convince her father that she would wed no one but Charles. If he lost his home there would be no hope for them ever.

And this was for the poor dowager baroness. Phaedra had been greatly saddened by the once-vibrant woman's frailty and descent into illness since her husband's death. What would being pitched from their family estate do to her?

But how was she to change Hardcastle's mind? He was an intelligent man, a logical man, but she did not think him evil. He was, perhaps, dispassionate to the point of coolness, but he had a passionate side. She had seen it blazing in his eyes. However, she saw no way to use that side of him in aid of her friends. Passion toward her—she still did not know whether to believe it, or whether it was all a part of his rake's bag of tricks—would not help them. No, she must find a way to appeal to his sense of justice and honor. She glanced over at him. He was sprawled at his ease, letting the sun warm his up-turned face. This was why God had sent him to her, to stop the horrible train of events that had started with Charles Fossey stupidly gambling away his ancestral home.

Think, Phaedra, think, she admonished herself. *Perhaps* . . . An idea formed in her mind, the result of a half-remembered detail that Hardcastle had told her in his relation of the story of the night he and Charles played that fatal game of cards. "I think, my lord, that you told me what the note Charles left for you said. What was it again?"

"The note? Let me see . . . It was some nonsense about needing time. If it were true, why did he not stay in London and ask me for it himself? That would have been the honorable thing."

"Perhaps," Phaedra said, doubtfully. "But you said yourself you did not know each other when you sat down to play cards. He could not know if you would acquiesce or not; perhaps he dared not risk it. After all," she added wryly, "I cannot imagine that you are well-known for your merciful side. Did you always do the exact right thing when you were three-and-twenty, sir? Were you always perfectly knowledge-able of the right thing to do or say?"

She had hit upon something, for he quickly turned crimson. He sat up straighter but remained silent.

"You do not know Charles," she said quickly, following up on her advantage, if that was what it was. "I do not know him well, myself, but he is well liked in this county, and the locals call him a 'likely lad'. That is high praise from some of them. He is thought to be honorable and promises to become a better landlord and employer than even his father. Do you truly think he meant to cheat you, or could it be that he raced home to try to arrange things, to try to prepare his mother and his sister for the necessity of their moving? Perhaps he is even trying to arrange it himself, to find some place for them to live that would not be too horrible for them. Could it be that was what he asked for time for?"

Reluctantly, Hardcastle said, "I suppose. But I am not an evil man, Phaedra. If he had told me that, if he had asked for time for that reason, I would have given him the time! As much, within reason, as he could need."

Carefully, Phaedra considered her next words. He said he was not an evil man, and he had a sense of justice. Perhaps . . . "Then you will admit that there was likely no intention to de-fraud you. I can tell you, he has not left the county. Does that not plead his case that he is just trying to do right by his family? By his mother who is ill and his sister who is poor?"

"I admit it, yes." Hardcastle gave her a twisted smile. "You have no doubt never been in a court of law, my dear, but you would make an admirable barrister. All right, I freely admit that the young man likely did not mean to defraud me, if, as you say, he is still in the county and has not fled in this week I have been laid up here."

"And isn't it that which really angered you, causing you to

race across country at night? You thought he was attempting to escape his rightful debt, to flee the country even."

"Yes. If what you conjecture is the truth, I am not angry at the pup. But he should have stayed to explain to me. Idiot."

"Then, knowing how desperate he is, knowing he is still an honorable young man, can you not make an exception this once? Release him from his debt, my lord. Let him go. He will be eternally grateful." *Blessed are the merciful . . .*

Sighing deeply, Hardcastle said nothing for a moment. He was going to capitulate, Phaedra thought, feeling a tiny welling of joy in her heart. He *must* see how important this was. He could not possibly want the estate at the cost of the dowager baroness and her widowed daughter.

"I wish it were that easy, Phaedra." His voice was quiet and he stared down at his hands, which were laced together over his leg. "But it is not as simple as releasing this young man from his debt. It truly is not."

"Why not?" she said. It seemed simple enough. All he had to do was send a message saying Charles would not need to pay. They could send one that very afternoon.

Hardcastle shifted in his seat and gazed steadily into her eyes. "My dear, you do not understand the code among men, nor do you know London society. Gambling debts are debts of honor, and honor *must* be served! If he could not afford to gamble, he should not have risked his family's fate on the turn of a card, but that is not my fault. I neither cajoled, nor bullied, nor entreated him to play. He challenged me. And now, in honor, he must pay his debt."

Frustrated, Phaedra said, "Honor! What honor is there in tossing out an elderly lady and a penniless young woman, along with the young man who foolishly gambled away their lives, from the only home they have?" She felt the tears well up, but she would not weep. He must see her side, must give in, but she would despise herself if she gave in to tears, and *that* was the reason he changed his mind.

His voice hard, his face grim, Hardcastle said, "What moralizing tripe! You know nothing of life if you think that it is as easy as just telling Charles Fossey that he is off the hook, that he does not have to pay his legal and rightful debt." He leaned over toward Phaedra and said, "That card game was a very public one. There were plenty of people there to witness it. Even if I were to forgo my winnings, Fossey would be ruined in London. Everyone would suspect some funny business. And I! I would not be welcome in my clubs. I would have let down the unspoken rules of behavior, the code of ethics that every young man learns, that your young Fossey knew before he engaged me to play."

"There must be some way," Phaedra cried, jumping up and pacing the length of the short flagstone terrace. She turned back and stared at the earl. "There must! It just isn't right that you who have so much should take away the only home Charles and his family have!"

"I am not 'taking' it away! I am not stealing it! For God's sake, why can you not see that?" Hardcastle clutched his head, jamming his fingers into his hair until it stood out in unusually ruffled spikes. He took a deep breath and passed one hand over his hair, laying it down flat again. When he spoke, it was slow and clear, much as one might talk to an idiot or an elderly maiden aunt tottering on the edge of dotage. "It is a debt of honor, and honor *must* be served!"

Exasperated, Phaedra threw her arms up in the air and cried, "You keep saying that as if honor is some kind of gorgon who will lash out and destroy society if her needs are not met exactly. It is ridiculous, *insane!* I *will* not believe it." She slumped back down in her chair.

"Now you are retreating to the last refuge of the loser, and that is ridicule. Do not deride what you do not understand."

Mr. Gillian, blinking in the late-morning sun, came out of a set of French doors to the garden terrace. "Hey, now, children; what is all this gibble-gabble about?"

"Papa! Did we disturb you?" Phaedra leaped to her feet and raced to her father's side.

He put an arm around her shoulders and she laid her head on his. Hardcastle felt a tug of regret. There was so much reliance between them, so much trust and love. What must that be like, to have someone run to you that way, knowing they were welcome, knowing you would love them and hold them, no matter what?

"You did. My library is right there, or have you forgotten?" He squeezed his daughter's shoulder while he pointed with a sheaf of papers in his hand toward the curtained window behind them.

"I am sorry, sir," Hardcastle said, struggling to his feet. "Phaedra and I have had a difference of opinion, and she was expressing herself, uh, vigorously."

"She always does." He chuckled, squeezed her shoulder again, and released her. "Good to see you up and about, my lord. How are you feeling?"

"Better, though not at full force. I seem to have bruised some, er, vital areas. It is good to be outside, though, and in clothing. I have never been a layabout type."

"Ah, yes, and there is nothing like an Oxfordshire morning!" The vicar looked around him and smiled benevolently at the brilliant scene of sun and blue sky.

Phaedra glanced over at Hardcastle and then back to her father. "Papa," she said slowly, as though she were thinking of what she was about to say. Then in a rush, she continued, "Papa, Lord Hardcastle and I have been having a difference of opinion over honor. Do you agree that honor can be used to excuse unpleasant behavior? That one must judge each circumstance on its own merits and not use 'honor' as some sort of feeble refuge?"

"That is not what I am doing!" Hardcastle turned to the older man and said, "I say, sir, that honor is inflexible, and must not be bent to one's own will. One cannot just change the rules where honor is concerned; it is immutable."

Phaedra turned to him and said, "I am not saying to change the rules, but merely to let compassion—"

"Stop!" Mr. Gillian held up his free hand. "I will not arbitrate this quarrel, children. I have other things to think about. But keep this in mind. Honor is real and important; no person has the right to judge another's sense of honor, because it is *not* a thing, like this table or that chair, immutable and unchanging. Every person's sense of honor comes from within themselves and must be respected."

Hardcastle nodded. "We may disagree on the nature of honor, sir, but I support your right to that view. And your beliefs buttress my argument, in this case. I cannot bend my own notion of honor to fit someone else's."

"However," Mr. Gillian said with a warning glance for the earl, "evil done to another in the name of honor is still evil; there is no way to ameliorate it with fine words and high-flown philosophies. Compassion will sometimes force us to rethink our code of honor and amend it, for we only live in this world once, and all of us depend upon one another to live. In some cultures honor demands that an insult must be returned by death; one must kill the one who has insulted your family or your name or your wife. Consider the dying practice of dueling in our own culture. It was once considered that honor had to be served, and that a slight must be served with vengeance to soothe honor. All that did was kill young men who had so much to live for. Now, though dueling is still practiced, we are more likely to let our quarrels be solved by the courts, thus saving lives."

"What are you saying, sir?" Hardcastle began to feel that the argument had gone far afield, and he was lost. No wonder this scholar's daughter sounded like a barrister.

"I am saying that I will not pronounce a victor in your quarrel. You are two intelligent youngsters. You will sort it out." And with a twinkle in his eye, he turned and started back toward the door. "But please, for my sake, sort it out more quietly."

The door closed, and they were alone again. Phaedra's face was turned away from Hardcastle, and he could not see her expression. He could not sort out what Mr. Gillian had really been saying. It was a matter of interpretation, he supposed. As a parson he understandably would come down on the side of people, of preventing the harm that would occur to them.

But one made a hundred decisions a day; if one spent all one's time rethinking everything to make sure it hurt no one . . . Surely the mill owner and the brewer and the landlord could not consider every man's good before he considered his own profits? If the landlord tossed out of one of his buildings the family of a layabout who would not pay his rent, did he need to consider that he would be putting a woman and children out of a home? What about his freedom to conduct his business how he chose? If a mill owner or a mine owner needed to modernize, to bring in machinery that would displace a hundred men, could he think about the impact that would have on every last one of his workers? No, that was ludicrous! He had to stay competitive.

And yet . . .

Hardcastle was not blind, nor was he stupid. He had heard about and even debated, in the House, the poor laws and the mill workers' strikes. He might be a rake and a gambler, but he also did his duty by his parliamentary position. Some compromise was always there, somewhere, if it could just be found and negotiated. The lack of such compromise in matters in the House had often frustrated him.

And too, *The quality of mercy is not strain'd.*

But still, it was the beliefs and values of a lifetime, and of hard learning that she was asking him to go against. He could not do it. Not even for her.

"I find myself without words, my lord," Phaedra said, her face still turned away. "I do not think there is a resolution here that will satisfy us both. And so you may hold on to your honor, and I hope it makes you happy. I shall feel it my duty to keep you abreast of what poor haven Lady Fossey and Anna Listerton have found, and how sadly their family is split up."

"That is below you, Phaedra. You have been quarreling by man's rules, and doing a damned fine job, and yet now you try to wound with a woman's ways."

Phaedra turned tragic eyes on him. "Unlike you, I have no harsh code of honor that I must live up to. If I cannot successfully entreat you to act like a human with compassion by 'men's rules', then I will resort to women's rules, the rules of compassion and caring and love. And guilt, if there is that feeble emotion in your breast. I will resort to tears, if I must. But I do not think that would move you, my lord. One needs a heart to be moved by tears."

Hardcastle saw the water build up in her eyes, the droplets spilling over and trickling down. "Ah, my dear," he said softly, desperately trying to ignore the slice of pain in his heart at the anguish he sensed in her. "Do you not know that every hardened rake has seen his share of tears, has been wheedled and implored with them for a new diamond necklace or an emerald bracelet?"

"If you cannot tell the difference between tears that flow for human need, and those that flow from avarice and greed, then I pity you." Phaedra stood and leveled a long, hard look at him. "It is time for me to prepare luncheon, my lord, and I think you should go back indoors as it has clouded over and threatens to rain."

Fourteen

The long morning in the garden had exhausted him and he had retreated to his temporary chamber, to rest his weary bones and muscles. He hated idleness, and yet he was forced into it by the abominable weakness he still felt.

Awake now, though, rested and well fed after a superb luncheon of pigeon pie, he stretched out on the bed and stared at the all-too-familiar ceiling. Phaedra . . . What a mystery she was, what a riddle. She was so young, if not in years, then in ideals. And she despised him. It disturbed him more than he cared to admit, more than he even would admit to himself. He had never met a woman like her. He was used to people, men and ladies, giving way in the face of his title, his intelligence, his reputation, a million and one advantages he knew he had and made use of every day.

But she would not capitulate, not one whit. She had beauty and sweetness, but also intelligence and a kind of rigorous morality he had only met with in one person before, his friend, Mercy Dandridge. Phaedra, like Mercy, lived the golden rule every day.

She was her father's daughter, and yet to the intelligence and moral rectitude of the father she added a compassion that truly connected with people. He did not have the feeling that she did things for people because it was a road to heaven or because she needed to feel superior, but because she honestly cared.

Restlessly, Hardcastle struggled out of bed and limped around the room. He had to push himself on to recovery. He must become physically the man he had always been. Phaedra was, no doubt, wishing him long gone, and his pride would not let him stay in a place he was not wanted. He hobbled over to the window and stared out blankly, not seeing the verdant hills, deep green with the rain sheeting down over them, nor the road winding into the distance, past Ainstoun and beyond, to other villages and estates.

There was so much in this household that he did not understand. For instance, it was clear that Mr. Gillian had heard, somehow, about his reputation as a rake, and yet he let him stay on even as he recovered, with a virginal daughter under his roof. Did he trust the gentleman's code Hardcastle lived by? As a man of honor, he would never force a lady, nor even cajole her against her morals. A woman must come to him freely or he would not bed her. How deeply he longed for Phaedra to come to him in that way he would never divulge to another living soul. But Mr. Gillian's apparent faith in him— it touched Hardcastle deeply to have the trust of such a man—would not be misplaced.

And yet, if she should come to him willingly, for her own reasons, would he not love her?

He folded his arms on the narrow sill of the window and stared out, watching the raindrops bouncing merrily off the wood. His friend, the finch, landed on the sill and shook himself, droplets of water flying off in all directions. He stared at Hardcastle for a moment, and then left again, to fly off to parts unknown.

The earl was deeply confused and could not find his way through the mess of emotion and logic and misplaced passion he was tangled within. Somehow his desire for her had become entangled with respect for her intelligence and regard for her sterling qualities. She was forcing him to spend as much time thinking about her conversation as about her personal attractions, and that was a rare thing indeed, where a lady was concerned. He had never before considered a woman's brains as important as her breasts.

He tried to contemplate with calmness Phaedra's arguments; they had some merit. What kind of code of ethics could state that a gambling debt, money acquired on the turn of a card, required payment that would ruin lives and destroy innocent people? But on the other hand, what was the use of gambling if it was not strictly required that bets, once made, were collected regardless of the hazard to lives? If one took the honorable resolution of debt away from gambling, it left merely cardplaying, with all the excitement taken out and no penalty for losing.

No. He stood by his reasoning. When both parties understood the penalty for losing, and in the case of himself and young Fossey they both had, for Hardcastle never ever gambled with someone who was drunk or whose mental capacity was not what it could be, then both parties must stand by the results. It was just. It was honorable. It was the only way to conduct society with any measure of dignity and grace.

Phaedra bustled in, a towel in her hands, and gathered up the dishes from his luncheon, which he had taken alone. He limped over to the bed and dropped down with a groan of pain.

"Phaedra, sit down beside me for a moment." A horrible new thought occurred to him as she obeyed. Was it possible . . . Could it be that she was betrothed or pledged to this young man, this Baron Fossey? She would never use that as leverage if that were true, but it would certainly explain why she was so concerned for him. But no, he knew her by now. If she were pledged to another man she would never have kissed him the way she did. Her heart was untouched, he would swear it.

"What do you want, my lord?" she said coolly.

"Have we not progressed beyond 'my lord'? Why do you not call me Hardcastle as my friends do?"

"Why do I not shorten it and just call you 'Hard'?" Her voice was velvety soft, but there was anger lingering under the tone.

"Do you think me hard and unfeeling, my dear?" He took her hand and felt it tremble, small and helpless like a pretty white dove in his hands. He turned it over. The palm had callused spots, and her fingers were puckered from hot wash water. What he wouldn't give to take her away from her toil, away to London where the best modistes could dress her elegant, slender limbs in costly silks, and the perfumier could mix a concoction of sandalwood and ambergris to perfume her perfect breasts and arms. He ached to touch her, and where their limbs met, where his leg touched hers on the edge of the bed, he felt afire. What a strange interlude this was that he should be so enchanted by a tuneless country sparrow when he had birds of paradise in London awaiting his every pleasure!

"I do not think you completely without feeling," she said after a moment. She glanced up and her eyes locked with his. "I just do not understand how, with the human emotion every man is given, you can still feel no pity for Anna and her mother. And for Charles."

"This Charles, do you know him well?" The flare of unaccustomed jealousy was unwelcome, and the words he had just uttered had not come from the thinking, reasoning part of him.

"I told you, I hardly know him. But Anna is of an age with

me, and we used to attend the same assemblies when we were girls."

That was good. Her voice was cool and unaffected when she spoke of Fossey. "Do you like to dance?" Hardcastle wound his fingers through hers, entranced by a vision of her floating around an elegant ballroom on satin slippers. How she would sparkle!

"I did when I was a girl. The local assemblies were not large, but a violin and a piano are sufficient when young people gather and are determined on gaiety. But we are far afield, my lord. What did you wish to say to me?" She pulled her hand away from his.

All right. He would have to tell her baldly. He put his hands on his knees and stared at the wall. "I have thought and thought on what we spoke of earlier, my dear, but I just cannot let it go. Charles Fossey lost a bet made in good faith, with full knowledge of the consequences. I cannot nor will I let him off."

Phaedra stood. "Then I guess that is all there is to say. I had hoped for a better outcome, my lord. I will not pretend I am not disappointed."

"I will send a note to my household staff in London by the next mailcoach to have my valet come down to help me back to London. I am sure you have long wished me hither."

"How strange you are," she said with a thoughtful frown. She cocked her head to one side. "Do you think that my hospitality is at an end because we disagree? I told you that you are welcome here. My father has told you that you are welcome here. And so you still are." She headed toward the door but turned back before exiting. "Constable Hodgins has a wish to speak with you this afternoon, along with Squire Daintry. They will be here within half an hour. After that, perhaps we may play chess."

★ ★ ★ ★ ★

Phaedra felt a calmness overtake her in the face of his definite answer. Argument was futile, she felt sure. Hardcastle was a man who, once he made up his mind it was done. And yet there were two warring sides to Hardcastle, she thought, as she mixed eggs into a flour mixture for the pudding she was making. One side of him was good and selfless and one was hard and severe. How did he choose which side would react to a problem or a person?

It was Sally's half day off, and she was gadding about the town in a dress Phaedra had altered for her, adding a few dressy ribbons and a furbelow to add length more suited to Sally's height. And so Phaedra was startled when a knock came at the back kitchen door. If that was Joe Mudge, the butcher's lad, she would give him a piece of her mind. He was entirely too forward, and too often distracted Sally from her duties. She wiped her floury hands on the cloth looped over her apron and headed for the door.

Unnecessarily, as it turned out. The door opened, and Deborah Daintry stumbled in, raindrops showering from her sodden bonnet. "Phaedra, I hoped you would be here," she sobbed.

Phaedra caught the girl just before she tumbled and saw the reason for her unwonted clumsiness; there were tears blinding her. "What is it, Deborah? What is wrong? Is it your mother? Is she sick?"

"No, she is fine. It is m-me!" The last word was an incoherent wail and she collapsed on a chair in front of the worktable and laid her head down in her arms, surrendering to a fit of weeping.

Crouching by her, Phaedra patted her back and whispered soothing words, then sprang up and got a cool, damp cloth to blot the girl's red eyes. Gradually Deborah calmed, and

Phaedra pulled a chair up close to her, kept the girl's hands in her own and said, "Now, tell me calmly, what is the matter?"

Sniffing and blowing her nose delicately, Deborah choked back one last sob, and said, "I s-saw him. I saw Charlie. He was riding through town, and I yelled for him; my mother would have a spasm if she heard me, but I did it and I don't care if it was unladylike. I yelled 'Charles', and he stopped and turned around. He saw me. I know he did, but he turned his horse and set him to gallop. Away from me. He has found someone new. I just know it. He found someone he likes better in London and he just cannot face me to tell me."

"No, Deborah, I do not believe that for a second." In an instant, Phaedra understood the scene. Charles Fossey and Deborah Daintry had a long-standing love, a childhood love that had matured as they grew up. Squire Daintry had demanded that no formal engagement take place and had bargained with his daughter for two seasons, two *London* seasons. If at the end of those two seasons she had found no one else she preferred—meaning in Squire Daintry's mind no one richer and better titled—then she and Charles would be allowed to announce their engagement. This being her second London season, Deborah had been looking forward to a summer wedding, even though Charles had never formally proposed.

But now, knowing that he was destitute, knowing he would have the responsibility of providing for his widowed mother and sister, Charles did not know how to face his sweetheart. And so he had left London, and he now avoided her back in Ainstoun.

More lives ruined by Hardcastle's wretched inflexibility. Or by Charles's stupid wagering! What had possessed the young baron? Was it his first season in London as the Baron Fossey? It was quite possible that the elevation to his title, the missing influence of his father, and the heady flattery of new London friends had all conspired to lead to his downfall, the ruinous wager.

"Then why else would he treat me this way?" Deborah asked. "What have I done? Did someone bear him false tales? I have been faithful; oh, I have danced and flirted with others, but that is accepted. That is London! He wouldn't think . . . Oh, Lord, I am so wretched!" She collapsed again in another fit of weeping.

Anger swept through Phaedra, as she accepted that even presenting Hardcastle with this terrible outcome would not move him. If a homeless widow would not touch his heart, then a pair of young lovers split asunder certainly would not. The future stretched out bleak and unhappy for four sad people. Deborah's heart would be broken. She had shown an astonishing fidelity toward her childhood friend and had never appeared to waver for an instant, even tempted by her success in London and a couple of proposals from young men much richer than Charles Fossey.

The dowager baroness would be forced, in her aging years, to live on the charity of some relative, as would Anna Listerton. Hardcastle was right; someone would take them in, and Phaedra very much feared it would be Anna's uncle, Sir Albert Vance. Anna had a terror of the man, and though she had never said so out loud, Phaedra suspected that the uncle had made advances to her, inappropriate suggestions— she could only pray it was nothing more. What a fate for her, to have to live on the charity of a man with such intentions toward her!

And Charles—what could a young man of three-and-twenty do when he had lost his livelihood? If he were very lucky he would become someone's land steward, for he knew farming and little else. But it would be a life of strictest economy, and he could not expect to marry until many years had passed, if he could ever afford it. And Phaedra very much feared Squire Daintry would absolutely put his foot down in this matter; Deborah would be beyond his touch forever.

As she thought, she had been mechanically patting Deborah's shoulder and murmuring soothing words. But coming back to the present, with new resolution in her heart, she said, "Deborah, dry your eyes, my dear. I do not believe Charles has been faithless. There may be some misunderstanding between you, but you must be patient. Do nothing for a couple of days, and I will see what I can find out." Hopefully that would stall the girl. Phaedra needed a little time. She needed time to enact a plan she had just concocted, a plan that had at least half a chance of regaining everything for the young couple, as well as for the baroness and Anna Listerton.

"Will you? Oh, Phaedra, I knew you would understand and help! I just knew it. That is why I stopped here on my way home." Deborah threw her arms around Phaedra's neck and hugged her.

"Go home. I will send you a note in a couple of days if I find out anything. I-I can't promise anything, you know. I just feel that Charles has not been unfaithful. He loves you too much."

It was later. Squire Daintry and Mr. Hodgins had come and gone, and Hardcastle had gone to sleep soon after. The luncheon dishes were done and put away, and most of dinner was prepared. Phaedra tiptoed into her father's library and waited for him to notice her. She had an enormous decision to make, and she did not know what to do. There was one path open to her, and she had almost determined to take it, but quailed at the thought of the risk she was taking.

"Papa," she finally said, gazing with affection at the gray head bent over the books on the desk.

"What? Oh, it's you, my dear. Is it dinnertime already?" He took his glasses off and laid them down.

"No, Papa. I just wanted to talk to you." She circled the desk and knelt by it, putting her arms around his neck and laying her head on his shoulder. As usual he smelled of books. It was odd, but there was a certain smell associated with books and paper, and that is how he had always smelled to her. He did not smoke, and he was an abstemious man; his books were his passion.

They stayed like that for a few moments, but finally he said, "What is troubling you, my girl?"

"I-I have a dilemma." She stood, moved his glasses over, and hopped up to sit on the edge of the desk. Her father leaned back in his chair and gazed up at her in the dimness. Again, the curtains were closed. Ever since her mother's death Phaedra had had the feeling that her father couldn't bear too much sunlight, as if it reminded him of his beloved, mourned-for wife. "Papa, is it justified, in God's sight, to risk something, to *sacrifice* something of great importance to oneself, for another's benefit?"

"It depends, I suppose." Mr. Gillian scratched his nose and furrowed his brow. "Are we talking a material sacrifice, or some other kind?"

"Some other kind." She could never tell him exactly what kind of sacrifice she had in mind.

He gazed at her steadily for a minute, and then said, "Are there moral issues involved?"

As always, her father could read her mind, or at least some portion of it. "Yes," she said doubtfully. "But . . . But there is a kind of biblical precedent for what I—"

He gave her a look of reproof. "Do not attempt to use the

bible or religion as justification for something you are not sure of. You must be sure in your own heart that what you are doing is right."

"I am thinking of a risk, the possibility of a great sacrifice, but an even greater reward, not . . . not to the uh, risker, but to someone else."

Her father's gaze stayed on her face and she felt him reading her, as if he were touching her heart and soul. He finally said, "I believe that God looks charitably on anyone willing to sacrifice greatly for others. But sacrifice is inevitably a risk, and one must be willing and able to live with all of the consequences. And live without blame, Phaedra, my dear. Live without blame. You must look deeply into your soul for the answers, and really and truly decide if your motives for doing what you plan to do are clearly understood. Are your motives pure? Are they truly known to you in your heart? Sometimes we do things for one reason, only to find we had a different expectation of the outcome all along."

She reached out and touched his cheek. No matter what, her father would love her; she knew that and it comforted her, for if her risk went wrong, if she failed, she would need his love and understanding. It would change her life.

"I will think about what you have said, Papa. And now I will leave you to go back to your books, for I have interrupted you for long enough."

He covered her hand. "I would give up anything for you, my dear, and not count the cost as too high."

"I know that. It is a comfort to me."

"I have been thinking about the *Codex*, my dear."

His rapid shift in topic did not faze Phaedra in the least, for he had always been thus. "Yes? And do you still think that Mr. Proctor is wrong, or have you come to see his point of view?"

"What I think is that I would like to go to Oxford for one day and sit down with him. Letters will never substitute for a face to face meeting. One day will uncover much of our disagreements."

Fondly she patted his shoulder as she slipped off the desk. "Then go to Oxford, Papa. I will man the guns here."

"How martial a metaphor, my dear. I will go, then. Within the next couple of days."

Phaedra slipped out of the room as her father went back to his books. She was almost convinced now that her intended path was the right one. With one grand risk she could rectify everything. Or lose so much. But what did it signify if what one lost was never much use in the first place? She headed up the stairs toward Lord Hardcastle's room.

Fifteen

"You are very good at this, my dear," Hardcastle said, laying down his cards in defeat. "Out of our last five hands you have won three, and very few people in London have done as much." He watched his opponent as she shuffled and dealt out another hand, trying to puzzle her out, a process he suspected might take a lifetime. She was so many layers and subtleties. His one complaint about women over the years had been that they were too uncomplicated, sometimes even brainless. They were necessary to one's bodily release, and there was nothing so pleasing to the eye as a beautiful woman, but beyond enjoying their charms and as far as carrying on a conversation, one might just as well engage one's spaniel in political talk. At least the spaniel would listen and not natter in one's ear about gossip or other trivialities. He had heard much made of political hostesses and their ilk, but it seemed to him that the level of talk that went on at their parties was tittle-tattle disguised as deep thinking.

He was prepared now to contemplate that he had dismissed a whole sex's intelligence based on faulty observation. Perhaps it was not the women who were at fault, but the milieu in which he had observed them, between the sheets or at balls. He laid down a card, which Phaedra took with a whoop of competitive zeal, and wondered how many women in the world were such an endearing blend of intelligence, sweetness, moral strength, courage . . . If his thoughts went on in that way, he would have her up for sainthood soon.

"And you win again, my dear," he said, as she took her third trick. "That makes game for you, I believe."

She smiled. "How many times have I beaten you? What is the percentage, do you think?"

"Enough," he said, laying aside the cards and leaning back.

"But how much? Has it been over half the time, do you think?"

Puzzled by her persistence, he paused before answering and watched her eager expression. What was behind this? "I think it has been over half," he said. "Perhaps, oh, three out of five times you beat me?"

"That is a good percentage for winning, is it not? If you were betting something of importance, you would bet it based on that chance of winning?"

"I like the odds to be significantly higher, but I will not play drunks and I will not play idiots, nor will I play anyone who I think is not a skilled enough player to provide a challenge, so that is about the best percentage I can usually hope for."

She crossed the room and put the deck of cards in the drawer of the table by the open window. She gazed out at the steady rain for a moment, and then turned back to him, her expression significantly altered. There was uncertainty in her eyes, he thought; she was unsure about something.

Lovely, sky blue eyes. The man who married her would always have a sunny day in his own home, even when the weather closed in and was as gloomy as this evening had become. The room brightened with her presence. He put that thought away from him like some noxious and insidious parasite.

She crossed back and sat down on the edge of the bed. He took one of her hands in his own and rubbed it with his thumb, caressing a raised callus, wishing he could do more. She was trembling. A longing to pull her into his arms and hold her swept over him, but he restrained the urge. He was not exactly in her good graces, no matter how fair and impartial she was attempting to be. She still did not see his side and likely never would. And he could not tell her why the ideal of honor was so deeply ingrained within him.

Or could he? Why could he not? It was not as if no one else knew the old story. Mercy Dandridge, his friend from school days, knew it.

"My father," he said, before he had consciously decided to divulge the whole sordid story, "was an odd mixture of terrible gambler and parsimonious miser. How he got that way, I will never know."

She was startled by his odd choice of subject matter, he could tell, but interest flared in her eyes. "Your father was a gambler?" She brought her knee up under her and gazed down at him.

"Yes. Oh, yes, indeed. He was addicted to it as some are overly fond of snuff and others secretly drink. He was a hard man, Phaedra, hard in ways that went bone deep. His heart was petrified like the stone shells one sometimes finds at the seashore."

"It could not have been easy, being son to such a man. What of your mother?"

"She died when I was very young." He looked away toward the white-painted wall, where a watercolor landscape, indifferently painted, hung over the small desk. "My father told me about her death in the postscript to a letter he sent me at school; it was my first term. I never forgave him for that, for . . . for the nonchalance of his delivery."

Phaedra squeezed his hand and held it in her lap, cradled in both her hands. "He may not have been comfortable with emotion. Some men are like that."

"No, you excuse him too readily, my dear. He just didn't care. She was a drain on his purse, you see. Had to have London physicians because she was sick, and so her dying provided him with financial relief. He never spoke of her again."

Phaedra examined his face. Twilight was approaching, and with the rain still pattering on the windowsill, the room was becoming dim. "I understand your bitterness. You have thought of her often over the years, I think."

Hardcastle shifted up higher in the bed and pushed away the old pain. They were off track from what he had intended to speak of. "I have a much older sister. The few times I was home before she married, she tried to speak of Mother, but I would not listen. It seemed to me to be of no use, for I could not bring her back. I was telling you of my father, though."

"Yes, you were," Phaedra said, her tone indicating that she was still puzzled as to why, but would go along with his chosen topic.

This was supremely uncomfortable for him, talking about the past in this way, and yet he felt some deep urge to present to Phaedra his genesis, the explanation behind his rigorous insistence on honesty in all dealings and the prompt and honest settlement of debts. And so he stumbled into speech again. "My father and I would occasionally fall into cardplaying when I was home from school." He pulled his hand from her grasp, finding it hard to concentrate with her fingers caressing his, twining around them tenderly like the soft green shoots of vines. "It was the only time we spent together. He usually had some woman he was sleeping with in the house—he was successful with women for some reason—

and other than that, he spent all of his time looking for something to gamble on."

"He doesn't sound like the ideal parent," Phaedra ventured.

Hardcastle leaned back on the pillow and closed his eyes. "You are the mistress of understatement, my dear." He missed her touch. Maybe it was better to feel her closeness, the connection between them making his confession easier. He took her hand in his own and when she would pull away clutched on to it tightly. Opening his eyes, he said, "This may seem like a strange rambling form of conversation, but I do have a point."

"All right," she said calmly. "I am listening."

Would she ever let him kiss her again? He did not think so. She despised him for what he was about to do to the young Baron Fossey, and he could not change that. His gaze traced the pursed outline of her rosebud lips, and he remembered their velvety softness. Would she still be vulnerable to him? Even against her conscience?

"My lord, you were saying?"

"Yes, yes. Uh, I was saying that we used to play cards on occasion, generally when he was trying to stay away from London and the gambling table. If he lost a great deal, his miserliness, always at odds with the wastefulness of gambling, would cause him to attempt a reform. It never lasted long."

"He sounds like a truly tortured individual."

"Do not feel sorry for him. He lived the life he chose, as we all do. One particular time we were playing cards, and we were gambling, as usual. I was doing reasonably well and he was becoming angrier by the minute. I think I was up a hundred guineas or more. There was a vein that would throb at his temple whenever he was reaching a breaking point. I knew it, and knew he was becoming incensed. I disliked him enough that I almost wished the vein would burst. And then he did the most extraordinary thing." Hardcastle paused.

Phaedra said, "Go on. What did he do? Have an apoplectic fit?"

"No. He asked me, how would I like to double my allowance?"

"Really? And yet he was a miser."

"Yes. He said, since I was doing so well, I might like to take a chance. He would wager me double my allowance until my majority—which was three years away, yet—on one game of cards."

"And should you lose?"

"I would lose my allowance."

"Ah," said Phaedra. "It must have been tempting."

"It was. I took the bet."

"And?"

"And I lost."

"Oh. You lost your entire allowance for three years?"

"Yes. When I returned to school I had nothing. No money for better food—the food at school was wretched unless you could go down to the bakeshop and buy a penny bun every day—no money for stabling my horse, no money for anything. I lived for a time like a charity student."

"Your father was a hard man," Phaedra said, her expression hidden by shadows. "You would think that pride of name would not allow him to let you live like that. How did you get through the next three years?"

"I gambled. I became very good, and I gambled. I was rusticated twice, almost sent down, but I just got cannier."

"And so you learned to live with the harsh realities of a losing wager," Phaedra said. "Just as you mean Charles to."

"There is that," he said, unable to tell by her voice if she understood or not. He had not really meant to equate his losing his allowance for three years with a young man losing his entire estate, and forever. "But there is more to the story. When he died, his mistress—you would know her if I said her name, for she was a notorious byword in the *ton*—she told me a story about that night, about how he had come to bed with her later and chuckled about how he had cheated me. How he had marked the cards and *cheated* me out of my allowance, and now he could go back to London and gamble more because it was like gambling free money. My money."

"So Papa was right," Phaedra said softly.

"What are you talking about?"

"He told me about a conversation you had with him, and that he advised you to live your own life, rather than living how you did to spite your father."

"But I don't live the way I do to spite him. I live how I do to prove that not every Hardcastle is a cheat, a-a bounder, a filthy—" He took a deep breath and wondered how the conversation could, again, have gone so profoundly off track.

"I understand," she said softly. "But still, even if it is not spite, you are living as you do in response to your father's behavior." She put out one hand and touched his hair.

There was gentleness in her touch, a world of forgiveness and sympathy. He turned his face and felt her caress his cheek. It was cold comfort to know that she understood, that she forgave him his hard and unyielding nature. He would have given much, at that moment, to say to her that now he could move past it, that he could let Fossey off from his debt. But he just couldn't.

"I have been hesitating," she said, "to offer this resolution to our dilemma, but after pondering it for a while now, I can think of no reason not to. Your story explains much about why you cannot let Charles go, why you feel you must persecute this debt to the end. I will not say I understand completely, but I accept that you feel that you cannot act in any other way without betraying some code of ethics. What if . . . What if someone were to wager Charles's freedom from his debt against something of value to themselves. Would that suffice? If they won, would that satisfy the debt?"

Hardcastle frowned into the gathering gloom. What on earth was she getting at? "Do you mean someone else would bet his freedom from the wagering debt against something of their own, some property?"

"Mmm, something like that," she said softly.

Her hand was still in his and she caressed his palm. He felt a thrill that left him breathless travel his body at that simple gesture. He could hardly think and he sternly quelled his body's response. Did she know her effect on him? He would wager that she did not.

"I would think that would suffice. But I doubt whether the young man has any friends with a possession of such worth to equal his estate." He felt her start.

"What . . . What would you consider equal to his estate? Would it have to be property? Or could it be anything you wanted?"

Hardcastle shrugged, not understanding the conversation. It made him irritable not to know what was going on. "It would be a subjective measure, indeed, but there are some things I would consider adequate exchange for the Fossey estate."

"Such as?"

"I don't know," he said. "How am I to answer that? Tell me what you mean."

He felt her get closer in the semidarkness until her body was pressed to his. He was startled by her lips on his, but then he was overtaken by the passion that surged through his veins and he pulled her close, taking her lips in a kiss of surprising heat and surpassing softness. Before he realized it, she was lying close to him and he was exploring her ears, the hollow of her neck, the soft peach fuzz near her hairline, while his body throbbed to life. He had been seduced by duchesses, had lain with courtesans of extraordinary beauty, had bedded a European princess once, but this simple country vicar's daughter was the first to stir his loins with a mere kiss, the touch of her lips to his. Did she have any idea of the intoxicating force of his desire for her? How much he would give at that moment if he thought she would give herself to him?

She pulled away after a moment, and then lit a candle from the tinderbox on the side table. Her cheeks were pink, her breath was short, and her tightly bound hair was adorably disheveled. He swallowed back his yearning for her.

"I would be willing," she said, her gaze directed at the table next to her rather than at him, "to wager you whatever you wanted in exchange for Charles's freedom from his lost bet."

His breath caught in his throat. "Whatever I wanted?"

"Whatever you wanted, my lord," she said softly. "If there is anything I have that would please you, I will lay it on the table as collateral for Charles's debt. Would that be a satisfactory wager?"

Sixteen

For a moment she thought he was offended. How horrible that would be, to offer him whatever he wanted, only to find she had misjudged his passion for her. She had thought about it long and hard, but had seen no alternative. She did not know men very well, but she knew enough to realize when a man wanted her. For some mysterious reason, Hardcastle found her pleasing. She had not understood how much until the kisses they had just shared. She watched his face carefully.

"You would . . . Let me understand this . . . this *wager*." His voice was hard and brittle, his expression enigmatic. "You would *barter* yourself for Fossey's estate?"

So that was how he saw it. Her chin went up. That was not how she had intended him to see it at all. "No. I will not sell myself. However, I will bet you whatever you want that I can win one game of euchre from you." It was a fine distinction; maybe she was deceiving herself and there was no distinction. Nevertheless . . . "*You* set the price, my lord; I have faith in my ability to win when I need to. In exchange, I want your pledge that, should I win, you will forgive Charles Fossey of his debt. I am not doing this for him, but for his mother and his sister, and . . . and one of whom you know nothing." He squinted his eyes. She thought of Deborah, and how improved her future would be if she could just win Charles's freedom.

His expression hardened. He shifted under the covers and appeared to think about it for a moment, but then he said, his voice like tempered steel, "All right. But let us be clear about the stakes. You said it is my choice. I will not trick you with some pretty words about what I will take in exchange. I think, perhaps, you already know that I want you. I did not think you would understand that—I thought you too innocent to understand a man's lust—but it appears that I underestimated you. You have a fishmonger's appreciation for and knowledge of her customer's appetites."

She flinched at that rough assessment of her wager. Was she being cheap? Was this the bet of a-a whore? She took a deep, steadying breath and would not allow her mind to fully digest what his words might mean. Her intentions were impeccable, and they must carry her through.

He continued. "But you are right. I have never had a pretty little vicar's daughter." He reached up and touched one curl that had loosened from her bun during their kiss, winding it around his finger and letting it go, watching it spring against her neck. His tone sardonic and cool, he said, "I find my jaded city tastes hunger for a country peach." He touched her cheek and cupped her chin. "I assume you are innocent of experience with men, so let me be blunt. I wish to make love to you. If you lose this bet, I will expect you to spend one night with me, to lie with me, to give me what I want. I expect to explore your soft, pink body with my hands and . . . and other parts of me."

His voice was harsh and he grimaced, perhaps at the blunt sound of his words in the hushed quiet of the bedchamber. His voice gentler, he continued. "It will not be unpleasant, my dear, I guarantee you that—or at least not past the first twinge. I am skilled and I genuinely like women, and I"—for the first time he faltered—"I-I like you very much, Phaedra, and I think you like me enough to enjoy the experience. If you do not, it will not be for lack of me trying. Understanding the full extent of the wager, will you still play me for Fossey's estate? Knowing the price of losing is your innocence?"

She would almost have thought, at that moment, that he wanted her to say no, despite just admitting that he desired her. "I—" She gulped back her hesitation, her fear. She knew him well enough to know that he would not hurt her. But still, she had been taught that her innocence was a precious cargo for a woman to protect, yielding it only to her husband on their wedding night. But she was not destined to have a husband. She was seven-and-twenty and would never marry. What would one night spent in his arms cost her?

And she did not intend to lose. No, she did not think she would. In a game this important she felt sure of victory.

"I understand what it means." She took a deep breath and straightened. "So, it is Charles Fossey's estate wagered against one night with you, to do as you bid."

She saw the surprise on his face and understood it instantly. "You did not think I would agree, did you? You thought that ultimately I would quail at the thought and would retreat in terror. That is why you made it sound so . . . so brutal and carnal. But this is important. If that is the only way you can let go of this wager, then we shall play one game for it. Shall we play now? Shall I get the cards again?"

He shook his head. "I am weary. You would not take advantage of me at less than my best, would you?" His tone had lapsed almost into sarcasm once more.

"No, my lord. I will not take advantage of you." She fully understood the irony behind her words and expected he did, too. "Tomorrow evening, then. Will that do?"

"That will do. Good night, Phaedra. Sleep well. If"—he

gazed up at her in the darkness, and his voice was low and quiet—"if you should decide against the wager, you can back out at any time up to the moment we start playing. But after that—"

She understood him. Rising from the bed, she said, "Good night, my lord."

The next day was full of odd moments for Phaedra. Miss Peckenham came to call just as Lord Hardcastle was climbing gingerly down the stairs to take a turn in the garden. She gave a shriek and a moan, and almost fainted, but then ended up spending a pleasant half hour in the garden with the earl.

He was at his most charming, and Phaedra watched with wry appreciation the way he mixed deference with flirtation in an alchemist's brew to turn the nosy and sharp-tongued spinster into a giggling ninny. A rake, it would seem, knew just how to charm and please a woman, *any* woman! Even one as set against him as the former governess.

He made a few sly, teasing allusions to bets and wagering, but Phaedra just frowned at him. If he was thinking to rattle her, then he was wasting his breath. She was sure that she had the power of right on her side, and that the evening would see her vanquish him and restore Charles to his birthright. She looked forward to the next morning when she would be able to summon Charles and tell him he was free from his disastrous bet. Before nightfall he would be back on good terms with Deborah, and the two young people could start planning their future together.

Miss Peckenham took her reluctant leave, eventually, and Lord Hardcastle, Phaedra, and her father took their lunch together, after which the elderly scholar played the earl a game of chess. Then her father went back to his books, as the earl hobbled awkwardly back up the stairs, and Phaedra went about her household chores with Sally's enthusiastic, if less than capable, hands.

But she found, as twilight grew near and the time for her game of cards, her fateful game of chance, drew closer, her stomach began to flutter. Would she win? Surely, if she had right on her side and prayed and kept her attention on the game, then she would prevail. Right over might, so to speak.

But what if he should win? Oh, Lord, what if he should? She knew him. She had no doubt he would claim his wager, and then she would join the ranks of "fallen" women, like Mrs. Jones, who had sold their innocence for lucre. For no matter how she dressed it up, it still came down to putting a price on her innocence. She had tried to find some other way to justify it, but it came down to the same in the end. And so be it. It was done. She would not be a hypocrite and mourn now.

Dinner was over and the dishes were washed. Her father was comfortably ensconced back among his books, not knowing that his daughter was soon to mount the stairs and find out if she was to maintain her virginity or give it to a rakish earl. She shivered.

And she was made of sterner stuff than this, she told herself. It would not be the end of the world if she lost the wager. But she was not going to lose; on the contrary, she would prevail and emerge triumphant, and on the morrow Charles would have his birthright back, Deborah would have her shining future as the adored wife of the young baron, and Hardcastle, well, he would go back to London. He was well enough to travel now and had been for a couple of days. He could hire a coach and be back by the day after next, and she would be left to go back to her own comforting, safe, stultifying, boring—

Phaedra shook herself mentally and told Sally she could

walk down to the village if she wanted to. The girl flew up the stairs to change into her new dress, and Phaedra followed more slowly and entered her former room, soon to be her room again, for, one way or another, Lord Hardcastle would be leaving within the next couple of days.

He was sitting up in bed waiting for her, the deck of cards in his hand already, and he was shuffling. He glanced up as she entered. "So, the moment has come," he said softly. "Have you thought about what I said last night, my dear? That you may back out at any moment up to the point of the first deal?"

She paused in the doorway. "Will you release Charles from his rash wager?"

"I cannot, Phaedra."

It almost sounded like sorrow in his voice. Would he change who he was if he could?

"Then we are playing a game of euchre." She glanced around. It was vitally important that she be comfortable during this game, and she supposed they should be downstairs playing in the parlor, in proper chairs. He was well enough to sit up for longer periods now, and there was no reason not to, she supposed. And yet, for some reason she would feel exposed down in the parlor, as if her wager were hanging in the air above them for her father or Sally to see, if they should wander through. No, they would play right here. It would end where it began.

She sat down on the edge of the bed and felt his legs behind her, touching her. She took in a deep breath and noted that he was doing the same. The look in his eyes was smoldering, intense; his dark eyes almost glowed in the twilit room. She still did not understand why he wanted her, but thought that perhaps it was just male need reasserting itself now that his injuries were healing. Or maybe, as he had suggested, his appetite was piqued by her very difference from the courtesans and ballroom beauties he was accustomed to. With a pang of something like sadness, she admitted to her self that whatever it was, it was transitory, fleeting, and that once he was back among his own kind he would forever laugh and shake his head, bemused at his lust for the country wren.

Even now, she knew she would never forget him. How much deeper would his impression be on her if she slept with him, if he became her only lover?

"Shall you deal first, or shall I?" he said.

"I shall deal first," she said, determined to snatch at any small advantage.

They played. It was going well, and Phaedra surged ahead to six out of the ten points she needed to win, while he was mired at two. She began to count the number of hands before she could announce herself the winner. Charles would have his estate, Anna and her mother would have their home, and Deborah would have her husband.

"My point," Hardcastle said, laying down his last card to claim hers.

Her heart thumped. She had let herself get distracted anticipating her win, and he had taken a hand that should have gone to her, if she had been wiser. She couldn't let that happen. "I must be more careful, my lord. I should have won that hand."

"So you should. If you had led with the ace on the third trick instead of the trump nine, that hand would have been yours. It is now six to three."

"Yes." She moved back a little on the bed, and felt his long legs bump against her bottom. She felt his body jolt and cast a swift glance his way, wondering if he was in any pain. But no, his eyes were not shadowed as they became when he was hurting; instead there was that fiery glow within them still.

She made a risky move in the next hand, and he euchred her neatly, gaining two points, bringing him up to five. They each in turn gained a point on the next two hands, and stood at seven to six, with Phaedra still leading.

"You are a very good gambler, my dear," he said, glancing down at her hands. He nodded toward them and continued. "They are steady, and you never give anything away by so much as a blink."

She dealt the hand and looked at her own cards. She felt a trickle of excitement. She could perhaps win two points on this hand, but it required concentration and logic. She looked at the card she had turned up and shook her head. No, that would never do. And so she would have to turn it down and risk him making it something she could not defend against. In the end, she prevailed, but won only one point, so she stood at eight.

The next hand went to him, with all of the tricks, so he took two points and they stood tied at eight apiece.

Lord, please help me, she almost whispered out loud, but she remained silent. He must not know that a trickle of perspiration raced down her back, feeling like an icy finger.

And then he won the next hand. He stood at nine, and she swallowed back a dry lump that sat in her throat like a fist. She must concentrate. She must win! The next hand went her way, but she gained only one point, and so they were both within one point of victory.

"This hand does it, my dear. At the end of it, either Charles Fossey will regain his estate, or you and I will become lovers, if just for one night." His voice was velvety, throaty, with deep undertones of excitement.

"I know that, my lord." Her stomach clenched and she shifted uneasily, dizziness overcoming her for a moment. It was just anticipation of winning, she thought. It was just the heady rush of knowing that Deborah and Charles would soon be able to plight their troth, perhaps a late-summer wedding in the garden at Thwicke House, when the chrysanthemums and the hollyhocks would be in full glorious bloom, and the new vicar would—

But first she must win. It was his deal, unfortunately, which gave him the advantage for the moment, if he could make use of the card he had turned up as a trump suit.

And he did. *Damn and blast.* Unpardonable language for a lady, even if it *was* just in her mind. She paused and hesitated over every turn of the card, watching his shadowed face, his hooded eyes making it impossible to read his expression. But long before the end of the hand, she knew the outcome. It was written in the cards, and it came about.

He had won. She would lose her innocence, and she felt a thrill of fear and excitement, and loathing and longing all at once. He would touch her in ways no man had, and she would be changed forever, without benefit of clergy. Is this why she had wagered as she did? Was this a sop to her conscience, for she recognized a trickle of anticipation within the nervousness and shyness. Kissing him had been a revelation, and she had known for some days that in the long stretch between Albert Deaville's kiss and the earl's kiss that she had ripened into a woman. She did not for a moment think she would hate what she and Hardcastle did, but she felt ashamed that she did not feel the horror that she should, being a well-brought-up young lady.

And yet she mourned sincerely for Charles's second loss. It seemed that he was not fated to be the master of his baronial estate for more than a little over the year since his father had died. And for generations to come he would bear the shame of the Fossey who had lost the ancient estate. There was no entail; family pride was all that had kept it in the

Fossey name for four centuries. And now he had lost it. And she had lost it a second time, though he would never know that.

He had not spoken. She looked up into his dark eyes, wondering if she would see pitiful triumph there, but there was no such poor emotion. He was watching her, with compassion, she thought, for he must know some of what she was feeling. If he thought her afraid, or reluctant, or bitter, she did not think he would force himself on her. She was sure he would not. He had shown himself to be kind and gentlemanly.

But she was an adult, too—she was not afraid of him, even now—and would own up to her wager. "You have won, sir."

"So I have."

"Will you . . ." Her voice faltered, against her own efforts. She cleared her throat. "Will you claim your wager tonight, sir?"

"No. No, I will not. I will not do you the injustice of making love to you while your father is down the hall. He is going to Oxford overnight soon, is he not? You and I will wait until then. I want you to myself, my dear, for the whole night long."

She shivered with a thrill of nervousness or anticipation, she was not sure which. "All right, my lord. We will wait until then."

Seventeen

She was his. She was to be his lover, his mistress, if only for one night. As she closed the door behind her and darkness swallowed the room, he took in a deep shuddering breath. One month ago—no, one *week* ago—he would have laughed to think any woman could leave him breathless with anticipation, but so Phaedra had done. He had wanted her with a kind of hopeless passion, not expecting any more than stolen kisses and sly caresses, but now he would make love to her once, or twice, or thrice, however much he could manage in one night, and have to leave after that. He would be the only man, perhaps in her whole life, to touch her body and drink of her nectar-sweet lips. He lay awake all night in a fever of desire and barely restrained yearning, wondering what it would be like, knowing he would remember in years to come the first touch of her flesh, the first taste of her breast, the first heady sweetness of her surrender.

He knew her well enough to know that she would pay her debt, and he did not think she would come to him with clenched teeth and a stiff body; he truly believed he could bring her to enjoy their lovemaking. It was why he had insisted on having her with him all night. The first time might be awkward; he could not remember the last time he had bedded a virgin. He rather thought it was in his teen years, and she a local barmaid, young but knowing and eager.

He was not a fumbling youth now, but a man with some experience. He had never known this anticipation, and yet it was not unmixed with guilt. She had fought hard for her friends, and he knew she was devastated by the loss. If there were only a way he could go back, would he lose the game on purpose? No. He could not do that in good conscience whether there was a wager at stake or no. Cheating to lose would be no better than cheating to win, after all.

And yet, there had been a point in the game when he looked up and saw her fierce concentration, her lip clenched between her teeth, her eyes fixed on her cards and her brow furrowed, when he wished she would win. There was every possibility that she might have, for she truly was a good and intelligent cardplayer. One mistake had made the difference, the one point she needed to prevail. Just one point. But he couldn't purposely give it to her. It went against every in-grained belief and hard-won conviction, to not fight to win.

When the door opened in the morning, after a night in which he had not slept, he was sorely disappointed to see Mrs. Lovett come in with his morning tray. "Where is Phaedra—uh, Miss Gillian?"

"Busy as always, me lord. Her pa is making ready to go to Oxford tomorrow, and y'would think he was a'goin' to see the queen, with all the preparations that must be made for an overnight trip! She be pressin' his best shirts, and his travelin' coat, and baking special for his lunch on the coach."

So, the next night would be theirs. As Mrs. Lovett bustled about the room, setting it to rights, he wondered how Phaedra was anticipating it. How did a bride feel, antici-pating her bridal night? And yet at the end of it they would not be wed, nor would they have more than just that one night. They would rise from the bed the next morning and he would politely and calmly take his leave of her, to return to

London—or no, first he would go to Charles Fossey's estate and claim his wager. All of his anger against the young man was gone now, dissipated in the time he had spent recovering in the Gillian household, but still, it was a score he must settle. For the first time he thought about what it meant to the young man, losing his estate.

His widowed mother thrown on the mercy of relatives.

His widowed sister, likewise farmed out as a poor relative.

And the baron's own life irrevocably changed—

Stop! He did not force the young man into a game. He remembered very clearly the events of that evening. He had been gambling, and winning, when the young man had been introduced to him by a mutual acquaintance. This was not an unusual occurrence at one's club. They played a few hands for money, and the young fellow proved to be more of a challenge than Hardcastle had anticipated. He was a fair cardplayer, though he was occasionally distracted by his group of friends who gathered around him, smoking and watching the action. They were urging him on to higher and higher wagers.

He was slightly ahead in the stakes when he threw down the challenge. He would bet anything Hardcastle liked, if the earl would put his stable on the table. To Hardcastle it was a calculated challenge, and he wondered if the group of young men had come up with it before Fossey even approached. A low hum of anticipation circled the room, and more gentlemen gathered around them. Everyone there knew what Hardcastle's stables were worth and what they meant to him. He had paused but ultimately agreed. It sharpened his interest in the game, which had lately begun to wane. He was not, he found, an inveterate gambler, and was beginning to become bored with the usual round of betting. *This* was living; *this* was betting something that really mattered to him.

He asked the young man what he could possibly have that was the equivalent of the finest stable in England and the finest-blooded horses outside of Ireland.

Fossey had drawn himself up as if mortally offended, and had said, "I am Baron Fossey. My estate is certainly worthy of this bet."

And Hardcastle, his interest piqued, had agreed. It had been a hard-fought game, but he had prevailed, just as he had with Phaedra. And all of that, with a couple of brutal bandits thrown into the mix, had brought him to this, to wagering a country damsel for her innocence, and winning it. What a story that would make upon his return to London.

A story he would never tell a soul. It was not something to be made light of.

His mind turned to the delicate duty he felt to repay the Gillians somehow for their outstanding hospitality toward him over this last week and a half. They had changed his life in some ways. He was not sure how, yet, but there was change coming. The impatient, restless urge to get back to London had dissipated, and he was not quite sure what he would do once he was there. Go back to gambling and drinking? Would the delectable widow, Lady Bosanquet, still be casting out her lures to him? He rather thought he would take a break from feminine companionship for a while, after making love to Phaedra. Going directly to another woman's bed would be like drinking from a mud puddle after quaffing from a cool, clear mountain stream. He did not yet know what it would be like, making love with Phaedra, but never had he approached an assignation with this kind of pulsing expectancy.

When Mrs. Lovett left, Hardcastle eased himself out of bed, used the hot water and towels the good widow had brought up with her, and dressed in the washed and mended clothes Phaedra had provided for him. He slowly traveled down the narrow, dark stairs, taking one step at a time and feeling every jolt, and stood at the bottom, wondering which way to go. Perhaps out to the garden. In London he would still be deeply asleep at this hour—it was not past eight, and yet he knew the household would have been bustling for hours—and he had a curiosity what the early morning hours would look like in Phaedra's pretty herb garden.

He stepped out the back door onto the flagstone terrace, after passing by the startled and motionless maid, Sally, who was in the act of scrubbing pots. It had rained much of the night and a mist lay over everything; it made the scene magical. The far hills were shrouded and sound was muffled. The cottage yard was fairly small, with a stone wall encircling it to keep marauding rabbits out of the garden, he supposed. Phaedra's herb garden was to his left, and he could make out, among the small plants, Phaedra herself, on her knees, doing something vigorous with a plant of some sort.

"What on earth are you doing?" he asked.

Suddenly, whatever she was tugging at gave way, and she tumbled backward with a soft *"Oof"* of surprise. She jumped up and wiped some muck from her hands, then tossed the stubborn vegetation to one side. "I am weeding," she said breathlessly. She rinsed her hands in a basin of water at the edge of the garden path and straightened.

Hardcastle limped toward her. The awful thought occurred to him that she was avoiding him now that the bet had been lost. After all, Mrs. Lovett had quite clearly said she was busy with preparations for her father's journey. "Do you . . . Do you require assistance?"

She laughed. "Are you offering your services, my lord, and do you know an herb from a weed? No, I did not think so. You would be no help."

Hardcastle gazed down into her upturned face. The dew

had settled on her crinkly coronet of golden hair, looking like a net of sparkling beads overlaying it. He reached up and touched her cheek, wiping a smudge of dirt away with his thumb. *Tomorrow night,* the refrain hummed though his brain. He would have her in his arms tomorrow night. She would not meet his eyes, and her cheeks had pinked. He moved away and sat down on a damp stone bench. "Do you never stop working, Phaedra? I have seldom seen you still, except when you were entertaining me. What do you do for leisure?"

"This is my leisure," she said, indicating the garden with a sweep of her hand.

"Why are you compelled to labor with such intensity?"

"I find pleasure in most of it."

"In the good deeds you do for the neighborhood?" He did not mean it, but it sounded almost like a sneer.

She cocked her head to one side. "I find pleasure in people's company. Even Mr. Ferguson—he is a curmudgeonly sort, I must say—gives me much more than I give him. He is a wise old man, with much to say."

Abruptly, he changed the subject. He had to ask. "Phaedra," he asked, gazing out into the mist and then back at her, "do you hate me for winning the bet last night?"

She gazed at him steadily and dried her hands on her apron. "How odd you are sometimes. What do you think of people, I wonder? That others are seething cauldrons of disapproval and dislike? No, I do not hate you for winning the bet. That would be foolish. I took a chance to help some friends, and it did not work. Chances sometimes do not, and that is why they are called chances rather than certainties."

"I—" He frowned off at the garden wall—he was finding it hard to ask what he really meant, and that was unlike him—and then looked at her again, standing in the garden in her

188

faded gingham dress and muddy apron, her still-dirty hands clasped in front of her. She was adorable and he wanted her, even now, even looking like some peasant garden helper. "I suppose what I am asking is, do you resent the price you will pay for losing that wager?" He had to know. Never had he asked that of someone who had lost a wager to him, but this time it was more than some guineas or a piece of property. It was herself she was bound to give him, and he dreaded seeing her flinch at his first touch. He could not bear that, for some reason.

"I do not resent it. I made a wager and I will stand by the terms, my lord."

He grimaced inwardly. He did not want her like that. And yet it was the only way he was ever going to have her, and his desire for her outweighed his doubts. He would bring her to pleasure, he swore it. She would not regret it in the end, and perhaps she would have a pleasant memory of him to look back upon—some sweet and tender moments among the passionate as they melded together in the night—rather than as the hard-hearted scoundrel who had taken away her friend's estate. That thought led to a vague memory of something Phaedra had said. "You said yesterday something about the loss of the estate to Fossey affecting someone of whom I know nothing. Who did you mean?"

"I am surprised you remember that, my lord. It is . . . The affected party is my friend, a young woman to whom Charles Fossey is betrothed—well, not exactly betrothed. There is nothing formal, as her father wished her to have two London seasons before committing herself to Charles. Now, however, he will not be able to marry soon, or perhaps ever." Her voice was cool, but there was trembling sadness behind it.

Like ripples in a pond, the effects of this wager were spreading out and affecting an ever-widening circle of people.

Her words had not been said with rancor, and yet how could she help feeling it? Hardcastle rose stiffly and said, "I should go back in. I do not think my limbs are ready yet for sitting on wet stone benches."

The day passed swiftly, too swiftly for Phaedra's liking. Her father was going the next day to consult with his old friend and adversary, Mr. Proctor, a don at Oxford. It was not far, and the trip could be undertaken in one day, but for his comfort he was going to stay one night with Mr. Proctor and come back the next day. And by the time he came back, his daughter would no longer be a maiden. She shivered and went back to her task, which was preparing the vegetable dish for the evening meal. Lord Hardcastle was going to be joining her father and her at the dining room table for the first time.

It was not something she looked forward to. It was getting too painful to contemplate how swiftly the next day or two would go, and the changes that would be wrought within those two days. Was this how a bride felt, reflecting on her coming nuptials? After all, the effect was going to be somewhat the same for Phaedra, except after the consummation, her "husband" would be leaving her forever.

Forever. A shock passed through Phaedra and she dropped the knife on the table and stood, shivering, staring bleakly out the window at the familiar scene of the back garden and the hills beyond. Why did it hurt so very badly to contemplate his leaving? She should be glad, for after all, he was taking away her friends' future. She should loathe him, despise him for his inflexibility, and yet she could not. She couldn't because—oh, Lord, because she had fallen in love with him.

Hardcastle chuckled to himself as he performed his ablutions prior to going down to join the company for dinner. How many times had he performed this ritual before dinner at a country house party? And how different this time was. In the normal course of his preparations he would bathe after the servants fetched up hot water for his bath, and his valet would dress him. He would wear a good coat of Bath superfine and a jeweled stickpin in his cravat. His Hessians would be shining, his nails would be trimmed and buffed, and his rings sparkling.

This time he was wearing a mended shirt and pantaloons, and homemade slippers. His rings had been stolen, and his Hessians, too. And apparently one could live without the luxury of servants to bring up one's bathwater. He had sent a note to his valet in London that very morning, to retrieve and bring to him at the Gillians' address some clothing and boots, as well as a purse full of guineas. How surprised Jean-Marc, his superior French valet, would be. Even more so when he traveled down and saw where his master had been living for the past two weeks.

A sobering thought. He had ordered Jean-Marc to come the day after the next, for then he could no longer pretend to have anything left to do in the Gillian household. And now he must go down and dine with the gentleman whose daughter he was to deflower on the morrow. In a sober frame of mind he descended the stairs carefully and entered the small, simply furnished dining room, to find the Gillians already there.

"Ah, Hardcastle, 'bout time, eh? We've been waiting on you. Have a seat. Have a seat."

Mr. Gillian's warm welcome did nothing to make Hardcastle feel any better, but he took the seat indicated, across the polished oak table from Phaedra, and sat.

"And now we shall say a grace. Will you do the honor,

Lord Hardcastle?" Mr. Gillian beamed at him kindly.

Feeling the utter hypocrite, Hardcastle murmured a grace barely remembered from school days, and finished with the "amen." "Thank you for welcoming me to your table, sir," he said as Sally came in with the first course, a clear soup. He was conscious of Phaedra's downcast eyes. There was something different about her demeanor, and its meaning eluded him. Was she just becoming more apprehensive about the next night? Surely she must know that he would never force her into anything. It did occur to him, though, that her fine sense of honor might not let her voice doubts that would keep her from fulfilling the wager. He would have to draw her out on that, reassure her as to his intentions. If she was truly afraid or if the notion of their lovemaking was abhorrent to her, he would know. He would take no woman against her wishes, no matter about the wager. It was one point on which there could be no second opinion.

"You are welcome," Mr. Gillian said heartily. "Our table is humble, but the fare is always superb, thanks to Phaedra's, and of course Sally's, skills in the kitchen."

They ate their soup and talked for a while about his trip to Oxford on the morrow, Phaedra adding almost nothing to the conversation. Mr. Gillian expounded a little on the abstruse point of contention between him and this Mr. Proctor whom he was to visit, but Hardcastle could only apply half his concentration to it. Most of his mind was filled with thoughts of Phaedra and questions about how she felt, what she was thinking.

The candles burned down as a raised rabbit pie replaced the fish course, and a ragout of vegetables was consumed. Sally retrieved the serving dishes and disappeared back to the kitchen.

"I have heard, my dear," Mr. Gillian said to his daughter,

as the door closed behind the maid, "that while I am gone you have allowed Sally a night away, to visit her mother."

Phaedra's cheeks pinked, and Hardcastle caught his breath. Entirely alone. He would have her for the entire night, alone, to make love to and to hold and to sleep with. To wake with in the morning and watch her sleep, the morning light sparkling in her golden, radiant hair. His heart thudded. He had never been able to bear a woman in his bed the entire night, but he wanted her beside him in that narrow bed upstairs.

"I . . . She has been wanting to go for some time, and I thought since the work would be less, with just Lord Hardcastle and I—"

"You must see, my dear, that it will never do," Mr. Gillian said, gentle remonstrance in his voice. "I do not doubt Lord Hardcastle's gentlemanly restraint. However, it does not do to give the old tabbies any more gossip material, as it would for you and the earl to be in the same house overnight with no chaperon, without even Sally to lend you countenance. To forestall that, I asked Squire Daintry if his daughter could come down to spend the night with you. She is young, yes, and perhaps in London would not do as a chaperon, but I felt she would be more to your taste as a companion than Miss Peckenham. He agreed and she will be coming tomorrow afternoon."

Phaedra gazed in consternation at her father and then at Hardcastle. Hardcastle shrugged, and was puzzled by the curious feeling of almost relief he felt. They would not be together as lovers, for he had pledged to himself not to embarrass her or expose her in any way. He had been surprised by the news that she had dismissed their maid for the night—unlike Phaedra, he had forgotten about the maid sleeping overhead in the attic room—but he had been even more amazed that Mr. Gillian had had the foresight to arrange a chaperon for his daughter.

And yet, if she were his daughter, he would do the same. To his liking for the older gentleman was added more respect than he already felt. He nodded and said, "You are a wise and careful father, sir."

Mr. Gillian smiled gently. "The Good Book says, my lord, that a virtuous woman's price is beyond rubies." He reached over and laid his hand over his daughter's. "My Phaedra is a ruby beyond price. It is not that I do not trust her virtue untended, but I would have no one take her lightly, nor would I have her reputation in this village tarnished in any way."

Was it a warning, or simply a statement? Quietly, Hardcastle said, "I agree with you, sir."

"So that is all settled," Mr. Gillian said, rubbing his hands together. "Is there any dessert, my dear?"

Eighteen

"I apologize for how things have turned out, my lord. I did not foresee my father's observance nor his uncharacteristic worry about gossip. I would think he would tell the old tabbies to go to the devil—he has been known to use that phrase on occasion—but for him to concern himself with it that way . . . I do not know what to think."

It was the next day and they were in the garden having lunch. The sun had returned to Oxfordshire and the air had a sparkling crispness from a breeze that had swept away all traces of clouds and had dried up all of the puddles and mud. Mr. Gillian had left just an hour before, with a kiss for his daughter and a handshake for the earl, and a reminder that Deborah Daintry could be expected in the early afternoon.

"I think him a wise man. You are in every way more precious than rubies to him. Your happiness and safety are important to him," Hardcastle said. "And a prudent man guards what he holds dear."

"As does a prudent woman," Phaedra said ruefully, thinking of the rash wager of her virtue. Her newly discovered love for Lord Hardcastle would have made the fulfilling of her debt both exquisite pleasure and horrible torture. To give him the rights accorded a husband could only have been pleasurable to her body—she felt flushed with desire for him just at the touch of his hand—but it would have left her with the bitterness of regret, that the occasion would be only an aberration in the smooth texture of her life. Was it better to never taste a delicious fruit that one could not have again, or was it better to experience the taste and live life while it was within one's grasp? It appeared the decision, or the opportunity, had been taken from her.

"You did what you thought right, my dear. I have never met a woman of such . . . such rigorous morality, and I do not think you wagered what you did lightly. It strikes me that for one who does not believe in an immutable rule of honor, you hold fast to the code in your own behavior. I respect that about you."

It was a relief, anyway, that he did not think ill of her. She looked over at him, sitting at his ease, the sunlight glinting blue-black sparks off his hair. His face was a study in hard planes and harsh lines, and yet his manner was gentle. At least toward her. He could not be so mild mannered if he tore down to Oxfordshire through the middle of the night to persecute a debt. What was she to think now, if his appearance on their road and attack by robbers was not part of some God-created scheme to save poor Charles's estate? Was it chance only that had brought Hardcastle into her life? It was that which she would ponder long after he had gone back to his life and his amours and his gambling.

"I have heard," Phaedra said, turning deliberately away from unhappy thoughts, "that Squire Daintry believes they have found the place where the robbers go with their booty. He is hoping to round up some of the locals and raid the den at some point when they know the men have just committed a crime."

"I wish them well."

"Do you not care? Do you not want your rings back, at least? They are family rings, I believe you said."

"I would like them, yes." Hardcastle frowned and stared down at his ringless fingers for a moment. "But I do not regret their loss as much as I would have thought."

He was unfathomable, she thought, watching the changing emotions passing over his handsome face. Every time she thought she knew him, he showed some other part of him, some new depth to his character. Far from being frustrated or angry that the wager could not be fulfilled, one would almost think him sanguine. Or was it resignation only? It would take a lifetime to plumb the depths of his mind and heart, but instead his valet would come on the morrow, and he would leave forever. How soon he would forget the vicar's daughter one could only surmise, but she would never forget her rakish earl. Ever.

It was peaceful in the kitchen with Sally gone, Phaedra thought, paring carrots for dinner. No sooner had she thought that thought, than the kitchen door flew open and Deborah rushed in.

Phaedra dropped her knife in surprise even though she had known the girl was coming, and was, in fact, late. "Deborah, why did you not come to the front door? You are my guest, not the kitchen help."

Deborah dropped her bag on the floor and moved to swiftly hug Phaedra. "I-I knew you would be back here, and I didn't want . . . I didn't want—" The girl broke down into sobs, standing in the kitchen in her pretty muslin dress and spencer, weeping dejectedly.

"Oh, my dear, what is wrong?" Phaedra pushed Deborah down into a chair and moved to put the kettle on the hob to boil for tea. She came back to her friend and took her hand.

Deborah wept quietly for a moment, large tears trickling down her cheek. "It is over. All . . . all my hopes are over!

Oh, I am so miserable!"

Phaedra took her in her arms and the girl leaned on her friend's bosom and wept out her whole story, how she had finally ridden, just that morning, over to the Fossey estate. She was determined to have it out with Charles, and she met him coming out of the house.

"And he was so c-cold! I asked him what was wrong, why he no longer loved me, and he j-just turned red and stammered that he had n-never asked for my hand and h-he was sorry I had misunderstood his intentions! M-misunderstood!" She broke down again, and filling the kitchen were the sounds of her weeping, Phaedra's murmurs of support, and the kettle hissing and bubbling over the fire.

Phaedra thought of poor Charles, and how he must have felt when faced with the girl he loved. How could he tell her? A stronger man would have told her the truth, but Charles was young and he adored Deborah. And so instead of telling her his weakness he was breaking her heart by pretending he didn't care. Foolish, but understandable. Should she tell the girl the truth? It was not her truth to tell, and it would be abominable interference.

"Hush, Deborah. All will come clear in time."

"No it won't. H-he will marry some other girl and I will be an old m-maid like you!" The girl stopped after saying that, and the consternation on her face would have been comical if it were not mixed with the evidence of her devastation. "I didn't mean—I wouldn't ever—"

"It is all right, Deborah."

Breaking down into tears again, Deborah wailed, "H-he says he may be going away! Where would he go? Why? I don't understand! M-mama says I should go back to London, but I don't want to, I don't want—" She broke down completely, then, incoherent through her sobs.

Phaedra felt helpless, not knowing what to do beyond patting the girl's shoulder and offering her tea. And she was angry. *Damn* Hardcastle anyway for his rigid "code"! Damn all gamblers and damn Charles Fossey, but damn especially Lord high-and-mighty Hardcastle who could not give an *inch* to help two young people in love. Charles and Deborah would break their hearts over each other, and their lives could be ruined. It was wrong, wrong, *wrong!*

"I w-want Mama!" Deborah was sniffling now, but her eyes were bloodshot, her nose running, and her whole body shaking. This time when she broke down in tears again, it was the deep shuddering sobs of heartbreak, of hopelessness.

"Then you should go home to your mother, my dear," Phaedra said. It was the only solution she could think of, because she did not know what to do for the girl, who was probably best off at home in her own bed, with her mother there to apply hartshorn and lavender water along with motherly love.

Deborah nodded mutely, and Phaedra picked up her bag and found, outside, that the Daintry pony cart was sitting by the back shed not even unhitched yet. She gave the girl a hand up and sent her on her way. Dobbin, her faithful and elderly pony, knew his own way home and would get her there safely. Deborah clearly did not even remember that there was a reason she was coming to stay at Phaedra's for the night, but her own needs at that moment far outweighed Phaedra's.

Phaedra went back into the kitchen and took up her knife, viciously chopping and slicing harmless cabbage. *How could he? How could he? How could he?* The phrase kept running through her mind. She threw the knife down on the counter, and, furious, raced up the stairs and flung open the door to her room. "I hope you are pleased with your work, sir, for you have ruined the lives of two very dear young people. You and your damned gentleman's code! How can you *live* with your-self?"

Hardcastle looked up from the cards he was playing. "What is wrong? What has happened?" he asked, frowning.

"You! You are what is wrong!" Phaedra paced up and down the small room, and then stopped in front of him. "Deborah Daintry—it is she who is Charles's sweetheart—was just here, crushed, devastated! She has been to see poor Charles, and he—the idiot—made a mull of it, of course. Couldn't tell her the truth, that he had wagered a hard-hearted aristocrat his estate and lost, and so he pretended he didn't care for her and broke her heart, and now the poor darling has gone home to cry her eyes out! And all because you—" Phaedra plunked down on the edge of the bed and put her hands over her eyes.

"I have done nothing wrong. I bet him what he asked and I won. Put the blame where it belongs, Phaedra, and not on me!"

It was too much, his casual denial of any blame, and even though she knew that in his eyes, in his world, he was right, she still felt the anger burning bright within her. Why did he have to be who he was? Why was he the Earl of Hardcastle, and not some commoner? "How can you be so cold?" she asked, her voice trembling. "Do you care about nothing or no one? Does nothing touch you? Are you so empty—"

She did not have time to finish before he grasped her in his arms and kissed her.

"Cold, you think I am cold?" he said, his voice grating hoarsely over the words. "Is this cold?"

Still stunned from the first kiss, she found herself swirled into a dark dream as he took her lips in a hard, almost brutal, kiss that quickly softened and became tender, loving, full of desire. Her eyes closed, she could feel his heart pounding against her breast and the strength of his arms, and yet she could tell that he was restraining his power; it was leashed, harnessed by his will.

Before she knew what was happening, she was kissing him back, and holding him, and threading her fingers through his silky hair. He pulled the pins from hers and it tumbled down, over her shoulders.

"I am not cold, woman; I am hot. I am an inferno! My sweet Phaedra, do you know how badly I want you? Need you? I have never felt this deep a need for any woman, but I want to be with you."

Her heart pounding, she could not speak. He had pulled her into his arms until she was lying with him on the bed, and he was looking down into her eyes, his own smoldering with desire. Gently, he kissed her again and pulled her close until her own slim frame was resting against his massive one on the narrow bed.

"Do you"—her voice was oddly breathless, but she continued—"do you mean to take your wager now, sir?" Did she want him to or not? She could no longer think rationally on the subject.

He touched her hair, spreading it out on the pillow with gentle hands, splaying it across a sunbeam that touched them where they lay together. He had never seen anything so beautiful in all his life. Her body was warm against his. He could imagine lifting her dress and taking off her stockings, one by one, caressing her dainty feet, kissing the sweet arch of her foot, letting his hands roam up to her slim thighs . . . And she accused him of being cold? And yet others had done the same. But he would show her he was not cold; she would experience . . . His breath coming faster, he asked, "Did I understand some part of your ranting? Miss Daintry, who was supposed to stay for the night, has gone?"

Phaedra nodded mutely. He was glad to see that her breast was rising and falling quickly, too. She might be angry with him, but she wanted him. If he knew anything about women it was that. She may despise him, but she wanted him. There was a pang in the region of his heart when he thought about her dislike for him, but triumph that she still, against her conscience, wanted him. He could only imagine what it would be like if she loved a man, what kind of luscious fire would course through her veins for that lucky bastard.

But he would take what he could get. If a physical semblance of love was to be all, then so be it. "Yes, my sweeting, I mean to take my wager, my precious, *precious* prize. Today, from now until tomorrow's morning light, you are mine."

She trembled and her eyes grew wide, their blue like crystal in the sunlight.

"Are you afraid, my sweet?"

"I-I am not afraid of what we are to do," she said, her voice coming in little gasps. "Every married woman does this, and many who are not. Mrs. Lovett says it is enjoyable, and she should know."

He chuckled, charmed anew by her sweet courage and ingenuous seduction. He kissed her nose, then her cheeks, then her lips. He nuzzled her neck and with quivering hands fumbled for the simple buttons that did up her homemade gown. He pushed the shoulder of the dress down, and nipped at her shoulder blade, the soft skin showing a tiny red mark. He kissed it better, and vowed to restrain himself, to hold himself back until she came to delight herself. She would have pleasure before him, and then she would have pleasure again, before he took his own.

He opened his eyes to find that hers were closed. Her sweet mouth was slightly open and her hands were caressing the nape of his neck. He had been right about one thing; because this was payment of a wager did not mean she would hold herself stiff. She would fulfill the spirit as well as the letter of the bet.

His angel. He remembered in that moment the first time he had opened his eyes, battered and almost unconscious as he was, and had seen her floating down the road to him. Dazzled by the sunlight behind her radiant hair, the glow like an aura, he had thought her a real angel, come to minister to him. His angel, his little savior.

Phaedra opened her eyes, wondering why he had stopped. His black eyes were on her, and she gazed up into their depths and then traced the hard planes of his face, the deeply grooved lines that told of a life of dissipation, the harshness that was erased at this moment, to be replaced by an expression of wonder, if she read him right.

What did this mean to him? For her it was the bittersweet culmination of her deepest desires and most hidden longings. What he would do to her she had dreamed of, a confused jumbled dream, to be sure, but in the end they had been one body, one soul, man and woman together.

How could she hate so much what he would do to Charles and Deborah and Anna and her mother, and yet—and yet love him? She reached up and touched his face, feeling the stubble of his chin, tracing the outline of his lips. When had it started, this love? Was it what was behind her wager? Had she secretly wanted him to seduce her? Could she have—dread the thought—deliberately lost the wager just so this would come about, this enforced acquiescence, unwilling to take the responsibility of freely giving him what he wanted?

No. She had genuinely fought to win for Charles's sake. And she still loathed that he felt it necessary to follow through with his original wager and take the Fossey estate away from the young baron. And yet there was a thread of trembling desire within her at the thought of being loved by him. "Loved" in only its physical sense, she reminded herself.

"And so, my dear little one, will you pay me the wager now? If you are afraid, or if you will hate yourself for this, I would have you renege. Do not do this if you will suffer irreparably. But I say to you, you will have nothing to be ashamed of. Man and woman are meant to fit together as we will; it is natural and beautiful."

"I will do this with you without hating myself after."

He swallowed and smiled, his face transformed by the gentle expression; even his dark eyes seemed warm. "I will be gentle, I promise, my dear," he said. He leaned down to kiss her again, and his whole body trembled against her. "The first time will hurt. I cannot make that different, though I would if I could. But I vow, I will give you pleasure. I want to show you how beautiful, how exquisite, is the love between a man and a woman."

With trembling fingers, he reached up to peel back the bodice of her soft, worn housedress.

Nineteen

He bent his head to kiss her again as he fumbled with her dress, and felt within their connection the wonder of all that was new to her. He was the first man to kiss her; he would be the first man to touch her breasts, to see her nakedness, to take her in lovemaking. And forever after, in her little village, she would know herself to be less than the pure, chaste flower everyone thought her to be. It would mark every day for one so upright. And the sadness was, she was innocent enough that she did not know what it would do to her.

By making love to her, he would mark her forever as his woman, and yet he would leave her behind.

It wasn't right. He pulled back from her and she opened her eyes and gazed up at him, unblinking, in the sunlight. He saw acceptance in her eyes, and something else he could not name, was *afraid* to name. It was nothing he had ever seen in a woman's eyes before, some deep strength and elemental force, the depth of a woman's love. No, not that. He was mistaken, for he had never done anything to deserve a gift of such magnitude.

He slipped off the bed and straightened, willing himself to ignore his arousal. "I-I find myself in the odd position of refusing your payment of your debt."

"Why? Did I . . . do you not want—"

Ruefully, he answered, "No, my dear. I very *much* want.

But you have no idea what our lovemaking will do, and I will not have you remember me with tears and regret. There is already one dark stain on my memory for you, that I am ruining your young friends' lives. I will not add shame to the mix. I-I care for you, Phaedra. And your father is right. You are a virtuous woman; I do not happen to think lovemaking incompatible with virtue, but I am not society, and you are a woman who lives for other people. Even if no one else ever knew about our wager and your surrender of your innocence, you would know and it would change you. It would change how you felt about yourself, and it would change your behavior. I will not risk the rest of your life for my pleasure."

Blushing, Phaedra sat up on the edge of the bed and pulled the shoulder of her dress up to hide her partial nakedness, though nothing beyond her shoulder had been exposed. Hardcastle smiled, though he did not feel particularly happy. He recognized that in making love to Phaedra, he had hoped to plunder some deep well of good, of purity. Was he hoping a little would rub off? Life did not work that way. His best friend for most of his adult years had been Mercy Dandridge, one of the best men he had ever known or known of, and yet Mercy's goodness had not transferred.

By leaving her innocence intact he was performing the first deed in his life that was solely for another's benefit. It felt good. It felt . . . it felt *very* good.

"I will be leaving tomorrow," he said, looking away from her. He limped to the door. "I will leave you to compose yourself, my dear, and then I will find someplace else to sleep this night, the local inn, or some other place. There is no point in you being condemned for a sin you have not enjoyed."

Phaedra was confused—*horribly* confused—by the feelings of almost regret that she was suffering. With unseeing eyes she stared out the back window, not taking in the landscape, seeing nothing beyond the pane of glass in front of her. Her vision was turned inward. She had offered herself to Hardcastle, body and soul, and yet in the end it was he who had the will to stop. She would never know what it was like, what the mysterious world of lovemaking was all about. And yet it was not so much *that* that she would regret. Embarrassingly, she had wanted the memory of him to cling to through the coming years, and would have welcomed the change in her body as a vivid reminder of that moment when they joined as one.

She had no illusions. He lived in a morally bankrupt world, and he had said enough during their late-night conversations to know that he had lived very much in that world. He had gambled and drank and made love with perhaps countless women. And yet ultimately, something that should have been easy for him was impossible. He could not take her, even though he had every right to and she had not come to him unwillingly. He had been extraordinarily circumspect. At that very moment he was packing a small bag to take with him down to the inn, just so he would not compromise her.

What did that signal? It was not fear of entrapment. As the daughter of a gentleman, she could, possibly, entrap him into marriage or a settlement just by virtue of their having been alone and in a compromising situation, but he knew her well enough not to fear that was her aim.

No, he truly had her best interests at heart, and she was deeply grateful to him. And proud of him, for she suspected that this was the first time he had done something motivated solely by another's interests. Dark angel though he was, there was yet a core of goodness in him of which she suspected he was not even aware. If only that goodness would shine out in the case of Charles's idiotic wager! Her melancholy thoughts were interrupted by a gabbling sound outside her back door, the sound of angry geese, or quarreling hens.

She went to it and opened it, to find on her back doorstep Mrs. Lovett with young Susan, Miss Peckenham, elderly Mrs. Jones, and Sally.

"What . . . what is going on?" she cried, as they flooded past her into the kitchen, filling its peaceful confines with their babble.

"What is she doing here?" Mrs. Lovett said, pointing at a red-faced Sally. "I thought as how she was gone to her ma's for the night."

Mrs. Jones, her querulous voice raised, complained that she had been sorely misled, and was turning right around and returning to her fireplace, which she promptly did. Miss Peckenham called after her, "Good riddance, I say. Nosy old woman. Now Phaedra, dear," she continued, turning back, "I saw Miss Daintry flying through the village earlier on her pony cart, and I thought she was to stay here for the night, but then I surmised that Sally must have changed her mind about going to her mama's, and yet I heard from Joe Mudge that no, she was gone to her mama's, and I realized you were likely all alone with that rakish earl and I said to myself, 'Delilah, you must go over and lend that poor girl countenance—'."

Into the midst of this gabble Lord Hardcastle came, with his small bag under his arm.

Miss Peckenham, though she had thawed somewhat toward the earl in their last encounter, said coldly, "And what are you doing, my lord?"

"Since Miss Gillian's chaperon was unable to stay, I was about to retreat to the inn in the village to preserve her stainless and well-deserved reputation." He bowed to her and smiled his devastating smile, flashing white, strong teeth.

Phaedra thought it made him look rather wolflike, but

Miss Peckenham thawed instantly, charmed anew. "Now that, young man, is something your father never would have done. I have been oft heard to say the acorn never falls far from the tree, but in your case I think it was carried some distance by squirrels."

With sparkling dark eyes, Hardcastle said, "Are you likening me to a nut, Miss Peckenham?"

No one wanted to leave, and so it was decided they would turn it into a party. Sally's return was accounted for when the girl explained her mother had insisted she return to help out Phaedra, mostly because she wanted Sally to come for her promised day off the next week, instead. And so Sally and Phaedra made ham and cress sandwiches, which they all ate in the garden while the sun descended, casting a mellow golden glow on the stone. Phaedra was astounded by the earl's ability to blend in with a gathering of women of such disparate character and class. And yet it was a congenial crowd. How different it was from the way she thought she would be spending the evening and night, she thought, blushing as she caught Hardcastle's eye across the small garden table.

He seemed to be thinking the same thing, for his look was rueful. How much she loved him, she thought, watching as his attention was recalled by Susan, who, at eleven, was just beginning to wonder about London and the great world beyond Ainstoun. His dark head bent to her fair one; he patiently listened to whatever her question was and answered gravely, as though she were his partner at a great London dinner party. He had proved himself to be so very different from what she had assumed an earl would be. Except for that one point of inflexibility, he had proved to be not only intelligent and articulate, which could be expected, but also good-natured and kind, and ultimately, thoughtful and caring. Did he even know that of himself? Did he even realize that there was an inner core of goodness to him that remained deeply hidden, except in extreme instances?

The evening passed merrily, with Mrs. Lovett and Susan finally heading home after eleven. Hardcastle eventually retired to his bed, while Miss Peckenham and Phaedra shared her father's bed and Sally retreated to her bed upstairs. All slept soundly.

Shortly after lunch the next day, Mr. Gillian came home, the stage letting him off near their door. He was surprised but pleased by Miss Peckenham's thoughtful gesture in protecting his daughter's reputation, and the two old friends took tea in the parlor, after which the former governess retreated to her own tiny cottage in Ainstoun.

And then the household returned to its usual routine. The earl's valet had arrived with clothing and a purse of gold coins for his master, but was being put up at the inn for the night. Hardcastle was to stay until the morn, and then leave, making his way to the Fossey estate to settle his wager, and then returning to London.

"You will have your room back on the morrow," Hardcastle said, as he looked up from writing a letter at Phaedra's desk in the corner of the bedchamber. She had come in just to bring fresh linen and to close the window against the damp breeze that foretold a quick spring shower.

"Yes," she said, pausing and gazing at him. "I hope you have not been too uncomfortable."

"No. Not at all. I could not have fared better in the best and most elegant of London hotels. It is the company, I find, that makes the visit. A lesson for one who has been accustomed, for many years, to luxury."

She smiled and was about to turn away, when he called her back. "Yes?" she said.

"Come here."

She came and stood in front of him. He spanned her waist with his hands and looked up into her eyes.

"Would you . . . would you come to me without that damned wager between us? Would you—"

She put her fingers over his mouth. "Do not spoil your magnificent gesture, my lord."

He kissed her fingers and said, "I'm not, my dear. I just—" He stopped.

She took his face in her hands and gazed into his eyes, then bent and kissed him. "I can't come to you that way, and we both know it. You were strong enough and wise enough for both of us once, and now it is my turn. It was wrong, I have come to think, to wager myself like that. It was holding something sacred and profound too cheaply. I would not have done what I did if I did not believe in my heart that I would win. It has shown me why Charles thought he could prevail in a game of chance; I will not be the one to judge him harshly. But I will never compromise myself in that way again. Not even—" She stopped.

"Not even? Not even for what?"

"Not even for you." She looked sadly into his dark eyes. "Not even for you." In her mind she added, *"my dearest love."*

"Sir?"

"Ah, ready to leave now, are you?" Mr. Gillian looked up from his book.

Hardcastle glanced around the stuffy library and hobbled over to pull open the curtains. "You should have more light when you read, sir. It is better for your eyes, and I think Phaedra worries about your preference for darkness."

"It is truly not a preference. I just forget about the sun, sometimes."

Casting a look at the open door behind him, where

211

Phaedra's off-key humming could be heard, Hardcastle said, "I don't know how you can forget about it when you have a little piece of it in your household, even on dreary days." He looked back at the vicar to see his shrewdly assessing eyes squinting at him. He hastily broke back into speech. "Did you and Mr. Proctor sort out your differences? Or will it require more conversation?"

With a regretful look on his saggy face, Mr. Gillian said, "I am afraid my only hope of prevailing in this argument is if I could copy from the original *Codex*, and that is locked away in London. A Mr. Bertram Conyngton is in charge of it, and though I have written to him, he will not send me a copy, nor will he answer my questions directly."

Hardcastle found himself smiling, and said, "Mr. Bertram Conyngton, eh? I believe I have heard of the gentleman. Mr. Gillian, your kindness to me has been so great, I would like to repay you, but I have not been able to think of a way to do so. Would a trip to London—I can send my coach at any time and you may stay in my London house, you know—would that help in your work?"

His face luminous, Mr. Gillian leaped to his feet, clapped the earl on the shoulder, and said, "That would be splendid, my lord! Do you, by any chance, have a maiden aunt or two around, or a widowed female relation?"

"Why, are you looking for a second wife?" Hardcastle asked, startled.

"Good Lord, no! But at the same time, you see, I was thinking that Phaedra has never seen London, and it is such a shame, for every girl should see London once, and she could go to the museums, and to the art exhibits. She would like that, you know. But London rules being so much stricter than country, you know, I was thinking that a maiden aunt or some other spare female would provide adequate chaperonage."

Hardcastle turned away and stared at the bookcases of elderly tomes. The thought of Phaedra in his London town house made his mouth go dry. How would he bear to know she was under his roof, and never approach her? He had thought of leaving as definite, that he would never see her again, and had not foreseen how Mr. Gillian would immediately think of his daughter when offered a trip to London.

"I will be on a trip to my estate in the near future. If I was out of town there would be no need for a chaperon other than yourself, sir." Master of his expression once more, he turned back to the older man.

Mr. Gillian nodded, but his expression was thoughtful. "That would do."

"I will be leaving this afternoon, sir."

"So you will. Get back to your proper life, eh? Got a woman or two waiting for you, I would wager, if I were a betting man. *Vino* to drink, card games to play, eh?"

"I suppose." Put baldly like that, his life seemed devoid of meaning or interest. And yet the vicar had accurately summed up the activities that filled his days and nights during the long season. Perhaps that hasty trip to his estates would be prolonged. Country air had become pleasant to him. He held out his hand to the older man. "It has been a pleasure to know you, sir. I will likely not see you, even if you take advantage of my offer and visit my London house. As I said, I have estate business that I fear I have neglected for far too long. However, my staff will take good care of you and—and Phaedra."

Mr. Gillian shook his hand heartily, and said, "We'll miss you, young man. I will miss playing chess and talking with you, and Phaedra, I think, will miss taking care of you."

"I doubt it, sir. I must go and say good-bye to her. Do you happen to know—"

"In the garden, my lord. In the garden."

Hardcastle gave a golden sovereign to a startled and over-whelmed Sally on his way through the kitchen, then exited through the back door, and made his way to the herb garden, where Phaedra was sure to be.

And she was. He stood for a moment watching her. She was not weeding nor digging; she was just standing by the low stone wall gazing at the distant hill that rose on the misty horizon. What was she thinking? he wondered. Was she wondering about the world beyond those hills? Oh, the sights he could show her! She could wander the Greek hills and pick wild basil while her father visited the museums and libraries. Her eyes were the blue of the Aegean, and he could picture her there, pretty dress fluttering around her ankles—

It was too real, and he started forward awkwardly, and said, "What are you thinking?"

She turned, her blue eyes widening, and smiled. "How . . . How handsome you look, my lord, in your proper attire. Though I confess the image of you in carpet slippers . . ." She trailed off.

He tried to smile, too, but was not sure how successful he was. What he did not say was that those humble carpet slippers were packed in his bag, even though his superior valet had sniffed quite audibly when he insisted on not leaving them behind. He looked down at his shining boots and proper breeches and coat and immaculate cravat. "Jean-Marc is the best. He awaits me at the inn with my coach. Pegasus looks marvelous by the way, if a little too fat. The Simondsons have been handsomely rewarded."

"You will be the talk of the village."

He paced toward her and sat on the wall so that their eyes were level. "I-I will miss you, my dear, and will often think

214

about what we did and even more often about what we did not do."

"Stop!" she said, putting her fingers over his mouth. "Now is not the time to speak of that. It—" Her voice trembled and she stopped and looked away.

"May I kiss you once more? Good-bye?"

Phaedra felt tears welling up in her eyes and resolutely blinked them away. She would not make his last memory of her one of a watering pot. She moved between his legs so she was close enough to put her hands on his shoulders and gaze steadily into his eyes. She could smell the spicy scent of his shaving soap and cologne rising to her, accoutrements his valet would have brought, she supposed. Until now he had been using her father's humble soap, handmade by her and smelling of nothing beyond a faint whiff of borage from her garden.

"Good-bye; it is such a sad word." Her voice broke and she took a long breath to steady it. "May we say *adieu* instead?"

"As long as I can kiss you again—" He broke off, too, and cleared his throat. "I find your kisses are rather addictive, my dear. Like your delicious bread. I shall be spoiled now for loaves and kisses from any other woman."

She laughed at his teasing. "My reputation shall be quite ruined, you know, if anyone sees us kissing in the garden."

"I will claim we have just discovered you are my long-lost cousin and that we were sealing our reunion with a cousinly kiss." He put his arms around her and pulled her close, nestling her in the V between his thighs.

She closed her eyes and surrendered to the sadness that surrounded her. When his lips met hers she relaxed into his embrace and felt the welling of love in her heart like a physical presence. It grew and blossomed and took root, and then, like a runner bean, made its way swiftly upward until it flowed out of her and into her kiss. She circled her arms around his neck as he bent his head to kiss her ear and her hair and her neck.

His hands wandered and soon she felt him pull her against him until she could feel the pounding of his powerful heart and the budding arousal in his form-fitting breeches. Heat coursed through her as she lost herself in the sensations he was arousing, the dark desires and longings.

She pulled away and stood apart from him. He looked dazed, and when he opened his dark eyes they were glazed. He swallowed hard and stood, too.

"I have to go," he said.

She shut out of her mind and heart the imprint he had made there. She must think rationally. She must! She had promised herself that once more she would try an appeal to the goodness he had shown on other occasions.

"Are . . . are you still going to Charles Fossey's estate?"

"Yes. I must settle this once and for all. It has waited long enough, and my valet says Fossey has sent no message to my London house. It is time to put an end to it."

"My lord—"

"Why do you still call me that, after all this?" he said impatiently, almost savagely. "After what we have been to each other, and what we have *almost* been to each other? Phaedra, we have almost been lovers; surely you can call me something other than 'my lord'?"

"What should I call you?"

"Call me Lawrence. Just once."

"Lawrence," she said softly, trying it out on her lips. "Lawrence, must you take everything from Charles and Deborah? And from Anna and her mother? It would be an act of great mercy, of charity, if you would leave them their home."

216

"I will not toss them from the doorstep. I will give them time to make arrangements, I can promise you that. If there is anything I can do to make their journey easier, I will do that, too."

"Lawrence, please. Is there no compromise? No way to work something out?"

"I-I don't think so," Hardcastle said. He had to leave. He had to go, because the sound of his name on her lips was doing strange things to his heart, and it would never do. Her mark was set upon his soul, but he could not have her any way other than marriage, and marriage he had long known was out of the question for a man of his tastes and habits. It would not be fair to any woman to saddle her with a rake who drank too much, gambled too much, and had an earned reputation as a heartless scoundrel.

And a woman like Phaedra—a lovely, artless *angel* like Phaedra—deserved a man of sterling worth and untarnished reputation, a man she could be proud of, a man who could give her a name of which to be proud. "I have to go," he said. He saw a tear start in her eye before she swiftly turned her face away, and he swallowed hard. If there was a measure of comfort in her pain, if the knowledge that she would miss him, too, gave him a moment of gratification, he pushed away the thought as unworthy. He would have erased himself from her mind if he could, simply to save her anguish of any kind. "Good-bye, my dear. All the promises I made, all the people I swore to help, I will fulfill those promises."

"I know you will." She turned back to face him and said, "Good-bye, Lawrence. I have come to care for you, and I will miss you."

"And I will miss you." With that, he turned and strode across the garden and out the gate that led to the road.

Twenty

"Take the carriage and wait for me at the crossroads, Jem," Hardcastle said to his coachman. They were in the yard of the Pilgrim's Lantern in Ainstoun. "Pegasus is fat and lazy, and I need to get both of us back into condition. I will ride to the Fossey estate to do my business, but I will return to London in the coach, I think, with Jean-Marc. I will be not more than three hours, so we should have time, if you meet me at the crossroads, to get halfway to London before dark."

Jem touched his hat with his customary surly obedience, and headed back into the stable to bring Pegasus around.

As he mounted, the ache in his back and legs a fading reminder of the beating he had sustained, Hardcastle reflected on how little, over the last two weeks, he had thought of the highwaymen who robbed him and left him for dead. His family rings were likely gracing the hands of some doxy at the moment, and his money had likely bought grog for half the hedgebirds in the county. And yet in some ways, he felt it was fair trade for the experiences of the last weeks.

He recognized that he had been bored and dissatisfied with his life for some time now, but he had not had the courage to confront that. After all, if he did not do what he did, then what was his life? How was he to live? He had never been one who needed the close company of others on a daily basis, and yet in the gentle rhythms of the Gillian household,

the daily converse with two people of such superior understanding and cheerful good nature, he had found peace and
contentment. At some future point he would have to ask him
self what that meant.

He rode out of the deserted yard and into the countryside,
the soft mist making quiet all around him. Soon he was gal-
loping along the unfamiliar road, breathing in deeply the
scents of ploughed fields and blooming heather. He no longer
looked forward to the confrontation he was about to have. He
thought that in the nearly two weeks he had spent in the
Gillian household, not only had his anger abated, but he had
gained some understanding of how his actions would affect
not just one hasty young man, but a circle of people he had
never considered. And even the county. The Fossey estate
was one of the principle employers and a center of people's
lives. With an absentee landlord like himself, things would
not be the same for the village and the tenants. It was shabby
treatment all around, but he still saw no way around it

Fossey had made a bet, lost it, and now must pay the price.
It was like crime, like those two highwaymen who had robbed
him, he thought. A goodly portion of society stayed away
from crime only because they knew the consequences of
criminal activity were severe. But there were some who bet
that they would not be caught. When they lost that bet, then
they paid the price. Action and consequence. It was nature at
its most raw form. The mouse might bet that the cat will sleep
through his incursions on the larder. If he lost the bet, he lost
his life.

And yet he could almost hear Phaedra's soft voice in his
ear whispering, "But, my lord, we are humans, not animals.
Should not human behavior be modulated by mercy and forgiveness rather than ruthless, mindless cruelty?" He shook
his head. How long would it be before he stopped hearing her

and seeing her and thinking of her?

The innkeeper had said there was a signpost indicating the crossroads, and that the Fossey estate was to be found a mile beyond that. And there was the signpost ahead. Grimly, Hardcastle trotted on until he came to the long drive that swept up between rows of beeches to the Fossey estate, an unimposing but attractive stone house of nice dimensions and size. His newest acquisition.

He rode around to the back, wondering whether he would have to go right up to the house and knock on the door, but as he approached the stable, Fossey walked out leading a dappled mare by its bridle. The young man stopped at the sight of Hardcastle, and his ruddy cheeks paled.

Hardcastle gazed steadily at him and then swung down off Pegasus. "I have come to settle our bet, young man," he said. "Is there some private place we can talk away from your family?"

He had been back in London for over a week, and yet this was the first night he had ventured out to his club. It had finally become too gloomy at the house, where the ghosts of what could have been haunted him. Too often he remembered the evening games of euchre with Phaedra, and the afternoon games of chess with her father. When a stray ray of rare London sun pierced the perpetual city miasma, it only reminded him of Phaedra and her insistence on sunshine.

And so this night he had ventured out to his club, and now he sat gloomily amidst the old men who sat reading papers and drinking port. He should be in the card room, and indeed that had been his first destination, but the moment his fingers touched a deck he remembered Phaedra, and saw her lips curve up in a shy smile as she made the wager that could have changed both of their lives. He had quietly put down the deck of cards and exited the room without a word to a soul, leaving behind many a puzzled glance, no doubt.

Had he backed away from taking his prize, the ultimate treasure of her sweet self, out of fear? He had begun to wonder about that. It occurred to him that as difficult as leaving Phaedra behind had been, how much more difficult would it have been if they had made love?

But he would not think of that. He sank deeper into the red leather chair and stared through the cigar smoke up into the vaulted reaches of the ceiling.

Why was everything so damned dreary? This was London, and not only that, it was London at the height of the season. There were a million pleasures, licit and illicit, just waiting for him. He was wealthy and could buy any indulgence he wanted; he need only name it. He could gamble 'til dawn, or make love for the same period. He could drink himself into a stupor, or—

"Hardcastle, old friend, it has been weeks!"

It was the one London voice he would welcome. He turned to see Mercy Dandridge gazing down at him. His friend's expression turned to one of concern.

"I say, it looks like you have been in a dustup. What happened?" Mercy sank into the chair beside Hardcastle and reached out, almost touching Hardcastle's cheek before remembering himself.

Grimacing, Hardcastle touched the healing reminder of his attack. If his friend remarked on the faint bruising and scab, he would have been appalled at how the earl looked in the early days following the unhappy event. He shrugged. "It is nothing. Waylaid by highway robbers, invalid for a couple of weeks, nothing important."

Mercy gazed at him steadily for a few moments. He cocked his head to one side in a motion painfully reminiscent, for Hardcastle, of Phaedra and her father, and said, "I would be very interested in hearing your adventures. I have an engagement this evening that I cannot evade, but may I drop in on you tomorrow?"

Hardcastle nodded. "I would like that, Mercy. Do that." He stood and stretched, then, and said, "Right now I am going home."

She should be glad he was gone, Phaedra thought, sweeping the kitchen floor. He had changed her life forever, and now it was as if he had never been there. She was back sleeping in her old room—not soundly sleeping, she could too easily picture his strong and enticing frame stretched out, taking up her space—but sleeping fitfully. Her father was back to his routine, and though he had said something about Lord Hardcastle making an offer for a visit to London so he could study the *Codex*, Phaedra had cautioned him that the earl might well forget the offer once back in his proper milieu. His proper milieu? Call it rather his highly *improper* milieu, draped with fair barques of frailty, soiled doves, as she had heard old Mrs. Jones speak of them, gambling at a faro table or over vingt-et-un.

Had some of those girls started like her, lured by a lusty lord into an improper relationship? No, it wasn't that easy. If she and the earl had made love, she would not have turned to the next man she met for the same relationship. For most of those girls, no doubt, it was not sexual desire but a desperate financial decision, made out of fear of starving, or a desire to live in some other way than abject poverty.

He was the only man who had ever appealed to her that way, and she would never forget him. Eventually, she hoped, she would stop tossing and turning at night, remembering his kisses and caresses and the entrancing force of his attraction.

And yet, for all of the physical attraction between them, and as much as she enjoyed that part of their brief relationship, it was not his body nor his touch that she remembered in the moments when she was baking bread or weeding the garden. It was his voice, and the way he would listen to her and talk to her, even argue with her, but without condescension. She had a feeling he really listened, just like her father did. It was the connection between them, an unspoken bond. She had felt they understood each other in some way.

And yet ultimately, she had not been able to convince him to see things her way. She remembered her shameful envy of poor Deborah, when she thought of all that that girl had. How different things were now. Mrs. Daintry had responded to a note from Phaedra with the news that the girl had made herself ill and would not eat, nor could she sleep. It was time to tell her the truth, Phaedra thought, now that Hardcastle was gone to London. She would not let Deborah keep thinking that Charles was unfaithful. Maybe something could still be done for the two young people, though she rather doubted it. Squire Daintry was not one to set his daughter's value cheaply. He would not countenance a son-in-law with no money, no estate, and no future.

A knock at the back door sent her scurrying to put away her broom, untie her apron, and answer it. As if she had stepped directly from Phaedra's thoughts, it was Deborah, and the girl fell into her friend's arms and hugged her fiercely.

In amazement, Phaedra pulled away from her and held the girl at arm's length. "I was just thinking of you! You . . . You look radiant! What has happened? Have you spoken to Charles?" What he could have said to put the roses back in Deborah's cheeks, Phaedra did not know, but it was the only explanation she could think of.

"Yes! He told me all! Oh, Phaedra, he does not love another girl! He is not so worthless." Deborah threw off her bonnet, tossing it toward the table, where it skidded and fell on the floor beyond. The girl danced around the kitchen, twirling on one toe and then stopped and hugged Phaedra again. "We are to be married!"

Wild imaginings flew through Phaedra's brain. Had there been some sort of error? Had she mistaken what Charles said? Or . . . awful thought, had something happened to Hardcastle, making the bet null and void?

"What has happened? What is going on? I thought—"

"I shall make tea," Deborah said grandly, "and tell you all about it. It is the most amazing story. You will never guess who is involved!"

The girl accidentally tipped the kettle over while trying to put it on the hob and the fire went partially out, and so it was some time before Phaedra could get the kettle over the fire again, and actually make tea. Deborah refused to talk before it was poured, though she hummed to herself, and kept jumping up to gaze out the window, down the road.

"Now," Phaedra said, impatiently, once the tea was sitting before them on the kitchen table, "what is this all about?"

Deborah then told Phaedra the story she already knew, about the euchre game and Charles's rash bet. So she would not have to tell Deborah that, anyway, she thought, relieved. But still, it did not explain anything. And the flighty girl had not yet mentioned Lord Hardcastle's name.

"I should be furious with Charles," Deborah said with a scowl that quickly turned back into a grin. "But I can't! I am so relieved it is not another girl. There were so many casting their caps for him in London, you would not believe. Miss Susan Debenham told me that a Miss Alistair was convinced he was going to offer for her, but that was all a hum. He told me—"

"Deborah! What happened with the bet?"

"Oh, yes. You will never guess who he made the bet with!" Deborah watched Phaedra's face avidly.

"I . . . Why don't you tell me," Phaedra said. Hardcastle had apparently told no one about her knowing, likely because he knew how her keeping that knowledge from the Daintrys would be viewed.

"It is your own earl, Lord Hardcastle. Can you imagine? Hard-hearted Hardcastle himself! He was on his way down here to settle the debt when the bandits waylaid him. All the time Hardcastle was convalescing here, Charles was trying to ready Anna and Lady Fossey for the necessity of moving. He had sent letters to their relations asking who would take them in, and was just waiting for their replies before he headed back to London to settle. He was so brave." Deborah sighed, swirling her tea and not noticing when it slopped over the sides of the cup. "He did not want to upset me, and thought that if I considered him unworthy of my love, I would be angry enough that I would forget him. As if I would! The goose."

Phaedra felt the urge to scream, but controlled her voice modulation well, she thought, when she said, "And so what happened when Lord Hardcastle left there? Did he . . . Did he release Charles from the debt?"

"Not exactly," Deborah said, frowning down into her cup. "He pointed out to Charles that a man's word was his pledge. And Charles responded that he was willing that moment to hand over the keys to the estate. He asked only that Anna and his mother be allowed to stay until they had time to pack and find a place to live. And he asked that he be the one to break the news to them, as he had not yet told them the truth.

"But Lord Hardcastle said he did not want the Fossey estate. And yet he could not just give up the bet, either. And so, he said that if Charles will just stay on the estate, with Anna and his mother, of course, and will remit twenty percent of his profits to Lord Hardcastle for three years, he will consider the bet paid in full! They shook on it, and it was done. Of course, the joke is on the earl! As I said to Charles, twenty percent of the profits over three years? That is a pittance compared to the worth of the estate. Charles cannot understand it, and says he believes the earl purposely let him off easily, but that is ridiculous. Everyone knows Hard-hearted Hardcastle's reputation. No, I believe it is simply that the earl did not stop to look around, and I suppose from the modest size of the house, compared to his own half dozen likely, he thought it would not be worth much."

Phaedra kept silent, but she knew in her heart that Hardcastle, as canny as he was, likely could estimate the worth of the estate. He had set a price he knew the baron could pay; it would be a bit of a hardship, but would serve to keep the young man on the estate and working to pay off the debt. He would have, for three long years, the twenty percent remittance to remind him of what he had almost lost.

She sent up a silent prayer of gratitude and said to Deborah, "And you settled things between you?"

The girl blushed and giggled. "We did. He kissed me in the most shockingly improper way! And he told me that if I would consent, we could be married inside of two years! Oh, I long to be married sooner! You being a maiden spinster will not know how—or why—I long to be married. There are things I have heard about—" She broke off, blushing. "But you, being a vicar's daughter, would not have heard of such things. I must not forget myself. I am in hopes of being able to convince him to marry sooner. We can live quite happily on the estate; I do not need London."

Privately, Phaedra thought that marriage would be a good

thing for Charles in giving him a motive for good behavior, and giving him an object at home to keep him there and happy. But the Daintrys and Charles would no doubt work things out. She was just happy and proud of Hardcastle— Lawrence.

He had listened to her, taken her concerns seriously; she had made a difference with him. And he had made a difference to her. She understood love, now. As Deborah said her good-byes, Phaedra's mind turned back to their moments together; now she could remember him with untarnished pleasure. She went back to her housekeeping, cooked the evening meal, ate with her father, sewed for a while, then read, and finally blew out her candle late that night in her narrow bed, but never once did her mind leave her rake, her Lawrence, her dark but ever brightening angel. She could think of him and dream of him now with sadness, but with no regret.

Twenty-One

Idly, Hardcastle noted that though the curtains were pulled back, there was no real sunshine streaming through the window of his library. There should be sunshine, he thought, remembering Mr. Gillian's tiny room in Oxfordshire. There should be Phaedra. He stretched out in the wing chair behind his desk and closed his eyes, remembering her bustling gait and off-tune hum, the smell of lavender and the image of her bottom pushing open the bedchamber door, signaling that his day was to get considerably brighter by her mere presence.

He opened his eyes again and toyed with his wax seal, twirling it on the silk ribbon that threaded through it. Silk ribbon. Would *she* like silk ribbons? He had never seen any adornment in her glorious hair, and it needed no decoration other than the sun glinting off of it. But still, a young woman should have ribbons and lace. And pearls. How pearls would glow against her skin!

He glanced at the clock on the mantel. What would she be doing at that moment? It was early in the day, yet. She could be weeding in the garden, or changing the bed linens, or any one of a hundred other chores. In the course of a normal London day, he would not be up and about at such an hour, but he had been home and in bed early, and so he rose early. He had become boring and dull, in other words, just like the fellows he used to laugh at who had families that interested them or wives they wished to spend time with.

But unlike them he had no object to focus his attentions on. He knew what he did not want, but he didn't know what to put in its place. What did a man do if he did not gamble or drink or wench? His own life had become tedious.

It was a strange and wonderful fact that the one brief, shining moment in his life, the moment he thought of with pride and joy, was the moment when, realizing what the loss of her innocence would mean to and do to Phaedra, he refused to use her for his own physical pleasure. He supposed it meant little when compared with the gesture of reconciliation he made toward young Fossey. Several lives could have been destroyed there. And he felt deeply that he had done the right thing. The disbelieving joy and utter relief on the young baron's face had told him how right it was. But that had left him with questions about how many lives had been ruined at the gambling table with him. How many wives beggared, how many children left without provision?

He could not look upon his one moment of humanity where young Fossey was concerned with anything more than satisfaction. With Phaedra it was unsullied joy.

Connor, his butler, entered the library and bowed. "A gentleman to see you, sir. He says he is expected; Mr. Dandridge?" He offered a card on a salver.

"Ah, early as one might expect. He is indeed expected; show him in," Hardcastle said, waving the salver away.

Mercy entered and the two men clasped hands. "Brandy?" Hardcastle said, and then chuckled. "A little early for that, is it not? I suppose we should have coffee." He rang, and within minutes coffee had been poured and both were comfortably ensconced in deep leather chairs.

Dandridge assessed Hardcastle boldly. "Something different about you, my friend. I mean other than the dashing scar."

Hardcastle frowned and shook his head, scratching at the scab. It itched furiously, but he supposed that was just because it was healing. "I am still the same, just a little worse for wear. I am going to send a Bow Street Runner down to Oxfordshire to ferret out those two miscreants, and then I am going to have them dragged all the way to London. I shall then give them a choice, Tyburn or the Colonies."

"Unlike you to give them a choice. So what happened after your unfortunate episode with the robbers? Did you hole up at an inn?"

Hardcastle found himself telling his friend—likely the only one he would tell the whole story to—the tale of his sojourn in the Gillian household. He talked about Mr. Gillian, his odd un-vicarish mannerisms, his love of chess and books, and his own intention of offering the older man his London house for the winter. And he talked about the tiny bed in the upstairs room, and told Mercy about Phaedra, her goodness, her nursing him back to health, her radiance. Her sweetness. Her unearthly beauty.

But he did not tell him about the bet, nor about Phaedra's willingness to risk her innocence for the good of a friend. That was a private matter between him and her, and would never be divulged to any living creature.

But Mercy was intelligent and curious and perceptive. "You would have liked to make love with her, I think, old friend. You were sorely tried, I surmise, to keep from offering her a slip on the shoulder."

"I did nothing of the kind," Hardcastle said, anger rising. "Do not speak of her that way or I will—"

"Hold," Dandridge said, with one hand up. "I meant no disrespect, my friend. I spoke only of your actions, not hers.

But I see how it is. There is a solution, you know."

"What is that?"

With a bland expression on his face, Dandridge said, "You could marry her. You could then, in good conscience, make love to her."

"Marry? I do not intend to marry. Look what happened to Byron, poor fellow. Rakes and rogues do not make good husbands, especially to ladies of unblemished virtue."

Shaking his head, Dandridge said, "Byron had other . . . complications in his life, and we both know that. I do not believe that he should ever have married. His proclivities make him spectacularly unsuited to marriage." With a sad frown, he took a sip of his coffee, and continued. "He did the only thing he could do by leaving England. I have some pity for him—I think he wanted to love Annabella and be true to her and kind to her, but found that he couldn't; his own nature would not allow him to be so—but I have more compassion for his wife. Annabella was never comfortable with the, well, with the sensualist in Byron."

"And why am I any different? Why counsel marriage for me? I will not ruin Phaedra's life with some ill-conceived marriage proposal. She is far too precious. I have never thought to marry, as I said."

Dandridge looked at him without speaking for a moment, and then said, gently, "But you never fell in love before."

Hardcastle felt all the breath pressed out of his body. It was like falling and having the wind knocked out of one. It was not that it had never occurred to him—he had heard friends moan about love often enough, after all—but he had dismissed it, as if it had no relevance to him, no chance of being his. "Love," he said finally, "is for farmhands and dairymaids. Even when an aristocrat feels it, he does not marry for it! That is absurd."

"Rubbish! Where have you been hiding your head? This is the nineteenth century, a new age! All around you aristocrats are marrying because they fancy a girl, rather than because she is of the right family or lineage. Any shameful connections in her family? Villains? Murderers? *Tradesmen?*"

Dandridge was teasing, of course. He was the most democratic of gentlemen, and had friends and acquaintances in every level of society. It was his mockery of snobbish behavior that Hardcastle appreciated in his old childhood friend, and yet the same quality that drove others away.

"Even if that were true, even if I did—even if I do love her . . ." Hardcastle paused for a moment, recognizing that his friend was right. He loved her. He had been in love with her for some time, but had confused the mixture of emotions that made up his love for her as quite separate elements of amity, lust, appreciation, respect, and any number of other sentiments. "All right, Dandridge." He took in a deep breath. "I do love her. And thank you for pointing out to me a hopeless passion that I can never find a way to express within the bounds of decency. I cannot marry her. Did I not tell you what she is? How innocent, how lovely, how . . . how good? I am tainted goods, my friend. I have a dark and varied history, some of which you know about, some of which I have been too ashamed to tell a gentleman of your purity. I have lain with prostitutes. I have gambled and debauched my way through fifteen seasons in London. I am not fit to touch her hem." As he ground out the last words, anguish stole through his heart. It was all far too true.

Impatiently, Dandridge banged his coffee cup down on the mahogany table beside him. "Good Lord, Hardcastle, you make her sound like a saint. No one is a saint." He leaned over, waggled a finger at him, and said, "And do not forget what you have just said, for when you are an old married man,

I shall remind you of your worship of her. And you will laugh, knowing all her little faults as you will by then. You are not Byron. Your propensities are not incompatible with marital harmony—not now, anyway. I saw you last night. You did not drink, nor gamble, nor even stay past eleven. You looked like you wanted to be anywhere but at the club. And if you are so unworthy, then why would you not take advantage of her even when she clearly had a preference toward you? I suspect there is more than just an innocent kiss between you, but I will not pry. Nor would you take the young baron's estate, though when I last saw you, before you left London, you fully intended to. I have never known you to work something out in that way before, with the loser of a bet."

Dandridge stood and stretched. "I must leave. I have another friend to see. But just consider this, Lawrence." He put one hand on Hardcastle's shoulder. "Against your will, against every intention of your corrupt old soul, you are being reformed. Your little Oxfordshire angel is in the process of redeeming your wretched soul. Or you are redeeming your own soul. One or the other. Give yourself over to her and let her finish the job, for God's sake. By this time next year you will be a boring old married man with a child on the way, quite content to sit at home on your Northampton estate and play chess with her father while she sews by the fire. At the end of the night you will say good evening to Mr. Gillian and carry your little angel upstairs where you will love her in the peace and tranquillity of your own bedroom."

A chill raced down Hardcastle's back at Dandridge's vivid depiction of married life with Phaedra. He could marry her. He could have her for himself, and with God's blessing, if she would have him. The purest moment of joy he had ever had in his life had come in a moment of torment. When he realized he could not take her even when she offered herself as the price of her wager, he had experienced an odd moment of quietude within himself, and a strange second of absolute, untrammeled joy. Why should he not marry the author of that joy?

The house fell quiet around him; he stared at the wall and thought about his life. Phaedra's father's words came back to him. What had the man said? That he was living his life in reaction to his father, which was the same as being controlled by him beyond the grave. So much had he abhorred his father's cheating and miserliness, that he had gone to opposite lengths, seeking to prove by rigorously upholding every agreement that he was a different Hardcastle. And yet he had slavishly followed in his father's rakish footsteps, gambling and wenching and drinking. Not once had he asked himself what he *really* wanted out of his life.

And now he wanted only one thing—to spend his life with Phaedra. Like a hard spring rain cleansed the foul and polluted streets of London, so her sweetness, innocence, and compassion had swept through his heart, cleansing it of corruption. No wonder drinking and gambling and whoring seemed tedious now. There was more to life. He wasn't quite sure what "more" consisted of, but he was sure it included Phaedra.

Would she have him? Was he deluding himself that there was more between them than just physical hunger on his side and awakening womanhood on hers? No, this time he was not deceiving himself. He was sure of his own heart, and he had some hope that she could, perhaps, love him a little.

"Thank you, Dandridge, I—" He looked up and realized that he had been quite alone for at least an hour. A precious hour that had just been wasted. He leaped from his chair and sped out of the room, shouting for Jean-Marc.

Another long and lonely night. Just one in the progress of the rest of her long and lonely life. And she was sleepless again. She stood at the window and looked back at the bed, the tumbled blanket and twisted sheets evidence of her restless inability to sleep. It was just a period of transition, she thought, this unaccustomed feeling sorry for herself. Would things be any different if she and Hardcastle had made love? Would she now be slumbering, welcoming sleep, perchance to dream? Of him? Moonlight glinted through the leafy trees, and she reflected that the moon was waxing again; it was almost one lunar cycle since Lord Lawrence Hardcastle had pitched into her life, upsetting the even tenor of her days forever.

The window was open and she moved closer, welcoming the cool breeze on her flushed cheeks. It was almost morning, and yet she had been unable to snatch more than an hour's uneasy rest. This could not go on. She must find a way to resolve the painful void in her heart. Why was her life not enough anymore? She was still the same Phaedra, without even an illicit love affair to regret—or remember.

The distant sound of a horse, and then a loud shout and following that a cry, split the quiet night. Phaedra stared out the window, down the road, trying to see what the commotion was all about, but she could see nothing. Had somebody fallen from their horse? Were they even now lying injured on the road?

Phaedra raced down the narrow stairs and out the door, bolting down the walk and toward the road without another thought. Old Mr. Brunton, the village drunk, had bought himself, against the advice of his wife, a spirited—some would say unreliable and nervous—horse, and she could not help but picture the poor old man lying on the road, his leg broken, or something worse.

But once out on the road, she could see that there was a scuffle of some sort going on. What to do? She clasped her hands in front of her and stood, uncertainly, poised for flight. What should she do? *Oh Lord,* she prayed, *what should I do?*

And then she heard it, *his* voice!

"You'll not get the best of me this time, you bastards!"

It was—No, she was dreaming. Was it—? She peered into the dim area by a clump of bushes and could see that a struggle was taking place. At least two, no, *three* men were tussling. Was he there? Was it him?

The struggle shifted out of the shadows and into moonlight, and she saw that one man was taller than the others, and with one booted foot he was kicking one of the others and drawing something out of his waistband while his horse careened around, snorting and flailing with dangerous hooves. One man got in the way and went down with a scream of pain under the battering hooves.

And now it was evenly matched, one man against one man.

"Lawrence," she cried out.

With one last kick of his booted foot, the tallest man subdued the last miscreant, and turned toward her. It was him! With a cry and no thought for her own safety, Phaedra flew down the road and threw her arms around him.

"My God, what are you doing out here?" he said, rocking back and holding her against him. "Why will you never learn to stay safely inside?"

She buried her face against his coat and it was if the floodgates opened or the dam burst; she wept the tears she had been holding back ever since he had gone from her doorstep. A commotion on the road behind her and the knowledge that Hardcastle was shielding her from the view of someone else made her pull away and wipe her eyes on her sleeve.

"What's goin' on here? Be these the thievin' arses we bin lookin' fer?"

A groan from one of the "thieving arses" was all the answer from those on the ground. But Phaedra recognized the voice and stepped out from Hardcastle's shadow. "Squire Daintry," she said, with as much calmness and aplomb as she could muster, given the circumstances—she being on a public road in her nightrail with an earl and two high-waymen—"I believe these are the two men you have been looking for. You remember Lord Hardcastle; he has been un-fortunate enough to be attacked twice by these fellows."

"Call it rather 'fortune' than 'misfortune'." Hardcastle bent over one of them and lifted his grubby hand. "Ah, just what I thought. Daintry, this, as you can see, is a ruby ring and is decorated with my crest. That it is on his hand is suffi-cient evidence that these are the same culprits." He roughly pulled his ring off the man's hand and slipped it back onto his finger. "I suppose my other ring is lost, though we may find it whenever we find where these fellows have been roosting."

Daintry, stubby and whiskery, was accompanied by the two Simondson boys, who grinned and pulled their forelocks at the generous earl, whom they remembered fondly in all of their toasts at the Pilgrim's Lantern. "Then we shall take them with us, right, boys?"

"Aye, that we will," Dick said. He bent down and hoisted one of the groaning robbers onto his shoulder, while his brother tossed the other one on *his* shoulder, and they made their way down the road in an odd procession.

Hardcastle turned and saw Phaedra starting back down the road toward the cottage. "Wait," he said. She turned back to him and he caught his breath. He must be getting older, he thought, that just the sight of a maiden in the moonlight was enough to take his breath away. Though this was not just any maiden. This was Phaedra Gillian, and she stood in a stream of moonglow, her golden hair glittering with captured beams, her nightrail skimming over sweet curves he would soon gain mastery over, if he had his way. All he wanted at that moment was the right to pick her up and carry her to a snug room somewhere, where he could whisper in her ear, make her blush, and then make love to her all night long. Dandridge had been right; this was the "more" he had been longing for in his life.

He hoped she would consent to a quick marriage. Or *any* marriage.

He strode to her side, cast away his pistol, and knelt on one knee in front of her. He took her hands in his and said, "Phaedra; that means shining one."

Her hair fell over one shoulder and caught the moonlight, glinting, sparkling. "As you know, sir, my father has a classical bent. He would not consent to my mother's choice of name, or I would now be a Margaret."

Her voice was breathless, he noted with approval and growing hope. From his angle he could see an enticing outline of her figure in her nightrail, and his heart thudded in his chest. "Phaedra, my beautiful, shining girl, I-I find myself in the worst of predicaments for a man of my reputation."

Her eyes widened.

"When I was in London, I found myself bored and restless, even though the entertainments of the city were all still there, for me to partake in if I so chose. Friends beckoned me to join them, and yet . . . and yet I couldn't."

"Why not?"

"I didn't want to."

"What entertainments, sir?"

"I do not think I shall answer that," he said ruefully, "for fear of jeopardizing the request I am going to make of you in a very few moments." The gravel-covered road was hurting his battered knee very badly, but he would not rise. He would remain the supplicant, for he had a boon to beg, and was unashamedly fearful of a negative answer. He looked up into her lovely eyes. "I have always been untamed, my sweet seraph—selfish, worldly, a hedonist in every sense of the word."

"Hedonism—pleasure as the ruling principle of your life," Phaedra said slowly, staring into his dark eyes.

He nodded and gazed up at her, afraid, now that he had her rapt attention, to pose his question, fearful of her answer. "I sought pleasure and I took pleasure, in brothels and gaming houses and taverns—I will be brutally honest with you after all, you see—and I gave very little thought to anything else. But pleasure, believe it or not, becomes tedious, and seeking it boring. What I found here in your village, in your home, is . . . is joy. Joy and pleasure are not the same thing, my sweet Phaedra, and I have learned the infinite value of one over the other. Joy has made me a different man, a better one, I hope. Joy has reformed me, redeemed me. *You* are my joy, and life will not be the same if you do not say 'yes' when I ask you to marry me. Will you? Will you be my shining joy, Phaedra? Will you marry me?"

A welling of relief and joy and love flowed through Phaedra, flowed from some deep, gushing spring. She pulled one hand free from his grasp and touched his coal-black hair, hair so dark it seemed to swallow the moonlight. "How can I say no? I would be denying myself the pleasure of loving you for the rest of my life." She gazed down at him knelt in front of her. She would remember and relate this moment to her daughters when the time came for them to learn about love and men and women. For no matter what he said about her redeeming him, she knew that the transformation started in his own heart. No woman truly redeemed a man; all she could ever do was love him. "Do you not think, that if I am to redeem you, I still have some work to do?" she teased. "I think it takes a terrible amount of effort to reform a rake, sir."

"Then I hope you take your time, for I have much to show you of what a rake does best," he said, a wicked gleam in his dark eyes. He stood and clasped her to him. "You have only just begun the process, my own dear little angel. It may easily take the rest of your life to reclaim my soul." He bent to kiss her and claimed her lips, lifting her against him, urgently moving against her body.

She gasped at his boldness and giggled softly when he released her. "Then you are lucky that I just happen to have the rest of my life free, sir."

"I think," he said, "I can find a way to fill it." He kissed her again, lingering over her lips, sucking the soft flesh into his mouth. His voice was hoarse when he spoke again. "We should start now. This minute." He wound his arms around her again, and she felt herself drift into a hazy world of love and joy as the landscape brightened with the dawn of another morning.